GIVEN

A village. A plague. An extraordinary love

CW00958308

Anna
JENSEN

Contents

Copyright

Just a short note about language. I am a most English author, despite having lived in South Africa for many years; I, therefore, use British English phraseology and spelling rather than American, so please forgive me if anything isn't clear or isn't spelt as you might expect.

Cover Art © 2021 Anna Jensen

Endorsement

M y great aunt (nine times over) and ancestor, Margaret Black-well, is part of this wonderful novel and, as a family survivor of this dreadful plague, I felt privileged to be asked to read Anna's novel.

The story unfolds as Kitty comes to Eyam to celebrate the annual Wakes Week and becomes isolated with the villagers as they try to contain the disease. It captures the real depth of sacrificial love, care and compassion and their heroism during the plague outbreak in 1665–66. The trust and hope the families had in God to bring them through this tragic time is a real testament to their fortitude, as Kitty constantly, with her family, looks forward to a brighter and happier future.

It's a great read. and my thanks to Anna for her factual insight and passion for our history. — *Joan Plant*

Dedication

To the people of Eyam, past and present.

Foreword

E yam (pronounced Eem) is a small hamlet in Derbyshire in the
north of England. I grew up in the city of Sheffield, a mere half
hour's drive away from this ancient village which we visited often on
school trips and family outings.

Stone cottages cluster around a central green, dominated by the
tower of St Lawrence's Church. Lush fields populated by sheep and
wildflowers, quiet woodlands and gently rippling streams create a
haven of peace and tranquillity.

Although it's a beautiful destination and a great place for a day out
in the country, that isn't the reason I climbed on a school bus as a ten-
or eleven-year-old and lurched out of the city clutching my lunchbox
and pencil case, headed for Eyam. Nor was it the reason why I have
returned again and again over the years. I go because I am drawn to
a story – a story of seventeenth-century England, of tragedy and of
triumph.

The mid-seventeenth century was a time of turmoil across England,
Scotland and Ireland. In January 1649, the reigning king, Charles I,
was executed and a new Commonwealth of England declared, led by
Oliver Cromwell. A bitter civil war was the result, with Parliamen-
tarians (Roundheads) pitted against Royalists (Cavaliers). Thousands

died on both sides; communities were destroyed and families torn apart.

On Cromwell's death in 1658, his son, Richard, took over the Protectorate, a move which proved unpopular and was doomed to fail. By 1660, the son of Charles I had been returned to England and crowned King Charles II. The Restoration had begun.

Not only was the monarchy restored and parliament put in its place by King Charles II's coronation, but the church was also reformed. During the Commonwealth period a new breed of preachers and church leaders had flourished. Their strict teaching and behaviour led to them being known as the non-conformists or Puritans. Orthodox church services and formats were removed, and the concept of the divine right of kings abolished – an idea that was understandably unpopular with the newly crowned king.

By 1662, all such ministers had been outlawed by the Uniformity Act. Everyone was required to follow the prescribed pattern of service as laid down in the Book of Common Prayer. Anyone refusing to do so was banned from the church and forced to move away from their congregations.

Amidst all this change and upheaval, an outbreak of a disease in the poor St Giles district of London seemed of little consequence at first. In May 1665 the number of deaths from the bubonic plague, or Black Death, was recorded as just 43. In June 6,137 died; at its peak in August some 31,159 people died, or fifteen per cent of the city's population.

Such events were far removed from the concerns of the inhabitants of a small village in the north of England. Although they had experienced the trials of the civil war, and although their own church minister had been banned and a new, unpopular incumbent brought in to take his place, happenings in far-off London were relatively unimportant. Life was a daily struggle of farming or mining, finding ways to work together or feed a family.

That is until September 1665 when the plague arrived in Eyam and left a community battling for survival.

This is the story of Eyam – the story that keeps me coming back to visit, the story that stirs my soul.

Each person mentioned in the following chapters really lived in Eyam, and each date recorded is accurate. Only Kitty Allenby and her Sheffield family and friends were birthed in my imagination. The Scriptures read on particular Sundays in my book were those required at the time, and a letter from Reverend Mompesson to his children, included in my manuscript, was written by an ancient hand.

Some details may confuse the observant reader. For example, New Year's Eve celebrations taking place in March. During the 1660s, different calendars were used in different locations – Europe used the Gregorian calendar exclusively, while London used a combination of both the Gregorian and the Julian. Away to the north, in the wilds of the Peak District, the Julian calendar was all that was known. Amongst other things, this stated that the new year began in March each year.

Truth is the outline and imagination the colour to this story. I hope you will be as captivated in the reading as I have been in the telling. I pray these given lives would touch your heart as you hear them speak down through the centuries.

Prologue

W e lined up on the playground clutching lunch bags and pencil cases, all ready to board the awaiting bus. Clattering down the stone steps to the pavement, I pushed my partner along to hurry her up. I wanted a good seat beside the window. Having climbed the few carpeted stairs into the dark interior of the coach, I joined the crush of boys and girls eager to start our school excursion. Mrs Bawcutt appealed unsuccessfully for calm as the cool kids commandeered the back row. At last we were all seated and ready to go. The doors closed with a gentle whoosh, the low rumble of the diesel engine roared eagerly into life, and we were off.

The driver drove to the end of the street where my school, Hunter's Bar Middle School, dominated the corner with its Victorian grey stonework and black railings, then we turned right and nosed onto the roundabout, taking the first exit leading out of the city. The bus lumbered past the park where we held our yearly sports day, past the fish and chip cafe my Nan, Aunty Betty and Uncle Ron frequented every Friday, past the rows of conjoined houses and past the strips of local shops.

The landscape quickly changed from city sprawl to rugged countryside, where the granite tors and soaring ridges of the Derbyshire Peak District came into view. Our route took us past lush green hillsides dotted with sheep prevented from escape by higgledy-piggledy dry-stone walls. Overhead the sun shone, and cottonwool clouds lazed across the blue sky.

After a while Mrs Bawcutt stood up, wedging herself between the two front rows of seats. Turning towards us, she began issuing instructions and information for our day out. Swaying to the rhythm of the bus, she occasionally lurched to one side or the other as the driver changed gear or navigated a particularly sharp corner.

'We will soon be arriving in Eyam,' she declared, glaring at any who were still absorbed in their own conversations. 'When we stop, remain seated while I hand out the worksheets and put you into your groups. You will then be able to get off the bus, making sure to stay together with your group and teacher. Please take a moment now to pick up all your litter and to collect your belongings. Don't forget your coats!' She sat back down, rustling through the backpack at her feet while we shrugged our way into coats and jackets.

'The crisp packet isn't mine so I won't pick it up!' someone yelled.

'Gimme back my pencil case!' wailed another.

Around a few more corners and we were there; the driver brought the bus to a hissing stop. We cheered and jumped up, full of pent-up energy after eating too many sweets. Mrs Bawcutt blocked our escape as she waved a fistful of printed papers aloft. 'Sit quietly and wait for the worksheets to be passed around.' She looked at me. 'Anna, please take one and pass the rest back.'

I grabbed the proffered papers, delighted that my favourite teacher had chosen me as her first recipient. I licked my finger and took one for me and another for my friend Alison sitting next to me. Stretching my arm up and over the back of the seat, I passed the sheets to the next pair. When I glanced at the page I saw there was a map, some pictures of a few cottages and space for lots of writing. It was going to be a busy day. Mrs Bawcutt eventually motioned for the driver to open the door and we were released. A shoving mass of noisy school children unleashed onto the unsuspecting streets of the village of Eyam. A story of tragedy and loss, of sacrifice and love, unleashed into my unsuspecting heart.

Like footprints in a dusty room, the villagers of Eyam have left their imprint.

It all unfolded in the summer of 1665

...

August 1665

K itty stood and waited as the rest of the family clambered onto the donkey cart. Ma, her skirts hitched high to avoid tripping, was the first to be seated. Pa passed her the baby, Oliver, already nearly asleep with his thumb plunged deep into his mouth. Joan was next, insisting that she climb in unaided, much to their father's irritation. Hampered by the straw doll she was clutching in one hand, she struggled to get hold of the cart's sides and would have landed in a heap in the mud if both parents hadn't grabbed her at the last minute. Finally settled next to Ma, she turned to regard Kitty with her solemn brown eyes, dark blonde curls sticking to the heat of her forehead. 'Isn't tha coming, Kitty?' she implored. 'I'll cry if tha doesn't.'

Kitty swallowed hard. She would not cry. She had vehemently asserted that a year away from family was *exactly* what she not only needed but also desperately longed for, and she would not now show herself to be wavering in that assertion. 'No, luv,' she finally managed to say, suppressed emotion causing her to sound a little less gentle than she had intended. 'Tha knows I'm not coming with thee now. I'm going to stay with Aunt Anne and Uncle Robert, and help them with t' cousins and farm. I'll see thee soon though, I promise. Now, mind tha takes good care of t' baby there while I'm gone.' She indicated the doll cradled in Joan's arms – a parting gift won at the fair by

Kitty's surprisingly accurate throw of a ball, dislodging as it had the one remaining skittle on the shelf.

'Alright,' snuffled Joan, clearly somewhat torn between bidding her big sister farewell and caressing her cherished 'baby'.

'Right, time we were going,' declared Pa from beside Kitty. 'Now, be good, be helpful, and don't forget to read,' he enjoined.

Pa had been a school teacher until five years before, imparting to young minds his love of words and contemporary theology. That was until Charles II returned from Europe and turned the country upside down. Again. Those deemed sympathetic to the old regime were immediately removed from positions of influence; Kitty's father was one of those who lost his job. Since then, he had been engaged by a string of wealthy Sheffield industrialists willing to turn a blind eye to his political and religious beliefs in their desperation that he teach their lazy children something of value. In his spare time, he had determined to teach Kitty to read and write. An unusual move, perhaps, in a city dominated by men, but one he hadn't regretted for a moment. Kitty had loved learning, finding joy as strange patterns on the page became words and phrases she could read and understand. Her own writing had become neat and easily legible – in her eyes a work of art to be perfected. They had both revelled in the camaraderie of learning, she in the focused attention she had received from him, and he finding her a pleasant antidote to the stream of disobedient and disinterested boy-children he frequently found himself saddled with.

'I've left thee something in t' bag which I dropped with Uncle Robert earlier.' He winked. Kitty gasped, guessing it would be the giant family Bible. She hugged him around the neck, breathing in the scent of home as she did so, drinking deep from his steadfast strength, his vibrancy and stability.'Thank you, Pa.' She smiled, aware of the sacrifice it would be for him, not having his Bible close at hand. However, she also knew that he had committed many passages to memory and seldom needed to leaf through its pages when in search of comfort or direction.

He raised his hand to her chin, holding her steady just as he had back when she was a young girl. Kitty felt the warmth, love and confidence contained within that one simple gesture and again found herself gulping for fresh, calming air. Pa said nothing more, just smiled and let his hand fall to his side as he turned, a sudden burst of energy released as he realised the lateness of the hour and the distance of the journey that lay ahead. He climbed on to the front of the cart, gathered the reigns and urged the donkey forward with a 'mst, mst' through his teeth.

'Goodbye, darling Catherine,' Ma called, waving her removed glove high in the air, a flag of farewell wafted for all to see.

'It's Kitty,' Kitty muttered, knowing it would make no difference, even if Ma could have heard. She would always be Catherine to her mother.

The cart lurched and bumped into motion, throwing Joan against the hard wooden side with a cry. Her wailing woke the sleeping Oliver, who in turn started up a great howl of indignation at the injustice of being woken so abruptly by his overly dramatic sibling. Ma ceased her exuberant waving, turning her attention instead to those offspring in far closer proximity than Kitty. Pa shook his head and seemed to settle lower in his seat, preparing himself for the road ahead and its upcoming joys. Even the donkey's ears had flattened against its head, and its braying laugh seemed to indicate it was enjoying the moment.

Kitty giggled, her eyes dancing in mirth as she watched them turn the corner, relieved that the tension of farewell had been broken by predictable Allenby chaos. Another group of friends tucked in behind the Allenby cart, following them on the road through the hills and back towards Sheffield. The Wakes Festival, the annual workers' holiday and fair, was over for another year; Kitty would only see her family again at the next one.

'Catherine – a pretty name.' Someone was standing at Kitty's elbow, having arrived quietly and unnoticed in all the confusion of farewells.

'Kitty, actually,' she muttered, not bothering to turn and address the newcomer directly, preferring to keep her eyes fixed on the road down which her family had now disappeared.

'Oh well, Kitty is nice too,' came the reply. 'Personally, I prefer to use my full name – Catherine.'

Kitty turned in embarrassed confusion, realising the lady at her side, another Catherine, had probably thought her disdain for their shared name was unfriendly at best and downright rude at worst.

'Ah, I'm that sorry...' she began, only to find any other words had flown from her thinking at the look of delighted amusement on the face of her namesake. The other Catherine's face was alive with the mischief of the moment, her already pretty features accentuated by the suppressed laughter Kitty could see bubbling under the surface. Dark, humour-filled eyes invited Kitty to join the merriment, erasing any of the awkwardness originally felt. Kitty let out a breath of relief and broke into a broad smile herself, grateful that this stranger had chosen kindness over offence.

'Pleased to make your acquaintance, Kitty. I'm Catherine Mompesson, wife to the newly appointed vicar of St Lawrence's Church. Is this your first visit to Eyam?'

The lightness of the exchange was suddenly engulfed in a cloud of shame and discomfort for Kitty. How could she not have noticed the careful accent, the fine clothes, the unmistakable symbols of a sort above her own? The woman before her represented all that

Kitty distrusted and, yes, feared. She was one of the privileged, the
well-connected, the ones who now ruled the world and, worse, the
church. And yet, even as memories of overheard conversations held
deep into the night between her father and his non-conformist friends
threatened to deprive her of even the most basic of manners, Kitty was
aware of something different. The look of concern that had replaced
the mirth earlier so evident on Mrs Mompesson's face hinted that
perhaps here before her stood one with a more sympathetic heart. She
could only hope so.

Kitty ducked her head, gathered her skirts and bobbed the slightest
of curtsies in outward response to this disconcerting revelation. She
hoped Mrs Mompesson would accept that as sufficient recompense
for her earlier presumption.

'Oh, no, please don't do that!' Catherine exclaimed in a rush, reaching out her perfectly gloved hands in entreaty. Kitty straightened, hiding her own bare and filthy hands behind her back. 'There's no need,
really. I'm sorry if I embarrassed you, Kitty, that wasn't my intention
in the least. It was so lovely to see a new face here in the village and then
find we share a name, that I quite forgot myself in my desire to greet
you. I do hope you'll forgive me and we can perhaps start again?'

'Yes ma'am,' agreed Kitty, still avoiding looking directly at Mrs
Mompesson. At that moment her aunt, Anne, arrived, carrying a
red-faced, angry looking cousin Sarah. Cousin Mary trotted behind,
trying to keep up with her mother's focused strides.

'Kitty dearest, we need to get going. T' children are hot and tired
and have had more than enough excitement for one day. Could tha
hold Mary's hand...' her voice trailed off into silence as she noticed
Mrs Mompesson standing next to Kitty. 'Oh, good day to thee Mrs
Mompesson. I trust you and t' reverend have enjoyed t' day?' she asked,
somewhat coldly, Kitty felt.

'Yes, thank you, Mrs Fox, it has been wonderful. Kitty, I didn't realise you knew Mrs Fox here?'

'She's my aunt, my ma's sister. I've come to stay till Wakes Fair next year. Help with t' kids and t' farm, that sort of thing.'

'Marvellous,' beamed Mrs Mompesson. 'Then I shall have the opportunity to get to know you after all. George, stop pulling your sister's hair. Elizabeth, don't scream so. Oh dear, I think it's time we left for home too. Good day, Kitty, good day, Mrs Fox.' And with that, she hurried after her warring offspring.

'Ma'am,' came Aunt Anne's muted response. 'Come now, our Kitty, we must be off.' For some reason Aunt Anne seemed cross and flustered, as though the encounter with Mrs Mompesson had unsettled her more than Kitty would expect. After all, the vicar's wife had been surprisingly friendly to her, a stranger in the village. Mind you, maybe that was just the good manners of a better position in life and not a real expression of warmth or companionship. Perhaps Aunt Anne knew something that Kitty didn't yet. She held her tongue and went to reach for Mary's outstretched hand. As she did so, she saw out of the corner of her eye a slight movement, as though the light had changed and caught someone standing in the shadows.

John.

Her breath caught and her hand dropped to her side, as Kitty forgot all about her little cousin who stamped her foot for the attention she had been so eagerly anticipating. Aunt Anne, ever attuned to the vagaries of her daughter's moods, stopped fussing with Sarah and looked up to see what could possibly have happened now. Her gaze took in her furious daughter, her frozen niece and the rapidly approaching young man.

'Oh, John,' she greeted the young man with a smile of welcome. 'Are thee getting ready for t' journey back t' town? Nice tha's had a break

from labour these couple of days. But I suppose tha must get back to
it, right? Well, we'll leave thee to bid Kitty here farewell, without the
musical accompaniment of our Mary's lungs and foot stomps!' She
grabbed the loudly protesting Mary by the wrist, hitched baby Sarah a
little higher up her hip, and took her young brood a discreet distance
away. 'See thee in a bit, our Kitty. But not too long, mind.'

Kitty hardly heard the commotion of her departing aunt and
cousins, so loud was the thump of her heart in her ears. She clenched
her palms, bitten fingernails digging painfully into the flesh as she
sought some degree of self-control. This was the moment she had
been dreading; had almost hoped wouldn't happen. She'd hoped Aunt
Anne would have needed her back at the house earlier and she would
have already left the fair. Or that, in the hustle and bustle of departure,
caught up with his friends and fellow labourers, John would simply
forget to find her. But he hadn't, and now he stood in front of Kitty,
looking down at her even though she herself was tall for the girl she still
was. His face was all red and freckly from the unaccustomed sunshine
burning his miner's skin. The smell of ale, slight but distinct, caused a
nose-wrinkling protest from Kitty as he drew closer. He grinned.

'Well, lass, we're off. Work's on again tomorrow so we can't be late.'
He tried for a jovial, *just popping down the road, back in a minute* sort
of approach, but Kitty could tell his heart wasn't in it. He was going
to miss her, and they both knew it. Oh, miserable were the rules for
apprentices! Even should he get placed with one of the cutlery masters
he desperately wanted to work for, he wouldn't be allowed to marry
until he was 21. Three whole years to wait! It seemed a lifetime for
the two of them, grown up and into friendship almost as soon as they
could walk and talk, now betrothed sweethearts.

Kitty knew that was the real reason behind Ma suggesting she spend
some time with Uncle Robert and Aunt Anne. Yes, of course, they'd

be grateful for the extra help, especially after Sarah was born just last Christmas, but she also knew they could cope perfectly well without her. This way, Kitty had something to keep her occupied while John worked his apprenticeship – not that he even had one yet. She sighed; it all seemed so unfair. A cloud covered the sun and a chill breeze lifted the dust at her feet.

'Don't be sad, Kitty, 'tis hard enough having to leave thee here. All this space and green grass and big skies – not right when tha's a town lad. And as for t' animals...' This as a chicken pecked at his boot and the sound of a desperately squealing pig caught their attention. 'Sounds like someone's just won t' greasy pig contest.' Suddenly he was laughing, the sound scattering the terrified chicken at his feet. That only made him laugh even harder, doubling over as he held his aching sides.

'Stop, stop!' Kitty cried, tears pouring down her cheeks as she too shook with laughter. 'Oh, my tummy hurts. Stop, oh stop!' Slowly John straightened, breathing deeply in an attempt to control himself. Kitty wiped her eyes and pressed her hands over her mouth to make sure she didn't get started again.

'Ah, Kitty, I'm going to miss thee, lass. We always have such fun together, don't we?' The mood changed, their hysterical outburst silenced by the reality that this was goodbye until the same time the following year. With his rough miner's fingers coarse against her damp cheek, he caught the newly flowing tears of a bereft heart as they traced their way down Kitty's face. 'It'll go quick,' he promised, trying to convince himself as much as her. 'And if tha needs anything, anything at all, tha only needs to get a message to me and tha knows, I'll get here – somehow. I need to go now, though. Don't hold me so – the lads are calling and will leave without me, tha knows they will!'

Sure enough, the other miners and apprentices were all shouting and jeering, whooping at John as he leaned closer to Kitty, whispering parting words of love and brushing her forehead with a kiss. She grasped his hand, willing him not to go, squeezing so tight her knuckles were white with the effort. Gently he prised her fingers open, blew her one last kiss and ran to leap onto the wagon that would take him away from Eyam – away from the treasure he held most dear.

Kitty watched the boys follow the same road her family had clattered down earlier. She stood perfectly still, alone for the first time in her seventeen years of life, trying to make sense of the torrent of feelings now rushing through her. Kitty suddenly remembered a day when she had been young; it had been pouring with rain for days, so much so that little rivulets and streams had formed in the street in front of their home. The water burbled and bubbled, forging a channel through the hard summer-baked earth. Swirling in a waltz of water, individual threads came together then parted, moving on to their next dance partner.

Once the rain had finally stopped falling from the leaden sky, Pa had grabbed a few sheets of paper, expertly folding and refolding them until there appeared in his hand, to Kitty's delight, three or four little boats. Perfectly triangular sails jutted proudly upwards, ready to harness the power of the air and toss, wild and free, to unknown worlds and destinations.

The two of them had gone outside, mindless of the cold and damp, and had released their vessels into the strongest flow of the deepest of the streams coursing past their door. With a squeal of excitement, Kitty had watched hers take to the high seas, tumbling and tossing its way to freedom and the end of the street. All of a sudden a gust of wind had caught its uppermost edge, and the boat flipped and flopped, dangerously close to capsizing. At the last second before disaster struck, the plucky little ship righted itself. Cheered and clapped on by Kitty, it continued down the street and around the corner.

'Where has it gone? What will happen to it now?' Kitty anxiously questioned her all-knowing father.

'To seek its fortune and find adventure,' Pa had responded.

'But it may get stuck, or break, or worse, sink.'

'Aye, but it may float and float and reach t' River Sheaf and then float some more and reach t' sea,' her father declared.

Kitty exhaled, releasing the tension in her neck and shoulders she hadn't even realised was there. Yes, that was it. She felt just like that paper boat, cast onto rough waters to be tossed whichever way they took her. Would she flounder and flail, be dashed upon the rocks of loneliness and difference and heartbreak? Or, as Pa had said, would she float and float and find the sea – her place and her purpose? She uttered a silent prayer for help and guidance from the Lord she had been told would always be there. *I hope He is,* she thought.

'Kitty, Kitty, look at me, Kitty.' The spell of introspection was broken. Racing towards her, on the unsteady legs of a chubby four-year-old, was Mary. Her dimpled cheeks were pink with exertion, her arms flailing wildly as she tried to keep her balance on the slippery slope of grass down which she was hurtling. Skidding to a breathless halt inches in front of a somewhat alarmed Kitty, Mary reached up and stretched her arms as far round Kitty's legs as she could. She burrowed her head deep into the coarse fabric of Kitty's skirts, her shoulders heaving from the effort of having run so far and so fast, and sighed a deep and contented sigh. 'I's loves thee, Kitty.'

'And I love thee too, darling Mary. Now, how about tha lets go of my legs and holds my hand instead, for I think it's time tha took me home. What say tha?'

Mary dutifully extricated herself from Kitty's skirt and began instead to skip in dizzying circles around her favourite cousin.

'Mary, stop doing that. Tha makes me feel all sick and wobbly just watching thee!' Aunt Anne had finally caught up with her daughter, slowed as she was by the burden of baby Sarah in her arms. 'Alright, Kitty, my luv? I know saying farewell is never fun nor easy, and I can see thee is mighty fond of that young John. And a find lad he looks too. Tha'll do well to wait for him.'

Kitty murmured a blushing word of acknowledgement. To prevent any further conversations of such an intimate nature, she tapped Mary's head and with shouts of 'Race thee!' she set off for the village. Going at barely more than walking pace, she was soon caught by a triumphant Mary.

'See, I's faster than thee!'

'That's the truth,' chuckled Kitty, grabbing Mary's hand to prevent her from running off again. Together they waited for Mary's mother to catch up, then they all clumped their way towards the little stream which marked the outskirts of Eyam itself. They stopped when they reached the brook, eager to take a moment to rest in the cool shade of the overhanging beech trees. Mary kicked off her small wooden clogs and wriggled her way to the edge. She dipped her feet in the gently flowing waters. Summer had been hot and rainless that year and rocks were clearly visible just below the surface.

'Any fish for tea?' asked Aunt Anne, with a wink at Kitty.

'I don't see any.' Mary, now leaning further forward trying to reach the waving fronds of waterweed with her fingertips, wanted to be certain. With a sudden 'splosh', Mary lost her balance and fell forward into the stream, frantically thrashing her arms around until she stood up in the shallow water. One second of stunned silence passed, then Mary filled her lungs with air and screamed. Kitty jumped up – Aunt

Anne still being hampered by the baby – and waded in, boots and all. Her skirts dragged and caught in the mud at the edge, but she soon reached the terrified Mary, who she whisked into her arms and back to the safety of the bank.

'There, there. Tha's alright, my precious. Just a little wet,' she softly comforted. 'And it has been a mighty hot day, so now tha'll be all cooled down ready for bed.'

Mary hiccupped, holding tight lest she fall and get wet again. Shaking her head at her daughter's antics, Aunt Anne pushed herself up off the grass, baby Sarah still nestling her head in her shoulder. Kitty reached down for Mary's shoes, now the only dry part of her, and together they waded across the stream.

'I'm so glad tha's here, Kitty.' Aunt Anne smiled gratefully. Kitty smiled back, feeling this had been a sign that she was here for a reason; she was here to help, and already she could see she was going to be needed.

They emerged from the cool of the trees into the early evening sun. To their right lay the cluster of stone and slate-roofed homes that formed the central street of the hamlet. Kitty noticed a group of men making their way to the Miner's Arms, intent on extracting every last moment of pleasure from the short holiday. Wives stood in small groups, chatting and remarking on the people they had met or the gossip they had overheard. Unsupervised children chased each other, the boys pulling the girls' hair, the girls, in turn, knocking the caps from the boys' heads. A glowing beam of sunlight graced the tower of St Lawrence's Church – a divine smile of approval brightening the countenance of this watchful sentinel.

The sight of the tower reminded Kitty of their encounter with Mrs Mompesson. She wondered again at the diffidence shown by her aunt.

'Aunt Anne, tha didn't seem to like Mrs Mompesson overly?'

'Ah, she's alright enough in herself I reckon. It's just, well, her husband is t' Reverend Mompesson isn't he?' As though that settled the matter.

Confused, Kitty pressed harder. 'And?' she prompted, shifting the weight of a sopping wet Mary to her other side; the child seemed to have dozed off after her fright.

'Alright, let me explain,' her aunt sighed. 'But tha mustn't say anything to t' others in t' village. I'm not wanting to make trouble or stir up an argument; there's been enough of that over t' last few years, as you well know.' She shook her head sadly. 'Did tha notice t' short, plump man at t' fair? He was on his own most of t' time, bit on t' outskirts of things? Well, he was t' previous reverend. Mr Stanley – Thomas Stanley. He was none too happy when t' king returned and changed all t' rules. He wouldn't use that new book of prayer they insisted on, nor would he agree with t' goings-on in church on a Sunday – kneeling and all that. He's such a lovely man, knows us and cares about us in t' village more than anyone else we've had.

'Anyways, Reverend Mompesson came and took his place. He's not from round here; he's not one of us, nor does he want to be. He just likes telling us what to do, preaching and praying from that book of his. Mr Stanley lost his job and his home, now he has nothing. They wanted to make him leave t' area completely, but a few in t' village insisted he stay. They found him a house and provide a small living for him. Some of us,' her voice dropped to a whisper that Kitty could barely hear, 'still have him come home and give a sermon or pray. But tha doesn't know anything about that if asked!'

Now Kitty understood. The civil war between Oliver Cromwell and the monarchy-supporting Cavaliers had been long and bitter. Her own family had been affected too; her father's brother had gone to support Cromwell's New Model Army and not returned. Dissenting preachers, as with school teachers, were removed from office and taken away from their precious flock. Many now found the open fields their pulpits, the painting of an early morning sunrise their stained-glass windows. It seemed even a place as remote as Eyam hadn't escaped the turmoil.

They walked on in thoughtful silence, speaking only to greet their neighbours or exhort a wayward child to 'get on home'. Kitty became aware of the song of a bird hovering high in the sky, its beautiful notes piercing the soft blue of an August evening. She stopped walking, arrested by such a glorious sound so unfamiliar to her town ears. Aunt Anne carried on a few paces before she realised her companion had left her side.

'What's up, luv?'

'That bird song – 'tis beautiful. What is it?'

Aunt Anne chuckled at her educated, uneducated niece. 'That's a lark. There are plenty round here. Tha'll hear lots of them while thee's here!'

They paused to enjoy the bird's song a little longer before continuing on their way. A bee buzzed lazily alongside them, attracted by the scent of pink foxgloves and white sweet cicely growing in profusion along the edge of the street.

Eventually, they reached Water Lane on the other side of the village and climbed the short incline to their destination. Kitty saw the small cottage, nestled in between two others just like it, its leaded windows winking in the evening light, welcoming them. Aunt Anne hurried on, eager to feed Sarah who was once again awake, hungry and grumpy. Mary too had woken and wriggled her way out of Kitty's arms, refreshed and full of energy once more. Kitty let them go ahead, turning away for a moment to reflect on her new surroundings.

Seeing Eyam spread beneath her, now quiet and itself resting from the day's activities, she wondered what the upcoming year had in store. Would she come to love these people, to call them her friends? Would she learn to embrace the way of the country – the wide sky with its opera of birdsong, the hum of insects, the scent of flowers? Or would she pine for the familiarity of town, for paved streets and narrow alleys, shrouded so often in the coal smoke of a hundred fires?

'Kitty, hurry.' Again it was Mary who disturbed her. Kitty inwardly rolled her eyes, realising here was a little imp determined to intrude as often as she could. And she'd thought Joan was a nuisance!

Giving herself a shake of admonition, Kitty turned and skipped the few steps needed to reach Mary. She wiggled her fingers, preparing to tickle and chase her young cousin. Mary retreated through the open door and tried to seek refuge at her mother's feet.

As Kitty followed Mary through the door, she immediately felt the embrace of home. She had visited the house a few times over the years, usually like now at the time of the Wakes Festival, when her mother would take the opportunity to meet up with her sister, but she had never stayed longer than a few hours.

The ceiling was low and hung with sweet-smelling herbs and dried flowers, ready for use by her talented aunt. In the grate, a small peat fire glowed amber and crimson, a pot of water already steaming at its edge. In the centre of the room stood a thick-legged wooden table, around which were tucked an assortment of small chairs and stools. In the far corner, a spinning wheel caught her eye. *I hope I get to try that out,* she thought, little knowing how frustrated she would become when she did get the opportunity. She could hear the contented snuffle of Sarah finishing her feed on her mother's lap, watched by a striped tabby cat that jumped off the windowsill and prowled towards the newcomer.

'Girls, really! Quieten down! I've just got Sarah fed and back to sleep. Time for thee to go to bed too, Mary. And Kitty, tha must be worn out from t' day. Let me show thee where I've put thee.' Hitching Sarah onto her hip. Anne nudged Mary up off the floor and shepherded her – complaining bitterly at the injustice of one of the greatest days of her life being forced to a close – up the narrow stairway to the bedrooms under the roof. There were only two small rooms, one for Uncle Robert, Aunt Anne and the baby, the other for Mary and, obviously, Kitty. Each had a window overlooking Eyam and the hills beyond. Kitty could just about make out the shapes of the last few sheep nibbling away at the grass on the hillside opposite. The sun was dipping behind the distant ridge, although she knew it would still be some time before full darkness drew a curtain over the magnificent view.

As she ducked under the low doorway, Kitty saw her bag neatly stowed in the corner of the room, and a small bed made up under the slope of the eaves. On the opposite side of the room was Mary's pallet. She was already dressed in dry clothes and being snuggled under a thin blanket by her mother. Aunt Anne covered Mary's tiny hands with her own work-worn palms and, kneeling down at her bedside, whispered quiet words of thanksgiving and prayer over her daughter. She watched as eyes heavy with a day of fresh air and excitement drooped closed, fluttered open again briefly, then closed again for the night. Long lashes rested peacefully on the little girl's cheek, and Mary was soon breathing the deep contentment of the young.

Suddenly exhausted, Kitty turned to Aunt Anne. Before she could say a word, she had been kissed and hugged and left blissfully alone. She plopped onto the bed, reaching up with arms almost too tired to lift, to take off her cap. Releasing her flow of wavy brown hair to cascade down her back, the girl leaned forwards to unlace her boots.

Stubborn fingers refused to comply, and it took what felt like an age to undo the knots. Finally, her feet were free, allowing her toes to stretch for the first time all day. She had needed new boots for a couple of months already, but they were not considered an essential household item, so Kitty had been left hobbling. Next, she untied the apron strings from around her waist and pulled her simple dress over her head. She stretched, lying back on the bed in her lightweight smock to stare at the beams of the roof above her.

As she lay in the twilight, watching the shadows lengthen, Kitty allowed her mind to recap the events of the day. Pa, Ma, Joan, Oliver and herself had risen at dawn and clambered up onto the donkey cart, waving at friends and neighbours who weren't lucky enough to get a day out in the country. Kitty had enjoyed the journey despite the early start and the bumpy road surface jolting her at almost every turn of the wheels. They had crossed the town boundary and begun the ascent into the depth of the moors. The fields and meadows were a patchwork of purples, greens and yellows spread before them. Others travelled alongside them, and there was much chatter and banter between all the families. Some she knew, others she didn't. Eventually they had arrived at the fair where they found Uncle Robert and Aunt Anne watching out for them.

After being helped from the cart, Kitty had gone on alone to explore all that was on offer. There was the skittle competition where she'd won the straw doll for Joan, and further along was a strong man contest – big, muscular miners and farmers battling it out to be declared the winner. The smell of roasting mutton enveloped the whole hillside, making her mouth water, and the stall selling ale was several men deep as they sought to quench their thirst. Children ducked and ran, chasing any sheep or chickens unfortunate enough to stray into the main arena. Women enjoyed the time to simply rest and chat with their friends and relations, while in the background choristers sang and troubadours played their instruments and told their stories.

The sun had shone all day with barely a cloud in the sky, but a gentle wind blowing down the valley prevented everyone from overheating. It had been a truly magical day. Kitty had lost sight of John soon after they arrived, until he had sneaked up behind her. He'd placed his hands over her eyes, blocking the light, and hissed a hello in her ear. She jumped with fright, then collapsed back against his chest as he removed his hands from her eyes and placed them briefly, instead, around her small waist. Then he was gone, only to be seen again at the end of the day when he came to bid her farewell.

At the rawness of the memory, Kitty slipped onto her knees and laid her forehead on her clasped hands where they rested on the bed in front of her. Asking for a strength beyond herself for all that the future held, tears collected in the cup made by her palms. Thou tellest my wanderings: Put thou my tears into thy bottle: Are they not in thy book? A verse she had recently read floated across her thoughts. A sense of peace and tranquillity which had eluded Kitty until then washed over her, and she knew she would be able to sleep. Moving quietly lest she disturb Mary, the young woman climbed back into bed, curled onto her side with her hand tucked under her ear and fell into a deep sleep.

Early September 1665

O ver the next few weeks, Kitty learned to adapt to country living. Uncle Robert got up early each morning, Aunt Anne rising at the same time in order to make him breakfast before he left for the lead mine a few miles outside the village. Once he had gone, Kitty would hear her aunt pottering around downstairs, clearing away the breakfast things, stoking the fire, shooing the cat outside. Then there would be a creaking of a particular chair and a few minutes of silence. Kitty knew this was Anne's time for prayers and quiet contemplation before the day – and the children – were fully awake.

Kitty had been surprised at how devout her relatives were. She knew from her own mother that they had been raised in a God-fearing home, but she hadn't realised how deeply personal their faith was. Her aunt and uncle seemed to hold regular intimate conversations with God, and emerge from the experience looking somehow lighter and more at peace.

Kitty's parents had become involved with some of the Puritan preachers who visited their local church back in Sheffield, and her pa was always bringing out the family Bible – the one she now had beside where she slept – when he sought guidance or direction. But neither he nor Ma had seemed to be special friends with God in the way that her uncle and aunt were. And although she herself knelt at her bedside and said prayers each evening – calling on God to look after her family back home, her uncle and the other miners underground, and the crops as harvest approached – she wasn't sure if anyone was actually listening. Except for that first night; that had been unusual.

Now, listening to the blackbird singing at the bottom of the lane, Kitty yawned and threw off the covers. The mornings were definitely feeling cooler. The trip to the nearby brook to fetch water was less appealing than when she had first arrived, but it was her job that needed to be done, and do it she would. The young woman glanced across at the still sleeping Mary, her arm flung above her head in

trouble-free abandon, little bubbles of moisture forming then bursting as she breathed in and out. Carrying her boots and outdoor clothes, she tiptoed down the stairs. Aunt Anne looked up as her niece descended, smiling wide as she saw Kitty.

'Morning, luv.' She got up from her chair as she spoke. 'Tha's off out to fetch t' water then?'

Kitty nodded and greeted her aunt with a kiss on the cheek before sitting on the recently vacated chair to put on her boots. Aunt Anne gave the girl's shoulder a gentle squeeze and started upstairs to wake Mary, then baby Sarah.

Kitty unlatched the door and went out into the misty September morning, grabbing the water pail from outside the door. The air was damp and full of the sound of birds not yet ready to leave for the winter. As the sun peered over the rooftops of the row of cottages, it burnished the slate with its glow. Collecting water was just one of the jobs Kitty had been assigned after the fun of the Wakes Festival was over. She also had to feed the chickens each morning, releasing them from their overnight coop before mixing together some grain and any leftover breadcrumbs from the day before, and scattering it in the yard. Once they were busy pecking and scratching for their breakfast, she foraged through the straw of their hen house in search of eggs; these all needed cleaning and preparing for sale later that day. After the eggs were packed carefully for their journey down into the village, Kitty would have a breakfast of ale and oatcakes while sitting at the large table with Aunt Anne and Mary. It was one of her favourite times of the day. Breakfast finished, it was time to attend to all the other chores that seemed to occupy her new country existence. To begin with, the sheep in the pen behind the cottage were led into the fields, expertly guided and cajoled by Patch, the farm dog. Once the sheep were happily nibbling away, Aunt Anne and the girls walked the mile or so to the strip of land on the other side of the village where their crops of oats and barley grew. Kitty could never quite understand why everyone's fields seemed to be randomly located rather than all grouped together in one place. She had tried asking her aunt and uncle, but they just looked at her blankly, not seeing a problem with the arrangement. As they walked, neighbours were greeted and eggs were sold. Mary taught Kitty the names of the flowers that still adorned the dry-stone walls they passed, and Kitty tried to teach Mary the alphabet – 'B' for 'buttercups' or 'H' for 'heather' helped both in their lessons.

By lunchtime they needed to be at the entrance to the lead mine where all the husbands would emerge, faces and hands blackened, sweat staining their shirts. The men lugged up the baskets of ore collected during their morning's work, exchanging them for parcels of food – bread, a couple of eggs, an oatcake or two, perhaps even some cold pie from the night before. After washing down the food with a mug or two of cold ale, they returned to their work like moles returning to their holes.

For the women, the hardest part of their day had just begun – the ore needed to be dressed and prepared for collection. The sound of hammers against rock echoed across the meadow as the large chunks were broken up and swirled through sieves of water. The heavy lead deposits settled at the bottom of the sieve, then they were retrieved and safely stored for the men to collect on their re-emergence from the mine later in the day. The older children helped where they could, the younger ones being left to play or doze in the grass. Kitty worked until her fingers were red and sore from the effort of prising apart pieces of rock and ore, or from fishing tiny pieces of lead out of the cold washing water.

As the women worked, they broke the monotony of the chore with gossip or singing, breaking off mid-sentence to admonish a wayward child or nurse a crying baby. Whether their own or not, it didn't matter – all were mothered by all.

The afternoon wore on, and when the tasks were completed the women gathered their belongings and began the slow walk home, children trailing behind them. Once home, Kitty would bring the sheep back in from the fields and fetch more water and firewood as Aunt Anne prepared the evening meal. It was usually a vegetable stew topped with fluffy dumplings, or pigeon pie with rich gravy, depending on what was available on the day.

By the time Uncle Robert arrived home, Kitty was ready to go to bed, but she loved the evenings spent with her uncle and aunt, enjoyed the gentle way they spoke to one another about their respective days, or exchanged news from the village. They often sat outside in the evening cool listening to the larks singing, just as Aunt Anne had promised they would. While the family relaxed, the cat prowled on her incessant search for mice, and Patch flopped at their feet, his tongue hanging out. Finally, Uncle Robert would declare the day over and, in his deep, dusty voice, pray for each of them in turn.

Once she was settled in her small bed under the roof, Kitty used the time to write letters home – if her stiffened fingers would allow. She regaled her parents and John with stories of her new life, marvelling as she did so at how much she had learned in a short space of time. She would have preferred the ease of face-to-face conversations, especially with John, rather than the stilted exchange of words on a page, but this was better than nothing. Eventually, the paper would slip from her lap and flutter to the floor, country air and hard work catching up with her at last. The young woman's sleep was sound, undisturbed by nightmares of the trouble that would stalk the households of Eyam in only a few days' time.

This measured pattern of their lives changed forever one early morning in September.

Kitty had left the cottage as usual to fetch the water. Swinging the pail backwards and forwards as she strolled along, she hummed a tune she had heard the women singing the previous day. Suddenly there was a great commotion on the road below her and a line of stamping horses pulling a large, covered wagon clattered into view. It came to a halt beside the stocks, empty at this hour of the day. The young woman watched as the driver helped a young man climb down; he then turned to drag a large, heavy-looking chest onto the grass beside him. Kitty was fascinated, not having seen this much activity since she left Sheffield. She wondered who the young man was, where he had come from and why he was here, in Eyam. Hoping to find out more, she continued to linger, waiting as the driver bullied the horses back into motion and took his place walking alongside them out of the village and into the open countryside beyond.

Returning her attention to the disembarked traveller, Kitty watched as he hefted the box onto his shoulder and wearily made his way back to the row of cottages behind him. The man pushed open the gate of one of the cottages and knocked on the door, which was soon opened to him. Kitty couldn't make out who had welcomed the stranger, but she did know the house belonged to the tailor, Alexander Hadfield.

Kitty suddenly realised she had taken far too long with her errand and, pulling her skirts high in one hand and clutching the bucket firmly in the other, she ran the remaining distance to the stream.

On her return, she shoved the cottage door open with her shoulder, being careful not to spill any of the water it had taken her so long to collect.

'Where on earth's tha been, our Kitty? Tha's taken an age and a half. I was thinking tha must have slipped and fallen or something!' Aunt Anne had never raised her voice the whole time Kitty had been staying there, but anxiety and irritation made her speech loud and edgy. Sarah wailed at the sound, and Mary joined her in protest; the calm of the morning was shattered. Kitty lowered the bucket apologetically, cross with herself for having upset her dear aunt. She pulled off her muddy boots and went straight to Mary's side, shushing her as she went. Aunt Anne, meanwhile, had successfully convinced Sarah that she was still the kind and gentle mother she had always known.

'Come and collect t' eggs with me, our Mary,' persuaded Kitty, knowing this was a task Mary loved because Kitty told her stories of pirates and buried treasure while they searched through the straw.

By the time that was done, breakfast eaten and they were all ready for their walk down to the village, Kitty had forgotten about the stranger's arrival. She only remembered the episode as they walked past the lychgate leading to St Lawrence's Church, the tailor's cottage being a few doors further on.

'Oh,' she exclaimed, 'I completely forgot. There was a reason I was so late with t' water this morning.' Aunt Anne raised her eyebrows, wondering what story she would hear from her niece's fertile imagination now.

'No, really, this isn't made up!' Kitty was stung, but persevered, so unusual had the actual event been. 'A caravan cart came in on t' Sheffield road, all huffing horses and bumping wheels. It stopped by t' stocks and a man got out, carrying a big box on his shoulder. He went in t' Mr Hadfield's place. It was ever so exciting.'

'Oh, that's George. He's come up from London to bring Mr Hadfield some cloth and do a bit of work for him. I was talking to the new Mrs Hadfield – Mrs Cooper as was, till her first husband died, God rest his soul – and she was telling me they were expecting George, with a parcel as well. I'm glad he's arrived then. Alexander – Mr Hadfield – was getting quite desperate, it was taking so long.'

Mystery solved, they carried on their way with Kitty somewhat crestfallen that the box only contained some boring old bits of fabric, and the stranger himself was nothing more than a tailor's helper.

After lunch at the mine site, they settled themselves in, ready for the long afternoon of hard, tedious work. Sarah snuggled into a bed made up of cast aside shawls, while Mary found her playmates and was soon happily rolling down the hill with them, getting dizzier and dirtier by the second.

Kitty wasn't the only one who had seen George arrive, and the village women were soon discussing the news he'd brought to Eyam along with the box of fabric.

'Did tha hear t' news from London? That fellow who arrived this morning to Tailor Hadfield's place was saying as everyone in t' city has been infected with a pestilence of some sort. All t' wealthy folks are leaving town and moving to their country places, and all t' poor folk are dying like flies. So he told them.'

'No, surely not! 'Tis London – streets there are paved with gold, so they say.'

'Tsk, get away with thee. My Samuel went there once and he said as how London is filthy; that river they have stinks, and there isn't a sight nor sound of gold anywhere.'

Kitty listened closely to the conversation, wanting to hear if the object of her morning's distraction had had anything else to say.

'Even t' king's left town, so Mr Viccars says. That's t' name of t' lad who's come all t' way from London with that parcel.' Bridget Ashe shared that final snippet; she was the mother of one of Mary's best friends, four-year-old Joan. 'He says so many have died, they can't even bury them properly. At first, they were taking t' bodies out at night, trying to hide how bad it was, but now tha's so many they're being carted around in broad daylight!'

Pausing for breath, enjoying the sensation of having everyone hanging on her every word, Mrs Ashe continued: 'Tis a terrible sickness, Mr Viccars says – starts with a hot fever tha' won't break, then big boils full of foul poison all over t' body. Nothing to be done to help t' poor patient, he says. Just a matter of time, and then they die. And t' worst is, if one in t' house catches it, everyone else also gets sick and passes.'

The women listening all shook their heads, inwardly grateful that they lived miles away from London and such problems. They turned their attention back to the more pressing and immediate needs their work presented, happy to dismiss such gloomy news from their conversation.

Kitty, however, was alarmed by what she heard. Growing up in the city as she had, she knew only too well the dangers of disease when living on a crowded street. She had seen a mere cough spread to the end of her own street, leaving each family touched by the finger of illness as it spread. She was grateful to now be living in the pleasant and open environs of Eyam but concerns about her family, and John, wouldn't be silenced. Would this disease reach Sheffield? Would it travel through the air, carried on the autumn winds like so much smoke from a fire? Or would one of the nobility flee the capital city, unknowingly carrying infection with him?

Suddenly the women around her broke out in raucous laughter, jolting Kitty away from the dark spectre of a city fighting for survival and back to the pleasant meadow where they all sat.

'Aye, so when they opened t' box brought up from London,' another woman – the tailor's next-door neighbour, Kitty thought – was saying, 't' cloth was all wet and damaged! Mary hung it out in t' kitchen, above t' fireplace, so's it could dry out, and as it warmed up, what should happen but a whole nest of fleas awoke and started hopping about all over t' house! I heard her screaming from my place.' Some of the women again laughed, others shook their heads in sympathy as they imagined themselves having to deal with an unexpected infestation of fleas.

Aunt Anne said little, merely whispering to Kitty, 'I's glad that we live at t' other end of t' village, away from t' tailor's and his visitors.' Kitty couldn't help but agree, grateful that they wouldn't now have to go home and clean in every corner to ensure no fleas had hopped over into their cottage. Imagining poor Sarah getting bitten, big red bites marking her delicate skin, and Mary itching and scratching all night in their shared room, she shuddered.

Soon enough it was time to finish for the day and return home. The women walked back together, waving farewell to Mrs Hawksworth as she went in at the house next to the tailor's where all the windows were flung wide and the sound of slapping and sweeping could be heard. The laughter was more muted this time, partly so Mrs Hadfield wouldn't hear them and think them uncaring, partly as they observed the enormity of the nuisance that had arrived with a simple bundle of cloth from London.

That evening Kitty took herself to her room early, for once not joining her aunt and uncle as they discussed their day. She didn't want to hear any more about the incident with Mr Viccars, the cloth and the fleas. Even more, she couldn't bear to listen as Aunt Anne related the details about the London sickness to her uncle. As she lay in bed, unable to fall asleep, Kitty could hear their quiet conversation – the soft whispers of her aunt and the low, deep answers of her uncle. It seemed he had already heard about what was happening in London but had chosen to say nothing for fear of alarming his wife. He tried to offer words of reassurance, saying that London was far away, and that it was unlikely such a distemper would ever reach their beautiful, wild corner of England. However, the tremble in his voice as he prayed his customary evening prayer seemed to Kitty to belie that confidence. She wondered what he knew that they didn't.

Late September 1665

✝

The next day was Sunday, a day Kitty half-loved and half-dreaded. She loved that they took the day off from most of the work of the week, except of course the essentials. She also loved the presence of Uncle Robert, his gruff miner's ways a welcome change in the predominantly female household of the weekdays. She marvelled at his gentleness with the baby, his huge hands enveloping her as he held her. Sarah clearly loved the extra attention as she gazed up at her father, burbling away at him as though it was the most important conversation of the week. Mary too thrived in the presence of her father, following him everywhere, eager to hear his stories about the birds they heard or the flowers they smelt. Aunt Anne also seemed to breathe more easily with her husband at home.

Uncle Robert even shared his time generously with Kitty, asking her about her life in the city or listening to her read from the Bible which he requested she bring downstairs. She would sit at the rough table while he stretched before the fire, smoothing the silky pages of the Bible under her blistered hands, reading whatever passage he chose. Occasionally she would need to pause and swallow hard as the smell of the open book transported her back to the front room of her home in Sheffield. She could hear her father's voice as he leaned over her, teaching her to identify the letters and words before her, and the rustle of her mother's skirts as she brought them a drink or slice of bread. She could almost feel the weight of Oliver in her lap and the kisses of Joan on her neck. Kitty loved her aunt and uncle dearly, but Sundays always made her feel homesick. She didn't dare allow thoughts of John to intrude as well – she knew that would be her undoing.

In addition to the waves of homesickness Sundays seemed to bring, this was also the day for church. Morning and evening they walked together into the village and through the great arched doors of St Lawrence's. Finding their pew halfway down one side of the aisle, Kitty would shuffle her way to the end of the row. Muted hellos echoed around the stone interior as villagers greeted each other with Sunday reverence, then there would be silence as Reverend Mompesson appeared from the vestry at the side. Taking his place front and centre of the church, he led his flock in the new rites of morning and evening worship as prescribed by the Book of Common Prayer. Kitty hated it.

Back in Sheffield, their church had been led by one of the new breed of leaders. Although they were strict to the point of harshness about singing or dancing or generally having a good time, there was an informality about the services which Kitty had always enjoyed. Now she had to endure the sound of Reverend Mompesson's voice droning on, repeating over and over the rehearsed phrases recorded in his precious prayer book. She knew she wasn't the only one sitting there who felt bored and frustrated; each time he stood and read the formal prayers from the book on the lectern in front of him, she heard the huffs and puffs of a congregation still firmly attached to their previous minister and his ways.

This particular Sunday was not likely to be an exception. However, as they approached the church gate, there seemed to be more people lingering and talking to one another at the entrance than usual. Kitty sensed something wasn't quite right, as though a window had been left open in a room and a breeze had blown through, disturbing the dust and the normalcy of the space it had entered. The change was only slight, but change was there. Absent-mindedly holding Mary's hand as they squeezed their way through the conversing adults, Kitty caught snatches of conversation.

'He fell ill just yesterday. Fever,' one was saying.

'I heard there were boils all over him,' another responded.

'He's not in his right mind, so I was told. Keeps crying out and moaning,' announced still another, intent on adding their own vital piece of information.

'Ssh, not in front of t' children.' One of the mothers Kitty knew from their lead-dressing afternoons admonished those gathered. 'Let's get inside; no more talk.'

Throughout the service, Kitty was distracted. She felt hot and un-comfortable, her skirts seeming to stick to her legs, despite the cool interior of the building. Aunt Anne kept giving her disapproving looks, her fidgeting attracting unwanted attention from those in the pews in front and behind them. Eventually the young woman pulled off her Sunday gloves in the hope that would cool her; somehow she made it through the service.

As they entered the lane to walk home, Uncle Robert pulled her to one side. 'What's got into thee, lass? Tha's not normally so uncom-fortable looking in church, even if tha doesn't like our good vicar too much. Tha looked like t' cat when she smells a mouse is close.'

Kitty knew exactly what he meant and couldn't help agreeing with him. That was how she had felt too – as though there were something nearby that she could smell but couldn't quite see or catch hold of.

'Who were they talking about, at t' entrance to t' church this morn-ing, Uncle Robert?' She looked sideways at her uncle's face, trying to

catch any unconscious reaction he had before he could arrange his features in the calm face of authority that he preferred to show her.

'Oh, tha doesn't want to go listening to those old gossips, our Kitty.' She had caught a look of concern on his face, she was sure of it.

'But was it that man who came up from London? T' one staying with Mr Hadfield? Is he sick?'

Uncle Robert knew it wouldn't be wise to hide the truth from his perceptive niece. He'd heard from his wife how Kitty was able to understand more than she should for her young age, that she seemed able to identify with the silent worry or fear of others as easily as others could hear a shout of alarm.

'Well, lass, just don't say anything to your aunt now, because tha'll worry her too much, what with t' little uns to think of. But yes, George Viccars, t' man arrived from London yesterday and who is staying with t' tailor and his family, he's fallen ill. Very ill, as a matter of fact. He has t' fever and can't eat nor drink anything without being sick. The boils are leaking and stinking, like his breath, and his belly's all swollen and hard.' Kitty's eyes widened in horror and her hands flew to her mouth as she listened to the list of ailments suffered by poor Mr Viccars.

'Will he live?' she whispered. The silent response of her uncle was all the answer she needed.

The rest of the day passed as every other Sunday had before it, but between Kitty and Uncle Robert there was now a new understanding, a secret held in their hearts which they tried their best to hide from Aunt Anne. Wise woman that she was, she kept her own counsel and didn't ask questions.

It was with some relief that they again hurried down the hill later that day and joined the rest of the village on their way to Evensong. The congregation seemed less full of gossip, more subdued than they had been that morning. Uncle Robert caught sight of a friend and, excusing himself from his family, accosted him for the latest information. He returned looking worried, and quietly relayed the news to Kitty that George Viccars' condition had worsened during the day. So much so, he said, that it was felt he might not last the night.

'Oh, poor man!' Kitty tried to cover her dismay by walking a little faster to catch up with Aunt Anne.

Kitty quietly took her place in the pew as she had that morning, and thought about the man she had seen for the first time just a few days before. Although understandably tired from an arduous journey, he had seemed healthy and vibrant, even though she had been watching from a distance. The way he had shouldered the box of cloth, striding purposefully towards the cottages; his knock at the door of the tailor's home, confident of his welcome; and the flourish with which he had removed his cap once the door was opened and he was ushered inside – all his actions portrayed strength and confidence. She hadn't seen his face, but somehow Kitty felt as though she knew him. Perhaps it was because he, too, was an outsider in the village. A man welcomed but not fully belonging, as she sometimes felt.

She turned her attention to Reverend Mompesson who had just stood to read the psalms allocated to that evening's service. She watched as he slowly turned the pages of the great Bible on the lectern in front of him, the crackle of rich parchment the only sound to be heard. Catherine Mompesson sat in the front row with her children, George and Elizabeth. Although her gloved hands rested calmly in her lap, Kitty noticed a tension in her neck and shoulders even from where she sat several rows behind. Catherine seemed to be willing her husband to read in the loud, clear voice the parishioners were accustomed to.

The reverend finally found his place and cleared his throat. 'The second psalm for this evening is taken from Psalm 32.'

Kitty realised she and everyone sitting near her had been holding their breath, waiting for some sort of reassurance from the pulpit. The strength of his voice, the unwavering look of his eye, even the way a shaft of early evening sunshine shone through the window at the exact moment he started speaking, seemed to offer what they had all needed. There was a muted shuffling as everyone settled more comfortably in the pews.

'Thou are my hiding place; thou shalt preserve me from trouble; thou shalt compass me with songs of deliverance. Selah.'

It was a verse she had heard and read many times, but not one she had ever needed for herself. Until now. Once again, similar to that first night when another psalm had filled her thoughts, Kitty knew these words were a special message for her. She listened to the rest of the service quietly, without the fidgeting of the morning. Later, on the way home, she hung back from her aunt and uncle as they carried their sleeping daughters home to bed, relishing the quiet of encroaching night.

Upon entering the house, Kitty was relieved to see Uncle Robert also seemed more relaxed than when they had left for the service. Maybe she had misjudged Reverend Mompesson – he seemed to know and care for his flock more than she had expected. Kitty was glad about that. She had so liked Mrs Mompesson – Catherine – when they'd first met that day at the Wakes Fair, and had been disappointed to discover she was the wife of the vicar at St Lawrence's Church. That had put her out of reach of Kitty, prohibiting any friendship from developing. They had seen each other every Sunday since, of course, and occasionally met in the streets of the village, like on market day, but they had exchanged little more than the politest of greetings. That had saddened Kitty, but after this evening, she felt a glimmer of hope that perhaps they could be, if not close friends, at least pleasant acquaintances.

Aunt Anne was coming down the stairs as Kitty walked in, sighing with the weariness of a day's end. She gathered the remains of a loaf of bread she had baked that morning, together with a couple of eggs and an end of cheese. As she poured a mug of ale for her husband, she ran through the plans for the upcoming week.

'Tha knows it will soon be harvest time,' she began. 'Kitty, luv, that's when we get really busy, with much to be done in preparation for t' winter months. Tha'll need to learn a few new things, like how to gather t' oats and take them down t' mill for grinding. Did my sister teach thee about jam and pickle-making? I trust so' – not giving Kitty a chance to reply – 'as we must make t' best of all that we can pick and gather over t' next few weeks. And then there's spinning. It's time you give that a try.'

As she pottered around the cottage, busying herself with domestic normality, Uncle Robert dozed by the fire. The anxiety of the day seemed to have been left behind, a welcome end to a troubling day.

Kitty got up from the stool where she had been sitting. 'I'd love to try, dear aunt, and I'd love for tha to teach me.' She kissed Aunt Anne on the cheek as she passed her on the way to the stairs, gave Uncle Robert a gentle tap on the shoulder, and climbed up to her room.

The moon shone through the still-open window, a stiff breeze now starting to blow. The branches of the tree closest to the house could be heard clacking and snapping together, and clouds were building, darkening the light of the moon as they scudded across its face. Kitty gave a shiver and reached to close the window. Looking down over the sleeping village, she was surprised to see the light of a torch bobbing along the street, held aloft by she knew not who. She lost sight of it as the walker passed under a tree or rounded a bend in the road, but she was sure of what she had seen. Who was out at this time of night? And in what was clearly a worsening turn of the weather. Kitty contemplated running back down the stairs and telling Uncle Robert, reassuring herself in the process. But the gentle murmur of contented, intimate conversation deterred her, and, giving herself a stern reprimand for being so silly and melodramatic, she turned back to her bed.

Still, her unease was sufficient that, once she had discarded her cap and Sunday clothes, she sank onto the soft rug next to her bed and tried to pray. With her hands clasped and pressed to her forehead, Kitty recalled the words of the psalm from earlier in the evening. *'Thou are my hiding place; thou shalt preserve me from trouble; thou shalt compass me with songs of deliverance. Selah.' You are my hiding place,* she prayed. *Or so Aunt Anne and Uncle Robert want me to believe. But I'm scared! Please let me find it to be true, for myself.*

Pulling herself from her kneeling position onto the bed, the young woman stretched and blew out the candle beside her. She watched the smoke curl upwards, lit by a brief appearance of patchy moonlight which had managed to struggle past the curtain of now dense cloud. Rather than diminishing with her prayers, Kitty's unease seemed to grow and bloom into a thousand fears as the night became darker and the whining of the wind louder.

She rolled over and curled onto her side, hoping the change of position would enable her to drift off into an undisturbed sleep. It didn't.

She heard her aunt and uncle tiptoe up the wooden staircase, trying their best not to disturb or wake any of their three girls. She watched as the candle wobbled past her own room, conjuring up leering ghouls and ghosts that were the embodiment of the wind rushing down the chimney, only to have them return to their lairs as the candle was extinguished. She lay awake long enough to hear Uncle Robert start to snore and baby Sarah release a plaintive cry as a newly protruding tooth made its presence felt in her tiny mouth. In her own room, even the usually motionless Mary was twisting and turning under her blankets, throwing her arm up above her head, mumbling an unintelligible conversation to herself. Patch barked at a foe of sorts out in the yard, growling and sounding the alarm for others to come and give chase.

Exhausted, Kitty eventually managed to fall asleep, although even in her dreams she seemed to be standing to attention, waiting anxiously for an unknown peril to reach and accost her. Suddenly she was wide awake, a loud crash sending her scurrying further under the blankets, eyes shut tight and body shaking. The girl's mind raced through all the possibilities, likely and otherwise, of the cause of the noise. With straining ears, she tried to hear more that might offer some clues. Hearing nothing further, she lay still once more before raising her head cautiously from the stuffiness of the blankets. It must have been one of the branches from the tree landing on the roof of the small outhouse. Uncle Robert had said a few of them looked as though they were turning bad and would need to be cut down, to be used for winter firewood. A sudden splatter of heavy rain blown against the window startled Kitty again. *Oh, what a dreadful night*, she wailed inwardly. She thought she had become familiar with country noises, even found comfort in the hoot of an owl or the rustle of a night-time animal on the prowl, but this, her first country storm, was something new and frightening. Sounds were magnified and distorted, echoing in the hills behind and swirling in the valleys beyond Eyam. Burrowing deep into her pillow Kitty muffled the sounds as best she could until tiredness won over fear.

Monday dawned and the rain continued unabated, only the wind having died slightly overnight. Kitty groaned, her body aching from

hours of restlessness and discomfort, her mind worn out with anxiety and fear. Forcing herself up, she roughly tied her hair at her neck and pinned her cap over the messy bunch. Grabbing her apron, she stumbled down the stairs, almost falling head over heels so leaden were her feet.

'What a storm that was!' exclaimed Aunt Anne as soon as she saw Kitty. 'Tha looks worn out, poor child. Tha's not used to our winds and rains, I think. Here, take this thick shawl and wrap it round thee to go and fetch t' water. Tha won't need to go far, though, t' river will be swollen and close t' road I should think.'

Kitty gratefully threw the rough woollen shawl over her head and shoulders, breathing in the smell of her aunt as she did so. Rubbing the rough cloth between her fingertips, she marvelled at the skill displayed in every knot and stitch.

'Did tha make this, Aunt? I wish I could make something so beautiful. And so warm!' Kitty realised she was beginning to overheat, so cosy was the shawl and so hot the recently stoked fire. 'I'd best be off, before I sit down and fall asleep.' She grimaced as she tugged the door open and was immediately met with a wall of water as it poured down the side of the house from the roof. *Ugh!* Aunt Anne held the door while Kitty struggled into her boots, picked up the pail and plunged into the weather.

'I'll have some milk all heated and ready for when thee gets back. And some fresh bread all baked too,' Anne called after her niece. 'Just be careful, luv – don't go too close where t' water's rushing fast. Find one of t' pools that will have filled up and take from there rather. And mind, t' bank will be full of mud and awfully slippery, so take care.'

With her aunt's warnings and concerns pursuing her through the gate and down the lane, Kitty trudged to the river. The cold, suddenly so pronounced this morning, pinched her cheeks and made her eyes water. Her boots were soon caked in oozing mud which crept through the holes where her toes had grown and rubbed the leather bare. By the time she reached the river her teeth were chattering and her hands almost too numb to wield her bucket. Misery taunted her as a bad night and the worst sort of autumn morning sought to get the better of her cheerful spirit.

Kitty wished there were someone who could help carry the water back to the house, someone she could confide in about her sudden rush of homesickness. As she stumbled along the pathway from the river, Kitty's skirt caught on a branch that had fallen overnight and she tripped, flinging the full water bucket from her hand as she tried to halt her fall. It landed with a clang, spilling the contents all over the prone Kitty, who lifted her muddy, grazed palms to her face and burst into tears.

'There lass, let me give thee a hand.' Kitty hadn't heard anyone approach, but the voice sounded caring. Peering through her fingers, she saw a short, stout gentleman leaning over her. He brandished a heavy walking stick which he used to push away the bucket and the branch on which Kitty's skirts had become entangled. 'Come on, easy does it. Tha took quite a tumble there. I was walking here beside t' river, on my way to see Mr and Mrs Fox. Well, Mrs Fox only by now, I should think, as he'll have left for t' mine already. I heard a great crash up ahead of me and, running as fast as these old legs of mine could carry me to find out what was amiss, what do I find but a young lass all torn and muddy sitting in a heap of unhappiness right here on t' path?' He stretched out his free hand towards Kitty, who grabbed it, allowing herself to be pulled up. His grip was stronger than she had expected, and he soon had her back on her feet.

'Thank thee, sir,' She bobbed a quick curtsey of thanks. 'I'm so glad tha were passing.'

'And where are thee from, lass? I don't think I've seen thee before. And let me help thee collect some more water so tha doesn't go home empty-handed – or empty bucket-ed.' He chuckled, amused at his own joke.

'I'm Anne Fox's niece, Kitty – Catherine – Allenby, sir. So I'm going t' same place as thee.'

'Well, then that's grand, we'll go there together. I'm Thomas Stanley.' The man extended a hand of introduction rather than rescue this time.

'Oh...' Kitty's voice disappeared in embarrassed silence as she realised who she was speaking to. She had thought he looked vaguely familiar but, having only seen him that once at the Wakes Festival, she'd been unable to place him.

Thomas Stanley, the previous vicar of St Lawrence's Church, stooped and picked up the bucket, graciously allowing Kitty time to recover her composure. She discreetly removed the leaves and twigs that had nested in her hair as she fell, while he moved ahead of her, striding to the water's edge and refilling the fallen receptacle. 'Right then, Catherine, let's be getting thee home and into some warm and dry clothes. If I know Anne Fox – and I do – she won't be happy to see thee in this mess on a damp September morning.'

He was right. Aunt Anne opened the door with a look of concern at first. However, that quickly evaporated and became as dark and stormy as the sky overhead when she took in the unhurt but bedraggled state of her ward. 'Upstairs with thee, and get out of those wet things,' she flapped. 'Take tha boots off first! Now, let me get t' water on to heat and tha can clean up. Mary's up there, she'll help thee find some skirts of mine that will fit thee.' This was followed immediately by a yell up the stairs: 'Mary, help tha daft, wet cousin, will thee, she'll catch her death otherwise! Oh Mr Stanley, am I glad to see thee. Thank t' Lord tha was passing and was able to help our Kitty. Come in, tha's soaked through t' skin.' She ushered her guest to the seat closest to the fire, taking his hat and cloak and laying them carefully over the chairs at the table. 'Let me get this water on, then I'll ask thee what tha's come for. Although I think I might guess,' she finished, looking at his now serious face.

Upstairs, Kitty surrendered to the ministrations of her young cousin, cleaning as much of the dirt from her as she could. While she dressed, she listened to the conversation downstairs.

'Yes, Anne, I'm sure tha does know why I'm here. Was t' young man over at Alexander Hadfield's place – t' one up from London. I was called out in t' middle of the night.' That explained the light Kitty had seen from the window. 'He was terribly poorly, Anne. I've not seen anything like that before. His skin was all black and swollen, an evil pus emitting from t' boils that were everywhere. He didn't know me, nor anyone else in t' room for that matter. He was too far gone. I prayed with him and left him for t' Lord to take him when He was ready, which wasn't much longer,' he sighed. 'He'll be buried later today. We can't wait for his family to get here. T' body's too...' He left the sentence unfinished, leaving Kitty to fill in the gaps with an appalled imagination.

Aunt Anne clucked and tutted, all the while preparing mugs of hot milk and plates of bread and cheese. 'Poor Mary.'

'But that's not the worst of it,' continued Thomas. 'Mary's son – Edward, t' youngest one – he was playing with Mr Viccars just before he fell so poorly. Loved him, apparently. Mary's worried about t' little chap; I told her I'd let tha know.'

'Poor Mary,' reiterated Anne, 'she must be out of her mind with worry, I'll try and call in on her later. Now, if t' rain would just ease up a bit! Oh, there tha is, Kitty luv, much better. Come and get warm here by t' fire.'

'I'd best be getting off,' Thomas said as he stood up. Anne passed him his outer clothes and he picked up his walking stick from the floor where he had let it fall. 'Make sure tha stays nice and warm now, young lass, and look more carefully where thee's going next time!'

'Yes, sir, thank 'ee, sir.' The still embarrassed Kitty kept her eyes on the floor until Thomas Stanley had gone, Aunt Anne shutting the door firmly against the weather.

Aunt Anne didn't mention her conversation with Mr Stanley, neither then nor over the next few days, but Kitty could tell she was worried. The usually cheerful, gentle and patient older woman was more impatient with Mary than usual and was irritated with Uncle Robert when he arrived home cold and dirty at the end of each day. She also complained about the weather, and how wet it continued to be. Her anxiety was infectious, and the sense of foreboding that Kitty had felt during Sunday night's storm increased.

Then came the news they had all been dreading. The rain had finally stopped, and the women were able to get back to their outside work. Sheep, goats and chickens were restored to their outside pastures and yards, free to roam once more after days of confinement. Of course their stalls and coops needed a good clean, the accumulated muck being collected and taken out to the fields for raking through the crops as fertiliser. The crops in turn had to be checked for damage and, where necessary, brought into storage to prevent further loss. The miners had continued with their underground extraction, but none of the ore had yet been dressed and made ready for sale, so that too had to be done.

Aunt Anne, Kitty and the two girls visited their field of oats to ensure all was well, then they climbed up to the head of the mine. To their dismay, Mary Cooper, Tailor Hadfield's wife, wasn't amongst the other women busily working alongside everyone else. The chatter was subdued. One of Mary's closest neighbours was sniffling into a rag, eyes pink-rimmed with distress.

Sitting down next to one of her close friends, Anne asked quietly, 'What's happened?'

'Ah, it's poor Mary's young lad, Edward. No older than your Mary, I reckon. He got sick, just like that man from London. He was crying something awful with t' pain and fever. Was nothing his mother could do but sit by his bedside and wait. They carried his body out yesterday afternoon.' The woman's face crumpled, her mouth no longer able to form any words beyond a low moan of sorrow.

Someone else took over. 'And now Mr Hawksworth — tha knows, Peter Senior — from next door, he's not expected to last out t' day.'

'But Mrs Hawksworth – Jane – she was only with us t' other day. Before t' storm.' Aunt Anne looked around, noticing Mrs Hawksworth's absence for the first time. 'And where's Lizzy? Please don't tell me...'

'Aye, 'tis spread over to t' Thorpe's house, for certain. Old man Thorpe and his Mary, they were heard coughing t' other day. And I hear Lizzy got it while she was trying to look after them.'

'And now t' little uns have it – Mary and Tommy,' chimed in another voice of despair.

It was all they could talk about all morning. The sun was bright in the sky, the storm clouds clear since early morning, yet Kitty shivered as the conversations continued around her. It was happening just as she'd thought it might; just as it always did in the city. One would fall ill, then the next and the next. She recalled stories of the plagues

God unleashed on Pharoah and the Egyptians in punishment for their harsh treatment of His Israelite children. There had been frogs and gnats, and, yes, boils. Was Eyam being punished for a secret sin she knew nothing about? Surely the children couldn't have done anything wrong, they were too young weren't they? She looked at Mary, playing happily and obliviously at her feet. How could God have taken one as young as her, so innocent? Or was it a punishment on the parents? Kitty felt faint as she tried to work through all the questions that pierced the safe havens of her mind and heart.

Just when she thought it couldn't get any worse, she noticed Mrs Talbot hurrying towards them. Her face was flushed and her hair hung loose around her shoulders. As she drew closer, she let out a wail and slumped onto the grass. Aunt Anne and the others sitting closest jumped up in alarm.

'Bring that jug of ale, child,' Aunt Anne called over to Kitty who seemed to have frozen to the spot. 'Quickly now. Ruth dear, let us help thee sit up. Slowly, mind.'

Together the ladies lifted Mrs Talbot into a sitting position, leaning her gently against the baskets and bags they had hurriedly put behind her.

'Drink a little of this. Now tell us – what ails thee, my dear?' Anne's soft voice elicited another torrent of tears from her distraught friend.

'Tis Betsy Syddall,' she managed between gulps. 'I went round to her on way out t' field. She'd said Sarah was taken weak, but we thought was t' age of her – her monthlies, tha knows – nothing else.' The women all nodded in understanding; they were desperate for her to continue telling her story but didn't want to appear to rush her. Kitty was horrified. Sarah was her one good friend in the village. 'I thought she'd be coming here today. Tha knows, there's so much to do after that awful storm. But she didn't even come t' door. She just called out from t' window that I mustn't come close, and that Sarah is... Sarah is too sick for us to even visit.' She hung her head, her hair falling like a curtain around her face as her shoulders heaved.

'And Betsy herself?' Aunt Anne spoke so quietly, Kitty almost didn't hear her.

'She's still feeling well, she said. But how long will that be for? Tha knows how it was with t' others.' Ruth stopped speaking, too drained to continue. Aunt Anne softly caressed her friend's hand, then she looked over at Kitty, noticing how pale she was.

At last the time came to pack up and head for home. Kitty was relieved to get away from the other women's company. Holding Mary's spare hand – the child's other hand clutching a fistful of late autumn flowers she had picked during the afternoon – Kitty led the way back down into the village. Calls of farewell rang out across the fields, seeming all the fonder after the sadness of their time together.

The sun hung low and golden, illuminating the ever-watchful tower of St Lawrence's as they reached the main street. Swallows and swifts dipped and rose overhead in search of supper on the wing, and the distinct hammering of a woodpecker could be heard as they passed a copse. Kitty and Aunt Anne walked in silence, reflecting on the day's sorrows, and relishing the tranquillity and comfort of one another's quiet company. Before long they reached the small row of cottages opposite the church, the doors of which were all closed. Candles could be seen flickering in some of the windows and curls of smoke rose from two or three of the chimneys. Only days before, they had all been laughing and joking about a box of wet cloth and a nest of fleas; now they pitied Mary Cooper with all their hearts, wishing on her behalf that George Viccars had never crossed her threshold.

Next door, more sorrow was unfolding in Lizzy Thorpe's home. Aunt Anne held baby Sarah a little tighter as they passed. She couldn't even imagine what Lizzy was going through. How do you watch your husband and children toss and turn, delirious with fever? How can anyone bear to watch the boils and sores grow by the minute as they filled up with the foul-smelling pus of disease? Add to that seeing your own body betray you with the spots and the start of the fatal rosy rash. Would Lizzy secretly be glad that she would be able to join her beloved family in the embrace of death, her faith giving her confidence that they would all be reunited on the other side of the cold grave? Or was she still clinging to life on this earth, desperate to try and save those of her children who might yet be made well?

Aunt Anne took one look at Kitty as they began the climb to their own home and realised she was going to need to find a distraction for the poor child. Terror seemed to have taken hold – Kitty's face was pinched and drawn, her eyes large dark pools staring out at a world she was suddenly afraid of. Anne was surprised Mary wasn't crying out in protest, so tight was Kitty's grip around her daughter's wrist. *Berry picking and jam making, that's what she needs*, Anne thought. *Time away from t' mine and t' women's idle chatter*

October 1665

S ure enough, Aunt Anne found plenty to distract her niece from
Eyam's woes. Kitty relished the days spent berry picking with the
weak October sun filtering through the trees above them. Accompanied by a chattering Mary and a dribbling Sarah, Anne, Kitty and one
or two of the quieter village women found bushes laden with bilberries
and blackberries, the plumpest Kitty had ever seen. Their skins seemed
to almost burst at the seams, full of the sweet juice which dribbled
stickily down the chins of the harvesters sneaking a taste as they picked.
Uncle Robert, together with the rest of the menfolk, had all left off
digging underground to help with the collection of the harvest above
it.

Kitty often wandered away from the others, grateful that her aunt
gave her some space to be alone with her increasingly distressing
thoughts. It was never for too long though. Kitty suspected her aunt
had noticed the effects of her lack of sleep. She knew there were dark
patches under her eyes, and her loss of appetite was evident by the way
she nibbled at her bread in the mornings. The looseness of her clothing
hinted at the weight she had lost. Aunt Anne didn't question or pry.
Rather she showed her kindness and compassion in the silent brushing
of her niece's hair or the softest of touches on the hand or shoulder as

they worked alongside one another. She seemed to know that Kitty would talk when she was ready.

Since the day they had heard that little Edward Cooper, Mary's son, had died, Kitty had struggled to find any peace or contentment. It was as though that one storm, disconcerting in its country ferocity, had tipped her over an invisible edge and she was now hanging on for dear life with nothing but her fingernails. Each morning she got out of bed drained and exhausted from hours of staring at the roof above her head. When she did sleep, she had the strangest of dreams, bright and vivid, often featuring members of her family – her beloved sister, Joan, or a grown up Oliver whose face she didn't recognise although she knew who he was. Each time, they were faced with some life-threatening peril which she couldn't rescue them from in time. Sometimes it was John, his familiar features distorted with distress as he bade her farewell, saying he couldn't be with her any longer – he had somewhere else he needed to be, and she couldn't go with him. She would spring awake with a start of alarm, unsure at first where she was or why she was shaking or, on a few occasions, weeping. Then she would hear the regular breathing of Mary next to her, or a bark from Patch under her window and her night terrors would be replaced by the waking nightmare that her new friends and neighbours were facing.

And indeed it was a nightmare. Each day as Kitty and Aunt Anne made their way out to the fields, more doors were closed shut, signifying the presence of the plague within that had come from London in the box with George Viccars. The same plague that was chasing the king and his courtiers out of the capital was decimating the poor who were forced to remain. Reports of the situation in London had filtered through to Eyam, communicated to Reverend Mompesson by his friend and benefactor, Sir George Saville. Mompesson had gravely informed his parishioners of the devastating news only that Sunday; it was clear that the symptoms of the victims here in Eyam were identical to those described by chroniclers in the capital.

The horror of the situation intruded amongst the thorns and brambles of the berry bushes. Fewer baskets lay on the ground waiting to be filled, fewer children hopped and skipped around, showing off their purple tongues to anyone who cared to look. Conversation was muted and a new distance could be observed between each of the family groups as fear of the contagion kept friends apart. Every now and then a couple of the women would be amused by something that had been said or done and would laugh out loud, only to glance guiltily around and press their hands to their mouths in an effort to contain the offence. At other times, one would be overcome with grief and exhaustion and collapse onto the grass at her feet, weeping. Those close by abandoned their caution in the rush to comfort, righting an upturned basket and collecting spilt berries. In these actions, however, there was a hesitation, a reluctance to draw too close lest the hysteria be a sign of something more sinister.

Evening prayers in the small cottage were a highlight at the end of each day. The fire flickered in the grate and candlelight danced on the walls and ceiling, the door and windows closed against the darkness of night. Kitty would turn the pages of the family Bible, usually to one of the psalms or some comforting words spoken by Jesus. The Scriptures she read in her clear, young voice brought hope not only to her uncle and aunt who listened, but also to her own worried heart. Promises of the Shepherd at their side as they traversed this valley of the shadow of death, reassurance that death has lost its sting and the grave its power, courage to overcome all that was thrown their way as they trusted in His love. Uncle Robert concluded each reading with a prayer, firstly for his family which of course included Kitty, then he named each villager he knew to be in need or despair, asking for the comfort and presence of the Lord. Wrapped in the warmth of these prayers, Kitty wearily climbed the stairs and fell onto her awaiting bed – only to find herself wide awake and alert, all sleepiness gone, listening to the whispered conversation continuing below her.

'Ah 'tis a terrible thing, Robert dear. There's more fallen sick that I've heard of even today. And now t' whole Thorpe family has passed from it, even t' Thorpe seniors! First Thomas and young Mary, then only eleven days and they were all gone.' The anguish in Anne's voice was plain, even to Kitty lying upstairs. 'Did tha notice how affected Reverend Mompesson was? I've never liked him much, but this seems to be hitting him hard. More than I expected at any rate.'

'Aye,' Uncle Robert's deep, calm voice held its own sadness. 'Thomas Stanley was telling me t' other day that t' reverend has been visiting everyone. T' two of them have gone to some homes together, as though they see that fighting and disputing with each other at a time like this is more than anyone can bear.'

'I heard that too,' came Aunt Anne's gentle voice. 'Mrs Mompesson has also been seen visiting, taking baskets of eggs or oatcakes to t' families where there's illness. I did hear she doesn't go inside, just leaves t' basket on t' doorstep, but that's fair enough, having her own young ones to think of.'

At the warm mention of Catherine, Kitty smiled into her pillow. She was glad the reverend's wife was becoming better liked, especially by her aunt but also by the other women in the village. The previous Sunday, after Evensong, Catherine had approached Kitty, laying a gentle gloved hand on her arm. There was a look of concern on her face.

'How are you, Kitty my dear?' she asked quietly. 'This must be a dreadful shock for you, staying here so far away from your family at a time like this. I trust you are taking good care of yourself, or at least allowing your wonderful aunt to do so. You must keep your strength up, dearest, so you can remain healthy and helpful to us all here in your temporary home.' She paused. 'I hear you can read and write very prettily – is that right?'

Kitty, surprised that Mrs Mompesson knew that about her and wondering who she could have heard it from, nodded. 'Yes, ma'am.'

'Yes, I did think so and I told my husband as much the other day. I feel you could be very useful to us at the rectory if this present trial is set to continue much longer. I will have a word with your aunt and see if you can be released from your duties with her – after the harvest is complete, of course. Oh, and please call me Catherine, at least when we are alone together. George, why do you always have to pull your sister's hair like that? Bye, Kitty darling.' With a smile and a swat of her hand at her unrepentant son, she was gone.

Kitty was too surprised by the whole conversation to be able to find her manners and respond. Had Mrs Mompesson really asked if she would go and work for her and her husband? What would Pa think – her being in the home of one of the 'enemy', a supporter of the king and devotee of the new prayer book? The wound was deep and bitter that cut her father's heart after the death of his brother, Albert. Anyone on the side of the king was not on the side of her pa, that she was sure of. And what of Aunt Anne and Uncle Robert? Would they even consider it, much less let her go? More amazing still, had she also been told to call Mrs Mompesson, Catherine?

Kitty wondered if Mrs Mompesson had already spoken to Aunt Anne. She suspected not; she was sure something would have been mentioned by now if that were the case.

'Has tha heard some of t' cures that's being tried by everyone?' Kitty's uncle was speaking again, amusement lightening his tone. 'There's t' one with t' berries, that tha must boil and crush up, then add to vinegar or strong wine to drink before going out and about. That's supposed to prevent tha getting sick in t' first place. 'T might work, I suppose. But then there's t' remedy with t' pigeon. Tha's supposed to catch a pigeon and pluck t' feathers of poor thing's tail, then put t' exposed flesh on t' sore of t' patient. Eventually, that poor pigeon will give up and die, and then tha's supposed to find another pigeon and do it all again! No wonder t' woods have seemed quiet t' last few days – those what are left have all flown to Sheffield.' He laughed.

'Ah, don't be too harsh,' his sympathetic wife replied. 'Folk are desperate and frightened and there's no one in these parts to tell them what to do. T' physicians have too far to come and charge too much, tha knows that. I reckon we'll all try anything, even if it does sound daft.' Despite her words of admonishment she allowed herself a little giggle too.

'By the way,' she continued, 'talking of Mrs Mompesson, she stopped me t' other day when Kitty was busy somewhere else and asked how I'd feel about letting her go and work for them at t' parsonage. Once harvest is over,' she added hurriedly on seeing her hard-working husband's look of dismay. 'I think she feels our Kitty could be useful to t' reverend while everything is going on. Especially that she can read and write so well. What does tha think?'

Robert humphed and coughed before replying, 'Well, as I say, I'm liking t' man more over recent weeks than I have all t' rest of t' time he's been here. He's not so full of his fancy ways now people need him. I say we both have a bit of a think, ask t' Lord for wisdom. And ask Kitty what she wants to do.'

Anne got up with a yawn. 'Righto. Well, I'm away to my bed, Robert, I can hardly keep my eyes open. Let's hope I sleep better and have no more of those dreams tonight.'

Kitty listened as her aunt climbed the stairs, heard the creak of the bed in the next room, amazed that not only had Mrs Mompesson already spoken about her plans, but that both her aunt and uncle would at least consider them. She slid to her knees, praying fervently that God would tell them she should go, and also pleading for a better night's sleep for her aunt who, she was sorry to learn, was also struggling with broken nights.

Chinese Knot outline

Over the next few days, Kitty hardly had a moment alone with her aunt or uncle. They had started collecting in the oats from the field on the other side of the village and were fully engaged with that task. First, the heads had to be scythed from the top of the stalks and gathered up, then be loaded on the cart for transporting back to the house. There they would be laid out on big sheets in the shelter behind the house and left to dry. The straw that remained also needed to be cut and gathered into sheaves ready to be used as winter fodder for the sheep, goats and dairy cow they owned. Once started, the job had to be finished quickly before any change in the weather damaged the vulnerable grain heads while they were still out in the open. The dried grain would later be taken to the watermill for separating and to be ground into flour the women used in cooking and baking. Of course, the Earl of Devonshire always took his tithe as payment for allowing them to farm in the first place and for the use of his mill.

Uncle Robert was working together with a few other men from the village, neighbours he knew well from their hours spent together underground. Once his field was cleared and stored away, they would all move on to another field to start the process again. The women, meanwhile, were fully occupied with providing food and drink to the workers in the field, carrying baskets of bread and cheese, oatcakes and ale from one centre of activity to another. On their return home, great pots of steaming fruit, sugar and water boiled over their fires as they transformed the afternoons of berry picking into sealed earthen jars of preserves. Apples, pears and berries all needed to be safely stored away.

Kitty had been tasked with caring for Mary and Sarah, releasing her aunt to the full-time work of harvesting. She continued to teach Mary her alphabet, and she helped the nearly-walking Sarah to stand and fumble her way around the small cottage. When the weather was fine, she would take the girls to watch the men in the fields, checking any bushes they passed for berries that might have been missed on their last outing.

So full were the days that little was spoken about the plague and the families it continued to ravage. By mid-October, Sarah Syddall's younger brother, Richard, had died, followed just a few days later by their father, John, and eldest sister, Ellen. That had been a dreadful funeral, Kitty recalled. Few villagers attended the funerals of the deceased anymore for fear of being infected by the disease themselves, but many hovered outside, keeping their distance while wishing to show their respect. For some reason, the service for the Syddall family had been different.

Even though the harvest was in full swing, almost every villager had made it to the church. Some remained outside, waiting to return to the fields and kitchens as soon as was decent, but several took their place in the pews. They tried as far as possible to sit in their own family groups rather than mixing with one another. Several of the women held posies of dried flowers wrapped in linen cloths to their faces, both to mask the sickly smell of death which seemed to have begun to seep into the very stones of the village and to ward off the evil illness itself.

Most were convinced this was a plague from God, punishment for the hitherto unseen sins of those who had been struck down. With the death of members of the Syddall family, the mood was different. They were known to be a generous, God-fearing family. They were liked by all, as the number who had arrived for the funeral attested. John had been a miner with Uncle Robert, a strong dependable man who had pulled his friend from danger underground on more than one occasion. In fact, Uncle Robert frequently mentioned the near misses he'd had and how, if it weren't for John, he might not be with them now.

Aunt Anne always hated the reminder. She and Betsy, John's wife, were the closest of friends. They were usually in and out of each other's gardens and kitchens, collecting vegetables or stirring pots while they chatted the hours away. The children too, were welcome in either home, loved and admonished alike by both women.

It was for this reason that Kitty had gone to the funeral. She had hardly known John, in fact, was slightly afraid of him when she had met him – he was so loud and large. His florid face would light up in amusement and he would throw his head back, mouth wide open, as his unconstrained laughter bellowed around the room. Kitty had, of course, met Betsy on many occasions, either in one of their homes or out in the fields. She hadn't joined in her aunt's conversations with her friend much, preferring instead the daughter Sarah's company as they were closer in age. The last time she had seen them was at the mine when they joined the other women in their pity for Mrs Hadfield and her visiting fleas. Kitty and Sarah had been sitting to one side, playing with the younger children. Sarah was clever and observant, able to teach Kitty the names of birds and flowers. She was also funny, able to mimic those around her or pull silly faces when everyone was becoming too serious.

When Kitty had heard that Sarah was sick, that day out in the fields, she had felt dizzy and faint. Back at the cottage, she had run up to the safety of her room. Tears blurring her vision as she stumbled toward the bed, she had banged her head hard on a protruding roof beam. Collapsing into her pillow and pulling the blanket over her head, she had sobbed into the evening. How could God be so uncaring as to take Sarah when she was just on the edge of life? What had she done to deserve to be on fire with fever, her bones aching, her head exploding with pain?

Aunt Anne had left her niece alone for a while, but then, full of tears herself, came and sat on the edge of Kitty's bed. She stroked Kitty's back just as she did when calming her own Sarah into sleep.

'Why?' snuffled Kitty, her cap askew, her hair a bird's nest tangle. Shoulders heaving and nose running, she implored her aunt for the answer no one could give.

'Ah, Kitty luv, I don't know. Why was little Edward t' first to go after Mr Viccars himself? Or Mary, a few days later? We don't know t' reasons for these things. But I know that God isn't mean like some are saying He is. I reckon His heart is breaking just as much as ours. So now, our Kitty, sit up and wipe tha face clean. Dear Betsy will need our prayers and practical helps, as does everyone in Eyam, more than ever before.' She reached over to kiss Kitty tenderly on her damp forehead before returning to her chores downstairs.

That had been less than three weeks ago. Since then, Sarah had passed away and Kitty had lost her only real friend in Eyam. She had taken her aunt's words to heart, however, and had found a new urgency to her prayers each night, imploring the Lord to help and heal. Sarah's death had affected her, but not as badly as the initial news of her illness. In the ensuing days she had helped Aunt Anne take food and other supplies to the Syddall household, as well as others they knew who were in need.

Now, sitting behind Mrs Syddall, Kitty looked on with concern. Her aunt's friend looked flushed and weak; she seemed to barely have any strength left, worn out from the trial of recent weeks. She had nursed her family through every hour of the day, barely leaving them to take some rest herself. Now she was thin and bony, her smart Sunday dress hanging from her shoulders like an old, discarded rag. Every now and then she let out a low moan, an animal in mortal agony, and rocked slowly to and fro. Kitty averted her gaze, feeling she was intruding in a private space she couldn't begin to comprehend.

A few days later, Kitty found Aunt Anne out by the chickens, the bowl of feed tipping out of her hand as she stared vacantly ahead, the again-pouring rain soaking her through and running in rivulets at her feet.

'Aunt Anne, whatever's t' matter?' Kitty cried, running to her aunt's side and taking the chicken feed from her dangling hand. With a feeling of dread, she felt she already knew the answer. 'Who is it? Not Mrs Syddall?'

As though waking from a deep sleep, unsure of her surroundings, Aunt Anne slowly turned her head towards the muffled voice. 'No. Lizzy. Lizzy Thorpe. Gone.'

Kitty dropped the bowl onto the ground, deciding the chickens would have to wait, and led her aunt back to the house. She struggled not to slip as she crossed the muddy yard, her aunt's listless arm heavy across her shoulders. The young woman pushed open the door with her hip, calling for Mary as she did so. 'Mary, lass, come here. I need rags and some water to boil up for tha ma. No, don't cry, she's fine, just got all wet in t' rain. But tha can be a big girl and help get her dry.'

A wide-eyed Mary scuttled off to fetch all that was needed, while Kitty helped Aunt Anne into the chair closest to the fire and gave the embers a poke to cajole them back to life and warmth. Throwing on a heavy log, she turned to take the cloths from Mary. 'Now, pop upstairs, there's a good lass, and check on Sarah. I think she's still sleeping, but just to be sure.' Kitty needed Mary out of the way for a moment, just while her mother recovered and regained something of her normal composure.

With shaking hands, Aunt Anne managed to hold the cup of warm ale Kitty offered her. Tears poured down her cheeks as she stared blankly at the flames burning orange in the grate.

'I thought He was going to make her well, tha knows. I'd been praying so much. We're friends since Mary's age. Grew up together. It was always me and t' two Elizabeths – Betsy and Lizzy. I was in t' middle, age-wise. Oh, Lizzy, what will I do without thee?' There were no words sufficient to ease the pain, so Kitty remained silent, kneeling at her aunt's feet.

Eventually, Uncle Robert came and relieved her of her role as chief comforter. By then the rain had eased to a soft drizzle, so Kitty got up and found shawls for herself and Mary, and took the child outside. They fed the now furious chickens, hunted half-heartedly for a few eggs, then wandered down the lane. Mary, not understanding what had happened, was full of four-year-old fun, jumping in puddles and dropping small sticks in at the edge of the river to watch them whoosh and toss out of view. On their return, Kitty was pleased to see that Thomas Stanley had arrived to visit; he sat opposite Anne, praying quietly.

No one is going to be left free from the scars of this disease, Kitty thought. It isn't just the boils and blisters that will leave their mark.

Aunt Anne slowly recovered from the acute distress of the loss of her friend, but Kitty often found her paused in a task of washing or chopping, her hands hanging loosely at her side. Her eyes would be unfocused, for that moment not present in the cottage but somewhere else entirely – perhaps wishing she had been at her friend's bedside for those last hours, or remembering an incident from their shared childhood. At those times Kitty would gently move her aunt to one side, leading her to a nearby stool, then taking over and completing the forgotten task quietly and efficiently.

Mary, young though she was, took on a few jobs of her own. Each morning she took out the bowl of scraps for the chickens and scattered the contents on the ground at her feet. She had taken to giving each of them names, something which concerned Kitty slightly, given that they would at some point be eating these new 'friends' for supper. Mary would squat down on her fat little legs and chat away seriously to each chicken in turn, telling them about the weather, or her mother, or even the plague with its unseen ghosts and ghouls. Acting out the latter, with much flapping of arms and wailing and moaning, she chased the creatures up and down the yard until they retreated back into their coop, traumatised. Kitty couldn't help but stop what she was doing and watch the display with a mixture of amusement and anxiety – amusement that a child could take something so disconcerting and strange and turn it into a delightful game, and anxiety at how much her young cousin had already observed and incorporated into her playtime.

The days grew shorter and colder as October continued. By the end of the month, Elizabeth Thorpe's son Thomas had followed his parents into the grave, leaving a teenage Robert to become the head of a household which even his grandparents had now departed. Under his care were Alice, nearly a young woman, and their younger brother William. The two older siblings could often be seen with their sheep out in the fields, or down by the mill trying to get their oats ground. Always alone, shunned by the active fear of those who had previously been their close friends, they seemed to be surviving on berries gleaned from the bushes, or a pigeon or two they had managed to capture in the woods. They were gaunt and dirty, matted hair falling onto their burdened shoulders, their clothes torn rags hanging from their skeletal frames. Rumours spread about the three of them – surely they were not for this life much longer; they would soon be reunited with the rest of their family.

Aunt Anne carried baskets laden with milk and eggs and portions of broth or pie to their gate every day. Often she returned home with the previous day's basket not even having been taken into the cottage, much less any of its contents consumed. Uncle Robert grew exasperated, imploring her to stop exhausting herself by taking the daily walk into the village and home again, all for no apparent purpose. But she was determined. She would show love and care to the poor mites as long as there was breath in her lungs, she would declare defiantly, ducking away from the hand that tried to touch her arm or caress her cheek.

At the end of October, on the eve of All Hallows, Uncle Robert returned from the fields with the news that Reverend Mompesson had called for the entire village to attend the following morning's All Hallows service at St Lawrence's. Although the more religious amongst them – or perhaps the more politically motivated, believed Uncle Robert – would be attending anyway, this was a special request of everybody. Even Thomas Stanley had been asked to attend, although no one expected him to accept the invitation. The reverend wanted to bring everyone together in a united cry for mercy from heaven, beseeching the Lord to bring this disaster to an end.

It seemed to Kitty that both her uncle and her aunt approved of the idea, agreeing that now was the time for the people of Eyam to come together perhaps more than they ever had before.

November 1665

The morning of 1 November 1665 saw the Fox family leave their cottage to join the rest of the community in the cold of St Lawrence's, even though it was Wednesday. Candles adorned the stone pillars and windowsills, doing their best to dispel the morning's gloom. Rain had returned to the moors and the parishioners sat in the discomfort of their damp clothes and wet hair waiting for the vicar to start the service. Furtive glances were cast around the church as quick registers were taken – who wasn't here today who had been just the other day? Who had fallen sick? Who was at home nursing another unfortunate member of an afflicted family? Eventually, Reverend Mompesson emerged from his vestry and took his place at the front of the church. His family – Catherine, George and Elizabeth – were already seated in their pew, loving support for her husband showing in Catherine's gentle smile.

'Good morning to you all.' He seemed to Kitty less stern than on other mornings, at other services. His voice remained low and measured rather than the loud, almost aggressive tone she was used to. 'Today we sit as a family, sharing in the sufferings of our brothers and sisters. We remember those who have already passed from this earth. Our sympathies and prayers are held out to those who are left behind, mourning the loss of their loved ones. And we remain steadfast and vigilant in our care of those who are, even now, falling prey to this deadly pestilence.' He paused, gazing around the building, allowing his words to sink in. 'And it is for this purpose we meet this morning – to come together in earnest entreaty to our Lord that He would stay His hand and remove this punishment from us. If punishment it truly is,' he added so quietly that Kitty barely heard the last words. The reverend seemed lost in thought, distracted and unseeing.

Realising an expectant hush had fallen on his bemused congregation, and that his wife was looking at him with some concern

showing in her unblinking gaze, Reverend Mompesson gave a cough and turned the pages of the book propped up on the lectern in front of him.

'Let us pray the special prayer written for times such as these.' Kitty and those around her fell onto their knees, bowing low, with their hands to their foreheads. Kitty could feel the cold stone of the floor through her skirts and shuffled, trying to ease the discomfort. Aunt Anne was beside her, clutching her rag of a handkerchief to her mouth in an attempt to smother the rising grief. Uncle Robert held a sleeping Sarah in his arms. Mary, on her other side, had her palms pressed together, fingers reaching to the roof in a look of pure angelic innocence. Kitty chuckled at the difference between appearance and reality, especially after an escapade just that morning with a cup of milk and said angel at her side. Closing her eyes quickly lest she have a fit of entirely inappropriate giggles, Kitty concentrated on the words Reverend Mompesson was now reading, his voice restored to its usual deep, well-projected strength.

'In the time of any common Plague or Sickness: Almighty God, who in thy wrath did send a plague upon thine own people in the wilderness, for their obstinate rebellion against Moses and Aaron; and also, in the time of king David, didst slay with the plague of Pestilence threescore and ten thousand, and yet remembering thy mercy didst save the rest; Have pity upon us miserable sinners, who now are visited with great sickness and mortality; that like as thou didst then accept of an atonement, and didst command the destroying Angel to cease from punishing, so it may now please thee to withdraw from us this plague and grievous sickness; through Jesus Christ our Lord. Amen.'

Kitty's 'Amen' was the most heartfelt she had ever prayed. There was a creaking of pews and a shuffling of feet as everyone rose for the next portion of the service, a reading from the Bible. Somewhere near the back a woken child wailed in surprise and cross indignation and was quickly shushed by his vigilant parents.

Reverend Mompesson waited until everyone was settled and paying attention. 'Let us read the first lesson. The Book of Wisdom, chapter three.' He cleared his throat. 'But the souls of the righteous are in the hand of God, and there shall no torment touch them. In the sight of the unwise, they seemed to die: and their departure is taken for misery, and their going from us to be utter destruction: but they are in peace. For though they be punished in the sight of men, yet is their hope full of immortality. And having been a little chastised, they shall be greatly rewarded: for God proved them, and found them worthy for himself. As gold in the furnace hath he tried them, and received them as a burnt offering.'

William looked around at his flock, observing the strain written in every pink-rimmed eye and gaunt cheek, every protective father and anxious mother. He noticed the empty pews and the missing families, knew the harrowing tales behind each vacant seat. How he wished for the right words to comfort, to reassure. It had struck him, during his preparation for this morning's service, that the prescribed passage of Scripture for the day could have been written for exactly this moment.

'Dearly beloved. We do indeed mourn the passing of our fellows, and perhaps even question the reason for the distress they have so recently endured.' As a man trained by the best theologians during his time at Cambridge, William had always held to the belief that a plague was God's punishment of sinners for their unrepentant sins; the Bible seemed clear on that. And yet now an uncomfortable doubt had crept in. As early as the funeral for little Edward Cooper, William had been crying out to God, searching the Scriptures and other books in an attempt to understand. He dreaded that he might be committing some sin himself, might be wandering from a truth he had embraced since a young age into a misguided act of heresy. But the disfigured face of an innocent child, swollen and marked beyond recognition, had broken his father-heart. *Surely, if God is really Our Father, He wouldn't want this for His children any more than I want anything like that to touch my own George or Elizabeth,* he'd contemplated alone in the dark of the night.

'Let us, however, be comforted by these words: where they now are, no torment shall touch them. They are free of the pain that wracked their bodies in their last hours, free of the fever and this foul plague. Indeed, they now rest in the arms of peace.'

The congregation sat silent as William concluded his homily. He allowed them a moment of pause, giving them the opportunity to comfort and be comforted. There were a few coughs and sniffs, and a whispered conversation in the back row before he completed the rest of the service. Finally, he stretched out his arms, the sleeves of his cassock hanging like wings. Everyone stood to their feet, ready to be dismissed.

'The grace of our Lord Jesus Christ, and the love of God, and the fellowship of the Holy Ghost, be with us all evermore. Amen.'

'Amen,' came the unified response.

Reverend Mompesson strode down the aisle and flung open the big wooden doors, ushering in a blast of freezing November air. Families gathered their children and their belongings, stuffing hands into woollen mittens and wrapping shawls around their shoulders. They took their turn in the line to leave the church, each shaking hands with their rector, thanking him for a special service. This was a marked contrast to their interaction with him only a few weeks before.

The reverend knew the villagers were angry with him for taking the place of their beloved Thomas Stanley; they'd also made it clear that they thought him stuck-up and aristocratic. 'Not from round here,' he'd heard on more than one occasion. As the congregation now made their way out into the rain-drenched churchyard, he heard in the warmth of the voices and the firmness of their handshakes an increased acceptance of his presence in their lives.

The plague had played its part in their change of attitude, he was sure, but he also knew he owed much to his wife, Catherine. He glanced over at her now, the children standing patiently at her side while she spoke to some young woman. He thought he recognised her as the niece of the family who lived halfway up Water Lane – the Foxes he thought they were called. She was the one Catherine had spoken to him about, urging him to take her on to help him with some of the duties of the parish now that there was so much more to do. She looked decent enough, he thought, and she certainly had an intelligent-looking brow. Her dark hair was gathered neatly in the cap she wore and the blush of delight on her cheeks as Catherine regaled her with some story or other brightened her otherwise pale countenance. Now that he came to think of it, wasn't her name also Catherine?

While William's eyes and thoughts wandered, a farmer from the other side of the village had asked him a question and was waiting for an answer. Something about a change in the weather, was it? William returned his focus to the man whose rough, weathered hand still squeezed his own more delicate one, and attempted to forecast when the rain would stop.

It didn't stop for the whole of that day, nor the next day, nor the next after that. The traditional service and festivities held around Guy Fawkes Day were muted. No one felt much like celebrating; children grew fractious and farmers fretful. There was limited time left to complete all the preparations necessary for winter, always a long and bitter season here in the middle of the moors. The ground would become hard with frost, a biting wind a constant companion as it billowed and blew from the great ridge to the north of them.

The advance of the contagion, while not completely stopped, did significantly slow. A teenager, Hugh Stubbs, fell victim to its deathly hold even as parishioners left the churchyard that Wednesday morning, but mercifully only four other people died that month – two of them were Hugh's parents.

Winter 1665 – 6

As winter took hold, Uncle Robert moved the sheep to other fields where it was easier for the fodder – already collected in October – to be taken. Patch seemed to relish the exercise, nudging and persuading the animals on their way each morning and back again in the afternoon. He sank low on his haunches as he prepared to spring if any should try to wander off in the wrong direction. Darting from one side to the other, he corralled the flock into a single unit of bleating moving white fleece. Kitty would often go with her uncle and his dog, running ahead to open gates.

The flowers in the dry-stone walls they passed along the way had all withered with frost, leaving only clumps of hardy heather and gorse. Skeletal trees loomed over them, giants in the mist reaching out to scrape Kitty's hair and face as she passed. Drips of water falling from their branches solidified into icicles as December progressed, colder than all but the village elders could remember. Redwings gathered in the now harvested fields, gleaning what they could from whatever had been dropped and left behind.

When it wasn't pouring with rain with the wind howling around, Kitty loved these excursions almost as much as Patch. A companionable silence existed between her and Uncle Robert – he absorbed with the task at hand, she delighting in the country surroundings, so different to those of a winter city. There, the snow and ice turned to a dirty slush within minutes of settling in the street; here the frost shone like diamonds throughout the day and the snow lay invitingly thick and untouched.

This outing through the winter wonderland was disturbed only by the sight of the shut-up cottages in the village on their return from the fields. Unlit windows gazed vacantly at them as they passed, piles of leaves blown high against their sills. Chimneys stood to attention devoid of any curl of smoke, there being no lit hearth in their grates.

On one occasion, Kitty noticed three more houses not yet abandoned but firmly closed and avoided. Hannah Rowland, a teenage friend of Hugh Stubbs, had died just a few days after him. The family had retreated to the isolation of their small cottage in the hope that the disease could be brought under control, but Kitty had heard just a few days earlier that Hannah's younger sister had taken ill and subsequently died. Her brother Abel was now said to be displaying worrying signs of also being infected.

Another day, flickering candles in the windows of the Rowbotham home indicated something of the torment taking place there as well. Kitty could make out the figure of Mrs Rowbotham as she sat slumped in a chair in the upstairs window. She held vigil over her sick husband and second son, allowing herself barely any time to grieve the death of her youngest, Johnny. Kitty turned away, not wanting Mrs Rowbotham to see her and think she was intruding on her sorrow.

The next cottage along was the most recently deserted. Kitty and Uncle Robert paused for a moment, remembering the young Mr and Mrs Rowe. It had only been a few weeks ago that they had come through to church with their new baby all wrapped in soft, knitted blankets. They had shown him off to any who wanted a peek, so proud and full of love were they for the bundle they carried. Their joy had been short-lived. Before he could even be christened in the great stone font at the back of St Lawrence's, he had drawn his last painful breath. Father and mother, their own bodies betraying them with the heat of fever, had called for Reverend Mompesson in desperation. Racked with guilt for having taken their baby out and so exposing him to illness, they were terrified lest he be damned for eternity due to their stupidity. They begged the rector to perform the christening service at home before it was too late. William had stood cradling the dying child in his arms while praying for his acceptance into God's everlasting Kingdom. Moments later, the child was cradled in Another's arms. Those watching from outside heard the wail of the child's mother, the low moan of the father; they watched as a pale and haggard Reverend Mompesson stumbled back out into the daylight. Mrs Rowe died the following morning, her husband just a few days later.

'Tragic, Kitty, there's no other word.' Uncle Robert spoke quietly. 'Let's be getting home, lass. Tha's aunt will be wondering where we've got to; she'll be sending Mary out to look for us if we don't get back soon.'

Chinese Knot outline

Christmas finally arrived. The cottage was filled with the mouth-watering smell of roasting meat. As she got everything ready for their feast, Anne sang softly to herself. She always enjoyed singing, especially some of the psalms of adoration that Thomas Stanley had introduced to them during his time as leader of St Lawrence's. She had been dismayed when the new incumbent, Reverend Mompesson, arrived and disbanded the small choir which a few of them had formed.

Mary and Kitty banged in through the door, dispelling the peace and bringing a great draught of freezing air with them.

'Clogs off,' commanded Aunt Anne. She had provided Kitty with a pair of the heavy outer shoes they all wore over their indoor slippers – far more practical than the silly boots she had arrived in. 'Does tha know how long I've spent making t' place nice?' Despite her gruff words Anne's tone betrayed the good humour she was in, much to Kitty's pleasure. She hadn't heard her usually cheerful aunt sounding so well for far too long; the difference today was a relief.

Seated around the big wooden table, Sarah banging her fists in demands for more and Patch at her feet waiting to catch the inevitable scraps that fell to the floor, Kitty rested her chin in her hands and breathed a contented sigh.

'Is tha alright, luv?' asked an immediately concerned aunt. 'Is tha missing everyone at home?'

'Oh no, not at all! Far from 't. This has been t' best day ever,' Kitty smiled. Lifting her head and reaching over to where Mary was focused on her carrots, she pulled a lock of hair that had fallen from behind the little girl's ear. 'And it's about to get better. Let's play!' The howl of surprise from Mary at the indignity of having her hair tugged so unexpectedly immediately gave way to a loud clapping of hands and heartfelt: 'Yes, let's!'

Scraping back her chair, she moved away from the table and then skipped to Kitty's side. 'What shall we play?'

From her lap, Kitty took a long scrap of fabric she had hidden from Mary. She wrapped it around Mary's head, with admonishments of 'Stop squirming!' until she could be sure that Mary couldn't see anything. Taking hold of Mary's shoulders, she gently twirled her around two or three times.

'Now,' she said to the confused Mary, 'I am going to move to another chair and when I say "ready", tha has to come and find me. Tha can't see anything, can thee?'

'No, it's all dark.'

Kitty moved quietly over to where Mary had been sitting just moments earlier. Sarah continued to bang her hands on the table, and Aunt Anne and Uncle Robert watched in amusement. 'Ready!'

Mary set off in search of her cousin, only to find her dizzied legs not responding at all how she had expected. She tripped and stumbled, arms stretched far out in front as she tried to feel her way towards where she could hear Kitty giggling. With much encouragement and directions from her parents, her hands finally connected with Kitty's face. The older girl laughed loudly, grabbed her cousin and pulled her close for a big wet kiss on the cheek.

Mary ripped off the makeshift blindfold and tried to wind it around her cousin's head. 'Your turn!' Gleefully she spun Kitty round and round before hopping off her chair. With cries of, 'Can't catch me!' she kept just out of Kitty's reach.

Before long everyone was persuaded to play, even Uncle Robert and baby Sarah – held aloft by her mother for safety. The day finally drew to a close, and just before it got dark outside Uncle Robert went out to check on the sheep and chickens. Aunt Anne took the younger girls up to bed, Mary protesting despite being so tired she could barely stand. Kitty poked the fire back to life and sat watching the flames dance and coil up the chimney. It had been a wonderful day, full of fun and laughter.

The following morning, yawning and rubbing the sleep from her eyes, Kitty plodded down the stairs. Christmas over, it was time for her to resume her daily duties. Although there were several hours until sunrise, and the stream outside would be frigid, water still need to be collected. She was surprised to find the fire already blazing, her aunt and uncle sitting on either side of the hearth. Had they not been to bed at all? They turned at the sound of her approach. Uncle Robert's eyes twinkled. Aunt Anne was smiling broadly.

'Morning, lass,' she said. 'I see my sister doesn't do things how we did when we were growing up then?'

Kitty had no idea what she was talking about. She mutely shook her head. *Am I still asleep and dreaming?*

'Tis t' day after Christmas – when we give each other a gift.'

Behind her, there was a sudden clatter as Mary flung herself down the stairs. 'Presents! Where's mine, Ma?'

Aunt Anne laughed as she pulled her daughter towards her, wrapping her in the warmth of her arms. 'Tha'll catch tha death, dressed like that,' she admonished. There was an awkward silence as she realised what she had said. It was a common enough phrase in normal times, but these were not normal times. Kitty looked at her in dismay; please would her aunt not burst into tears again. The day before her mood had been so happy that Kitty was sure her aunt had turned a corner in her grief. She held her breath, waiting.

'Silly me.' Two pink spots flushed Anne's cheeks as she struggled to regain her composure.

'So, where's t' boxes, young miss?' Uncle Robert tugged one of Mary's ears, breaking the tension. 'Tha knows how it works – tha needs to look. Come now, let's help Kitty.' Mary hopped off her mother's lap and ran to Kitty's side, oblivious to the awkwardness of the moment. Aunt Anne smiled gratefully at her husband who gently squeezed her shoulder in sympathetic response.

The next few minutes were taken up with a hunt throughout the small cottage for the gifts that had been hidden for all three girls. Sarah, woken by the squealing and banging about, howled a protest at being left out; Anne hurried up the stairs to fetch her.

'Thank thee, Aunt, for t' beautiful shawl.' Kitty held aloft a delicately knitted shawl made of soft wool. She wrapped it around her shoulders, hugging it tight.

'Tis a pleasure, child. I couldn't bear t' think how cold tha's going to be over t' winter with just that old cloak tha brought from home!' Anne smiled, pleased that her hard work was so well received. She had sat up late on many nights making sure it would be a surprise for her niece. Kitty flung her arms around Anne and Sarah in a grateful embrace.

'Water. I must go fetch t' water...' Kitty pulled away from Aunt Anne. Turning quickly so no one would see the tears which were suddenly glistening on her lashes, she pushed open the door. 'Back in a sec!' Overcome with a turmoil of emotions – happiness at being here, homesickness for those left behind, surprise at the beauty of the gift – Kitty was glad for the rush of icy air and flurry of snowflakes in her face.

Chinese Knot outline

After the excitement and joy of Christmas, life settled back to its normal winter routine. The cold intensified, snow falling thick and heavy on the moors and in the streets of Eyam. Children cried as chilblains bloomed on their fingers and toes, the constant change of temperature from outside to in and back out again exacerbating the inflammation. Time slowed to a tedious progression of short days and long nights. The windows rattled and bitter draughts blew through every crack in the roof above Kitty's bed.

Kitty grew bored with the tedious monotony of the winter months. At first she had relished the fairy tale that was the countryside in winter, but now the monochrome palette of gun metal skies, glistening white snow and frost, and the stark outlines of silhouetted trees had lost much of their appeal. Sheep huddled together around clumps of fodder, their white fleeces and faces blending into the background. Jackdaws, crows and redwings scavenged in hopping, squabbling groups. Even the deep green holly bushes were no longer studded with the bright red berries that had hung like jewels from every branch.

The relentless cold pinched her cheeks and chapped her fingers, and her toes ached from being squashed despite the clogs she wore. When the sun's rays did manage to peep over the distant hills long enough to be felt, the melting snow made conditions underfoot treacherous. Kitty still had grazed palms and a bruised knee from slipping on a patch of ice in the lane – a puddle she hadn't seen hidden under a layer of sun-blushed snow. How she wished for the return of spring, its promise of new life blossoming as clusters of snowdrops and bluebells pushed their determined way to the surface.

She wished too for the return to a normal working day that helped occupy the hours and her thoughts. Kitty had come to dread the long periods of inactivity sitting beside the fire with her happily domesticated aunt. Fumbling with needle and thread or wheel and wool, the young woman was finding it increasingly difficult to remember why she had come to Eyam in the first place. She could have been helping her own mother, rather than Mary and Sarah's. She could have been reading to her pa, who would correct and help her when she found a new word that she didn't know, rather than to Uncle Robert who just nodded encouragingly but unhelpfully whenever she paused.

In those moments of tedium and irritation, even her little sister, Joan, was remembered as being more well-behaved, more angelic than Kitty's cousin could ever be, and she was sure Oliver too was the quietest, happiest baby she had ever known. And John – dear, patient, ambitious John. Why couldn't she have stayed at home to encourage him as he worked his way as an apprentice? She would have waited patiently for him to complete his training, wouldn't have entreated him to give it all up and marry her instead. At that point in her musings, Kitty would stop and chuckle to herself. She knew she was no saint, and patient waiting had never been one of her stronger virtues.

She did miss the vibrancy of her first months spent with her aunt and uncle though. Now, the mine was silent, the drip of slowly melting water the only echo through its deserted chambers. No men's voices rang and sang as they hammered out the precious seams of lead. Above ground, no women worked side by side in the field, no children played or danced. Meetings between friends were infrequent. Wrapping up in layer upon layer of warm woollen shawls and knitted caps was so cumbersome it was impossible to be comfortable.

The only high point of each dreary week was Sunday, when all would ready themselves for the outing to St Lawrence's. There at least there would be conversation and connection, an opportunity to hear news of others. Before the service began the men gathered outside under the trees, stamping their feet and clapping their hands as they tried to stay warm. The women and children hustled inside where, although not much warmer, there was at least somewhere to sit while they gossiped.

The gossip which passed between them that winter was wonder-
fully unremarkable. Since December, only two families – the Wilsons
and the Blackwells – had become newly infected with the dread disease that had so dominated everyone's conversation just a couple of
months previously. If the plague was mentioned at all, it was with
words of relief and gratitude that it seemed to have left them alone.

'Tha knows, it was t' prayer of t' reverend that has made all t'
difference,' one would start.

'For certain,' another would reply. 'I'm so glad he came to us after
all. We wouldn't have survived otherwise.'

'Well, I'm not so sure,' a third would respond. 'Mr Stanley would
have prayed too!'

'But not with so much learning,' countered the first to speak.
'Maybe 'tis right that t' whole country is using the same book every
Sunday.'

The others would nod in general agreement as the conversation
burbled on to the next thing. 'T' chickens aren't laying well in this
weather...'

After a while, the men would all troop in through the great doors,
find their families and hustle them to their pews. Soon afterwards,
Reverend Mompesson would appear from his vestry to read the day's
service with great authority and presence, in spite of his cold red nose.

Nothing more had been said to Kitty about the possibility of going
to work for the Mompessons. She wondered if that would still happen
when the weather warmed up, or if they had only thought they might
need her help during the crisis at the end of the previous year. She
watched Mrs Mompesson, composed and serene despite the chill.
Kitty liked the idea of helping at the rectory; it would be a pleasant
change from the domestic chores and backbreaking farm labour her
aunt gave her to do. However, she was mindful that the Mompessons

were only likely to call for her assistance if their workload stretched them beyond their own capacity, and she knew that would only be if the plague resurfaced in Eyam. She fervently hoped it would not.

Spring 1666

S pring delayed its awakening from hibernation longer than every-one was accustomed to. February and March continued cold and barren, with snow lying thick and untouched on all the hills surrounding the village. Towards the end of March, the sun stirred itself into action and put on a display worthy of an early summer's day. Kitty had woken early, the brightness of the light waking her from a deep and restful sleep. She could hear Aunt Anne moving around below her, although the young girls slept on oblivious to the dawn of a glorious day.

Kitty threw back the covers and moved straight over to the window. The air danced and sparkled as the sun caught every dust mote and diamond drip of melting snow and ice. Judging by the big tree out in the lane, Kitty knew a stiff breeze was blowing – the tree's topmost branches waving ecstatically in delight at a bright spring morning. A wood pigeon cooed – one of Kitty's favourite summer sounds – and the cat stretched on the wall below her. A surge of happy energy sent Kitty tearing downstairs and almost into disaster as her aunt crossed the small living space, laden with breakfast things.

'Careful, lass, where's tha going in such a hurry?' Anne remon-strated. 'It's early still, tha doesn't need to be racing and running already.'

Kitty just managed to stop herself from colliding with Aunt Anne before striding towards the door. 'But it's such a beautiful morning!' she sang. With that she was gone, leaving a smiling Aunt Anne shaking her head at the girl's retreating figure.

'I'm glad to see thee full of life again, my luv,' she called after her rapidly disappearing niece. Anne had become worried about Kitty as the winter had persisted. Her sombre mood and restless frustration hadn't escaped Anne's notice, but she had felt powerless to help in any way. The beauty of the morning and Kitty's lively exuberance caused a new hope to bubble up within her. Singing happily, she returned to preparing breakfast for everyone.

For her part, Kitty ran on through the gate and out into the lane. She breathed in the sweet green smell of new shoots and warm earth. Moving on past the dancing tree and along the pathway towards the river, she marvelled as she noticed tiny flowers protruding from the retreating snow. How had she not seen them earlier, she wondered. And how had they managed to grow despite the blanket of white that trapped them underground?

Delicate white snow drops drooped on slender, deep green stems. A sprinkling of blue dusted the dips and hollows where she had seen nothing but decay for weeks. Kitty chastised herself for not having made the effort to come into the woods more recently so she could observe the transformation of the landscape as it happened. *But then*, she thought, *it wouldn't be nearly so magical if I'd seen it bit by bit.* This way, the impression of sudden resurrection life was beautifully painted in her memory.

There was more excitement to come. That afternoon, Uncle Robert returned breathless from a longer than expected walk into the village.

'There's going to be a bonfire!' he bellowed, startling his family. 'T' biggest there's ever been. Up on t' hill, behind t' church. Bigger even than for Guy Fawkes.' Kitty remembered the disappointment of that missed event, celebrating the downfall of Fawkes' plot to blow up the Houses of Parliament. Too many families were held captive by the then raging plague for it to be acceptable in November. But this? This sounded even better.

Throughout the rest of the week groups of children could be seen searching all across the village for material for the New Year bonfire. They disappeared into the woods, emerging soon afterwards laden with branches and sticks. These were all dragged to the site of the celebration where the men were building a pile that seemed, to the children's young eyes, to reach the sky.

New Year's Eve finally arrived. Everyone met at the church, where Reverend Mompesson led a heartfelt prayer of thanks. Although the words were not his own, being those contained within the pages of the official prayer book, William's voice rose with the conviction of one certain of the saving power of his God. The people cheered in unison, then, with lit torches held high, they proceeded out to the site for the bonfire. Children ran on ahead, mothers following behind with baskets laden with apples and cakes and jugs of ale for the menfolk.

Watched by every family in Eyam, Uncle Robert stepped forward and lay his torch at the base of the great pile of wood. The dry grass and leaves soon caught and, with a surge of hot air, the flames took. Sparks leapt upwards accompanied by the oohs and aahs of the assembled villagers. Clouds of smoke from some of the damp branches suddenly chased some of the crowd from one side of the fire to the other, its acrid smell causing eyes to water and throats to constrict.

Someone took out a fiddle and began to play, everyone clapping and dancing in time to the jaunty melodies. It was the happiest time Kitty had known since her arrival. It seemed the whole village was determined to shake off the horror of the previous year and instead embrace the promise of a better one to come. Those who were no longer there to enjoy the festivities were of course missed and mourned, but gone were the terrifying questions of 'Who's next?' and 'Why me?'.

It was a hopeful time of new beginnings. By Easter, later in April than the previous year, the days were a bewildering combination of early sunshine followed by intense downpours, to be followed in minutes by more sunshine. Mary followed Kitty everywhere she went, sheltering under trees when the showers came, and splashing in puddles when they departed. Delicate blossoms flourished on every tree and branch, with bees and insects returning to buzz and flit between the flowers. Sparrows and blue tits gathered material for nests, flying hurriedly with beaks laden with straw and twigs.

Mary had built a small bird house over the winter, hammering bits of wood together under the guidance of her father's careful hand. They had wedged it in a low fork of a nearby tree and a couple of tits had taken up residence. Much to Mary's pride and delight, the female had laid eggs inside the little house, and each day she anxiously peered in to see if any of them had hatched.

'I can hear 'em!' she cried excitedly one afternoon. 'They've hatched. Come, Kitty, tha must listen. Can tha see 'em? Lift me up so I can look.' Mary's stream of commands nearly drowned out the sound of the chicks inside the box, but their demands for food were greater, and Kitty could make out their chirps as soon as she drew close. She lifted Mary up to take a peek. The little girl turned to her cousin, wide-eyed, as she spied the open beaks and fluffy heads of the baby birds.

Signs of the new season were all around. The sheep had been moved from their winter fields and were enjoying the lush new growth of the hillside. The oat field had been cleared and made ready for ploughing and sowing with seed for another year's crop. Uncle Robert and the other men had returned to their jobs underground, replacing the long dark nights of winter with the long dark days of mine work. Aunt Anne, now accompanied by a toddling Sarah, spent days washing and drying and cleaning and airing the cottage, eager to capture the warmth of spring in its cold stone walls. Afternoon strolls into the village, for so long a hurried, unpleasant task, bundled up against the weather, were once again a pleasant pastime. Friendships were reignited and strengthened, smiles of greeting replacing the grimaces of chattering teeth.

There was just one large cloud that threatened this spring idyll. Some of those who everyone thought had recovered from the plague had once again fallen dangerously ill. Members of the Wilson, Blackwell and Thorpe families had either never recovered or suffered a relapse as the weather turned warmer. By the beginning of May, just one week after the Easter holiday weekend, all the remaining family of Aunt Anne's dear friend Lizzy Thorpe had perished. Even more worrying, members of other families – those who had remained untouched by the disease until now – were reported to be sick.

'It's back,' Kitty overheard Ellen Bocking whisper to the lady sitting beside her at the Easter Sunday service.

'What is?' replied her distracted friend, busy as she was trying to persuade her two young children to sit still and be good.

'T' sickness.' Ellen leaned forward. 'I hear all t' Thornleys are down with it. Their door's been shut up tight for t' last week. And see, none of them are here today!' With a triumphant glance around the church as confirmation of her point, she looked at her now anxiously observant friend.

Kitty took a quick look around. Sure enough, none of the Thornleys were sitting in their usual place. As she looked more closely, she noticed other empty pews. *No!* She gasped, a shiver running through her despite the warmth of the sun streaming in the windows. *It can't be. Please Lord, surely that is over with. Maybe it's something else that's kept them away – planting or some such.*

Even as her mind voiced the explanation, she knew it was wishful thinking. No one missed the main Easter service. Over the winter months, every person in Eyam had become vocally thankful to God for His intervention, for His healing of their village. It was inconceivable that this year of all years anyone would voluntarily miss what would be a service of great thanksgiving. Moreover, the Thornleys were a large extended family; any farming emergency would be taken care of without them all needing to be absent from church.

Kitty glanced at her aunt to see if she had heard the whispered conversation behind them. By the slight tremble of her lips and a stare fixed determinedly ahead, Kitty could tell she had. She tried to get her attention, but Aunt Anne was deliberately avoiding her niece's eye.

Kitty heard little of anything else that morning. She watched Mrs Mompesson and her children file into their seats at the front, wondering at their unaccustomed lateness. Catherine looked flustered and out of sorts, the peace of her usual serene countenance broken. She noticed Reverend Mompesson hesitate as he read, heard the rustle of the pages of his prayer book as he shakily turned them. He kept pausing to cough and clear his throat, or to take a handkerchief from his pocket and wipe it across his forehead. Was he also unwell? Kitty hoped and trusted not, but she did wonder what was causing such obvious signs of strain in the rector and his family. Coupled with the conversation she had overheard, she could hazard a guess. A dreadful, terrifying, mind-numbing guess. Had the plague really returned?

After the service, Kitty, still deep in nervous thought, was surprised to see Mrs Mompesson approach her aunt. Aunt Anne bobbed a small curtsy, which Mrs Mompesson immediately reached out to prevent. Kitty was too far away to hear what was being said, but she could tell the tone was serious and the matter urgent.

On the walk back to the cottage, Aunt Anne encouraged Mary and Sarah to run on ahead with Uncle Robert, making some excuse for lagging behind with Kitty.

'Mrs Mompesson came to speak to me this morning, after t' service,' Anne began. Kitty nodded but didn't say anything in reply yet. 'She was asking again if tha' be free to go to work at t' parsonage. Help t' reverend with some of his duties, she said.' There was a pause as Kitty waited for her aunt to continue.

'There's trouble coming, Kitty. Reverend and Mrs Mompesson are worried. They've been visiting and are seeing things in t' village which aren't good. Did tha see how many were missing from this morning's service?' She peered at Kitty. 'I knew tha'd heard Ellen talking behind us, I could see it in tha face. She must learn to keep her thoughts to herself that lass. In church too. No point in getting everyone all worked up.'

'Is it true then? Are t' Thornleys all sick?' Their cottage was at the opposite side of the village to Water Lane where Robert and Anne lived, and so Kitty hadn't had reason to walk past the Thornleys' homes for weeks. If she had done so, she would have no need for her questions now. Each of their cottages displayed the all too familiar signs that the plague was raging within. Gardens that were normally kept neat and pretty were overgrown with a proliferation of spring weeds. Doors were firmly shut. Fabric was draped across all the windows preventing anyone from seeing inside. Occasionally a shadow could be seen moving around an upper room, but for the most part there was an unnatural stillness.

'T' Mompessons and Thomas Stanley have been visiting them. And a few other families too. They say they are just as poorly as dear Lizzy was before she passed. That's why they want you to go and help out – they are fearing t' worst and want to make sure they can be ready for whatever comes. Tha doesn't have to go, tha knows? Tha can stay helping us with Mary and Sarah, especially now t' mine work will get going strong again. But I can see tha likes Mrs Mompesson and maybe it would do thee good to have tha days filled with books and learning again.'

'But what do you think, Aunt? Can tha manage without me, really? Uncle Robert will be out until late each day, and Sarah needs more attention now than when she stayed in her crib for most of t' day. And then there are Mary's lessons – she's doing so well learning her alphabet, it would be fun to start her with writing now too.' Kitty meant what she said, knowing that she was here to help her relatives more than the village parson, but she couldn't quite keep the hope out of her voice as she spoke.

'Our Kitty, tha's a terrible liar,' laughed Aunt Anne. 'I know tha likes Mrs Mompesson and have done ever since tha first arrived here in Eyam. And I know tha's not terribly taken with t' reverend – and nor was I to be honest – but I can see he's made an effort these last months, trying to get to know us all better. Who knows, maybe tha can help him with that, tell him what people in t' village really need. And yes, of course, tha must go and work. We'll miss thee, but tha'll be with us at t' end of every day, and sleep under our roof. Tha won't get out of tha chores round t' house that quickly either – I'll just save them up for thee! Oh, and tha starts there tomorrow!' finished an exultant Anne.

She saw the look of pure happiness flash across the surprised face of her dear niece. Yes, she would miss having her at home with her all the time, she'd got used to her light-hearted company, but it would be good for her to help the reverend. Besides, if Mrs Mompesson was right and things were going to get as bad as she suspected, it would do no harm to have someone bringing news home from the village each day.

Anne had already decided that she wouldn't go into the centre of the village as often, at least not for the time being, and she would leave Sarah and Mary at home together as much as she dared. Should she be worried for Kitty? She thought not as she wouldn't be going out visiting herself; rather she would be asked to write letters and teach George and Elizabeth, that kind of thing. Anne wasn't entirely sure what her sister back in Sheffield, Kitty's mother, would say, but for now, she didn't need to know anything. Kitty could tell her all about it later.

Kitty barely slept that night. Each time she closed her eyes and began to drift off, dark shadows floated through her thoughts. Funeral processions with everyone dressed in flowing black robes that made her think of crows hovering over their carrion prey; nosegays turning rotten and putrid even as she held them under her nose; her own flesh turning black and peeling away as she watched. Not only were her dreams stalked by the spectre of death once more loose amongst the villagers, but her waking hours were also full of worries about going to the Mompessons in the morning. What if she did fall asleep, but only just before dawn, and then didn't wake up again until it was late? She quickly dismissed that as silly; Uncle Robert was up with the singing of the first birds every day, and she had never yet failed to wake on hearing him clattering around below her. What, though, if she was delayed finishing her own morning duties here with Aunt Anne and was late because of that? Or what if she got to the parsonage and they were all out, visiting the sick or something? Round and round the questions nagged.

What if Reverend Mompesson gave her something to read that she didn't understand – something that was too hard for her limited learning? He would immediately realise he'd made a grave mistake bringing her into his home, and he would send her away. The look of disappointment on Aunt Anne's face as she returned home before lunchtime would be unbearable. She would never be able to face Catherine at church again; she would be so ashamed!

As the deep indigo of night faded to the paler blue of early morning, Kitty gave up trying to sleep. She slipped out of bed and down the stairs, up even before Uncle Robert. Tiptoeing to the door, she grabbed her boots on the way out. As the young woman stepped into the distilled clarity of a cool May morning, an opera of birdsong filled the air, choristers too numerous for Kitty to identify all performing in divine harmony. Patch woke from his sleep as soon as he heard the creak of the door and sat up eagerly, tail wagging and ears pricked, hoping for a dash through the fields.

'G'morning, old boy,' whispered Kitty. 'We'd best be quiet so as not to disturb t' others. But come, let's walk!' Patch let out a delighted bark, keeping his voice low on account of the young mistress's injunction to not wake anyone, and bounded along beside her as she strode down the lane. Together they made their way across the fields at the back of the lane, climbing to the summit of the ridge, from which Kitty could survey the whole village below.

Few were stirring, although some of the men from the mine could be seen making their way out of the village on the other side. Curls of smoke rose in the clear air from several chimneys; others stood silent and cold, sentries guarding the memories of those who had warmed their hearths. Standing proud in its permanence right in the centre, the tower of St Lawrence's welcomed the morning sun as it swept over the horizon behind it. All would be well, Kitty felt.

When she brought her gaze closer, she spotted Uncle Robert moving about in the yard outside the cottage. That meant she needed to get back there herself and get started with her day. With a call to Patch who was snuffling around in the grass behind her, Kitty raced off down the hill. Hair streaming behind her, arms spread wide, she felt like the eagle spoken of in the Bible – soaring wild and high, flying without fear or fatigue.

'My, where's tha been so early?' questioned a surprised Uncle Robert as the breathless Kitty rounded the corner of the lane and came back through the gate. 'Tha looks bonny for it, anyway!' He smiled. He was glad to see his young niece full of vibrant life again. It had been a hard and bitter winter for her, and this idea that Mrs Mompesson and his wife had come up with seemed just what Kitty needed. It was a new season for her, filled with the same hope of life and promise as the woods and fields around.

'I need to go! Mustn't be late!' Kitty had dashed into the house, given her face a quick scrub and was already rushing back out through the gate, crunching on the apple she carried while trying to pin her cap onto her head in some semblance of respectability.

All that excited energy had evaporated by the time she reached the gate of the parsonage. She'd had to pass the Thorpes' cottage on the way, and its neglected air had unnerved her. The menace was still prowling, and she felt its shadowed presence in every closed door, every unlit window, that she passed.

Smoothing her skirts before knocking on the door, Kitty tried to calm herself. She didn't want to seem all flustered and nervous, even if the butterflies in her stomach knew she was.

'Kitty, dearest!' The door was pulled open before Kitty could lift her hand to knock. There stood Catherine, arms stretched in welcome, a broad smile lighting her face. 'You came! I knew you would. William – the Reverend Mompesson – thought you might decide against it. I'm so glad you're here! George, Elizabeth, come down and greet Kitty. Come, come in, don't just stand on the step.'

With no time to feel either flustered or nervous at such an encouraging tone, Kitty stepped into the parsonage. She breathed in the smell of the herbs hanging over the recently lit fireplace, so similar to how it was at Aunt Anne's, and she felt more at ease. This was a household like any other, with a woman at its helm who might be better educated or wealthier, but still a woman who wanted her hearth to offer the friendly greeting of home.

Right at the outset of their introductions to one another, Kitty had felt Mrs Mompesson would perfectly fit her role as village parson's wife. She was gently spoken and calm, tender in her attitude towards the parishioners. Kitty had often noticed her quietly standing alongside one of the widows, discreetly giving a gift of a pot of preserves or a carefully wrapped loaf. She had watched as Catherine caressed the calloused palm of one of the older women, had seen her tousle the hair of the youngest ruffian. Now, stepping into the orderliness of her home, inhaling the scent of the herbs, watching her twirl Elizabeth around as she jumped the last stair into her mother's arms, Kitty was filled with gratitude that she had come to this dear woman's attention.

'Please, Catherine darling, keep them quiet while I'm working,' groaned a voice from a second room Kitty hadn't noticed, off to her right. Reverend Mompesson's tiny study. She heard a chair scrape and a creak, footsteps across the stone floor. The door was flung open, and around it appeared the agitated face of the man himself. Kitty froze. She felt the sudden clammy sweat of her hands as she pressed her palms together, felt her chest tighten and restrict her ability to breathe. She knew her ears were burning, could hear the rush of blood as her heart pounded in panic. The reverend caught sight of Kitty, but, having never met her for longer than a handshake, didn't recognise her.

'Oh, what now?' he spluttered. 'Catherine, there's a woman from the village here to see you. Where are you?' His wife had gone upstairs to find George and persuade him to come and meet Kitty. Overhead, the clumping of feet revealed her whereabouts as she hurried to return to her husband and guest.

'That's Catherine Allenby, I told you she was coming. The niece of Robert and Anne Fox of Water Lane? She's come to help us in case things...' her voice tailed off, not wanting to say anything further with the children standing nearby, ears flapping to try and catch every word that she spoke.

'Oh, Miss Allenby! I do apologise. Yes, of course, I see that now. The light behind you, you know. You're the lass from Sheffield, isn't that right? And you can read? And write neatly?' Faced with all the attention and the sudden barrage of questions, Kitty had to fight the desire to turn around and run straight out of the door and back to the safety of the Water Lane cottage.

Looking down at her feet, she replied, 'Yes, sir, I'm Catherine Allenby, from Sheffield. And yes, sir, I have been taught to read and write, by my pa. I prefer Kitty,' she ended, lifting her head slightly as though to defy her interlocutor any objection. She was startled by the sudden bark of laughter that erupted from the reverend.

'Well, then, Kitty it shall be.' He smiled, stepping forward with a handshake of welcome. 'Catherine, could you and Kitty perhaps take the children out for a walk or something, and then I can spend time with Kitty when you get back. I really have to finish these notes before Sunday.' And with that, he retreated to the peace and quiet of his

personal domain and left the two Catherines to spend the morning
however they wished.

Catherine called for George and Elizabeth to get their boots and
the basket of eggs they would be delivering to one of the homes of the
recently sick while they were out, then she linked her arm in Kitty's
and headed for the lane.

'Let's get to know each other!' For all her refined upbringing,
Catherine showed a girlish enjoyment of life. She chatted away happily
as they walked, telling Kitty about her own childhood spent further
north, in the city of Durham, a place Kitty had heard of but never
dreamt of visiting. *Imagine travelling so far*, she thought to herself
as Mrs Mompesson continued to regale her with stories from her
younger days. 'And now to you, Kitty dear. Tell me about yourself.'

'There's not much to tell.' Kitty was so embarrassed. What could
she say? Her life was so small, so insignificant when compared to that
of her benefactor. Besides, all she could think of that was even remote-
ly of interest was connected to years of war between the pro-monar-
chist Cavaliers and their Parliamentarian enemies, the Roundheads.
Given that Catherine's husband was the present incumbent of the
church, and therefore by definition on the side of the monarchy, she
didn't really feel that was a suitable topic for polite conversation on a
sunny May morning.

'My father was a teacher, but now he works for different families,
teaching their boys. My mother takes in sewing, but nothing fancy like
Mr Hadfield made.' The conversation was going from bad to worse.
First, she had sounded angry and self-pitying at the mention of her
father's change of position, then she had spoken of the tailor here in
Eyam — the man many held responsible for the arrival of the plague
to this remote corner of countryside. The mention also reminded her

that poor Mr Hadfield's young brother had died of the dreaded disease just days before.

'Ah, these haven't been easy years,' Mrs Mompesson noted kindly, astutely aware of Kitty's discomfort and understanding the reason for it. 'It was very hard when we first came to Eyam, you know. No one liked us or trusted us. They thought we had personally asked to replace Reverend Stanley; I think someone found out that Sir George Saville – oh, never mind, you wouldn't know who he is would you? – was William's sponsor. They seem to have assumed we pulled strings to get this position. Which isn't true,' she added hastily.

After a pause, she continued, 'Although I can see why some would think that. William loves order and rules. He couldn't abide the state of the church – chaos on all sides, preachers choosing their personal favourite passages of Scripture instead of methodically teaching their congregants the whole Bible. He sympathised with some of the arguments, agreeing that Papist ceremonies and practices should be removed from services, that sort of thing. And yes, perhaps the king does have divine rights, but he also has divine responsibilities.

'I think William felt he could change things better from within, rather than being an outsider. He thus became closely connected with Sir George, which enabled William to influence and guide him. When the position at Eyam became available, William saw it as his chance to make a real difference – to bring the sort of discipline he thrived on into this small community. "Be faithful with the little and God will honour you with much", is one of his favourite sayings.'

They continued their walk in silence for a while, George and Elizabeth trailing behind them, kicking stones as they walked. 'I wish they wouldn't do that; it ruins their boots!' Catherine sounded dutifully annoyed, but no more.

'And so we came to Eyam,' she continued. 'No one spoke to us for the first few months, you know. They came to Sunday services, sat down and then left at the end. Barely anyone shook William's hand, or kissed my little ones. It was horrible! We wondered if this was the biggest mistake we could possibly have made. William tried to find a way to leave, to go somewhere else, but nothing came of it. So we stayed. We learned the ways of the country and how to get to know our neighbours. We planted alongside the others in the spring, reaped a harvest together in autumn. We celebrated every birth, mourned every death. And slowly – oh, so slowly – they started accepting us. I'm not sure if they liked us much better, but accepted, yes.'

Kitty was saddened by this revelation. She had found everyone here to be so friendly, so welcoming and accepting of her and her strange city ways. But perhaps that was thanks to the good standing of Uncle Robert and Aunt Anne. Uncle Robert's family had lived in Eyam for generations, they were admired and respected by everyone, and Aunt Anne was deeply loved.

'But you know, maybe the Lord has brought us here for just this time, Kitty.' Mrs Mompesson stopped walking and turned to face Kitty. Suddenly she was eager, excited instead of melancholy. 'You know Queen Esther in the Bible? She came to her royal position to save her people from certain disaster, and the Lord used her mightily. Perhaps the Lord will also use us – William, me, and you, Kitty – to save this village from the disaster that could strike at any moment.'

Kitty was doubtful that God had brought her to Eyam for any grand purpose of salvation, but she didn't want to be impolite and quash her new friend's enthusiasm. She merely nodded, hoping that would be enough to get them walking again. 'T' eggs? Who're they for?' she enquired.

'Oh, I almost forgot! We'll take them for the Thornleys; so many of them are very poorly.'

When they arrived at the Thornleys' cottage, Kitty remained standing at the gate with George and Elizabeth while Mrs Mompesson carried the basket up to the cottage. A large cross was daubed in the centre of the door, the symbol of despair now disfiguring several previously unadorned cottages throughout the village. Kitty wasn't sure who was responsible for their appearance, whether it was the householders themselves warning their neighbours not to come near, or if it was someone else highlighting the dreadful plight of those indoors.

Catherine knocked gently on the door, laying the basket on the unbrushed step. She moved back slightly and waited, her head bent forward in the concentration of listening. Would anyone come, or were they all too sick to move? Eventually, the door opened a crack. Catherine involuntarily covered her mouth and nose with the handkerchief she held and recoiled a couple of hasty steps further back. Quickly recomposing herself, she dropped her hands slightly and called out a greeting.

'Mrs Thornley, how is everyone? We brought you some eggs; we thought you could make use of them.' Kitty heard no response from the cottage, but watched transfixed as the door opened a little further. The hand that reached through the gap would give her nightmares for the next few days. What had once been the strong fingers of a working woman's hand were now more like the claws of an animal. The nails were long and yellowed, the skin taught across the bones. Even from where she stood next to the gate, Kitty could make out the blackened pustules covering the hand and wrists. Open sores oozed a sticky liquid that glistened wetly in the sunshine.

Kitty was horrified. She had heard that the disease ate away its victims' flesh, leaving the sufferers raw and painfully disfigured, but she hadn't expected what she now saw grasp the handle of the basket and pull it quickly inside.

'Such suffering, Kitty.' Catherine was back at her side, her voice trembling slightly. 'Let's get back, I'm sure William will be ready for you now.'

He was. As soon as they were through the door and into the cottage, Reverend Mompesson emerged from his study. 'Ah there you are, good, let's get to work Miss Allenby – Kitty,' he remembered.

Kitty spent the rest of the afternoon in a state of such combined delight and anxiety that she could hardly put one foot in front of the other as she made her weary way back home. The study in which she sat smelt warm and safe, reminding Kitty of her father. Books and papers were stored haphazardly on the shelves of a magnificent piece of wooden furniture that filled one entire wall. Clearly, this was something brought from a family home of more prosperous aspect and bigger proportions.

A small fire smouldered in the blackened grate, clouds of smoke and ash billowing into the room each time the door was opened. A couple of chairs were positioned to either side of the fireplace, and a large desk was under the window. Dappled green light danced across yet more papers strewn across the desk as the overhanging branches of the large tree, growing at the entrance to St Lawrence's opposite, cast their shade.

Reverend Mompesson had been as kind as could be expected of a busy man burdened with the responsibilities of a parish in the midst of a crisis, but his brusque, quick manner intimidated Kitty. She had stumbled over the reading he had tested her with, and blotched ink on the pages where he asked her to write a short note. For hours she had perched on the edge of a chair, not daring to relax her guard lest she make any further mistakes, and now her back ached, a dull throb between the shoulder blades.

It was with relief that she set off for the cottage, her home. Kitty swung her arms as she walked, trying to release some of the tension which remained. Halfway down the lane she was greeted by an excited Mary who raced up to her with hair flying and arms whirling.

'Tha's home!' she cried ecstatically as she pulled Kitty the rest of the way.

After supper that evening, once Uncle Robert had returned from the mine and all the work around the house had been completed, Kitty sat outside, her stiff back easing as she leant against the warm stones of the cottage walls.

'So, how did t' day go, lass?' Kitty knew her aunt had been dying to ask her that ever since she walked through the door. She was grateful the questions were only starting now, after she'd had a bit of time to recover. 'What was Mrs Mompesson like? Did tha get on well with her? And t' reverend? Was he ever so stern? I'm sure he would be? George and Elizabeth – they're good children, aren't they?' Aunt Anne finally stopped to draw breath, giving Kitty opportunity to reply.

'Mrs Mompesson is lovely! We went for a walk and took some eggs to t' Thornleys' place. Oh!' Kitty suddenly remembered the morning's experience and the monstrous looking hand that had emerged. She paled. 'It was terrible. Someone – I think Mrs Thornley – came to fetch t' basket from t' step. All I saw was her hand, but it looked nothing like any hand I have ever seen – black and rotten like a piece of old meat. And I think there was a terrible smell. I was too far away, but Catherine – Mrs Mompesson – had to take a few steps away when t' door first opened. It was horrible!' Her face crumped. The lack of sleep and early morning start, the nervous excitement she had been nursing all day and now the shock of remembrance was all too much.

'Ah, there luv,' shushed Aunt Anne, rising from her seat and going to Kitty, embracing and comforting her. 'Tha's had enough for today. Tha needs to get rested and then tomorrow is another day which will seem all t' better after a good night's sleep. *His compassions fail not; they are new every morning.* It was only yesterday tha read that to us and 'tis just as true today as 'twas then.'

*Chinese Knot out-
line*

'Hurry, we'll be late!' Aunt Anne was standing at the bottom of the stairs, twisting her hair into a thick plait. 'I don't want to miss Betsy's big day.'

'Coming!' chorused Kitty and Mary. They appeared suddenly, both wearing their best Sunday clothes. The two had been out and collected dainty blue harebells from the lane earlier that morning, and the flowers were now tucked into Mary's hair and arranged in a small posie which she gripped tightly.

Mary beamed at her mother. 'Does I look pretty?' she asked.

'Tha looks beautiful. A perfect princess!' Her father had come in from outside. He bowed and blew her a kiss before scooping Sarah up off the floor. Mary giggled. 'Let's get going then!'

Amidst the horror and the devastation, this day was to be a bright moment of joy and happiness. Elizabeth Syddall – Betsy – was getting married. Some whispered that it was far too soon after her husband's death, but the majority of the villagers were delighted for her. After the grief she had suffered before Christmas, many felt it was only fair that she should be allowed to start again, away from the straw-thatched cottage and all the memories it held. John Daniel, himself a widower with a son, had asked her to marry him. Ten years Betsy's senior, he had shown himself kind and caring after the death of her husband and her children. Now he and John Junior were to welcome her, together with her last surviving daughter – Emmott – into his home. A new family formed at a time when so many were being torn apart – little wonder there was such excitement.

The flowers in Mary's hands were already wilting in the heat, and those in her hair were falling loose, leaving behind a path of petals as she walked with her family to St Lawrence's. A brief ceremony was to be held in the church before the new Mrs Elizabeth Daniel would be cheered home. Neither she nor John had wished for a big party, but they had wanted their closest friends to witness their vows in the church and to bless them on their way.

When they entered the church, Kitty noticed it was decorated with softly burning candles and flowers from the hedgerows which had been arranged in borrowed jars and pots.

John Senior stood stiffly at the front of the church awaiting the appearance of his bride, John Junior at his side. Reverend Mompesson stood before them. Once everyone was seated he beckoned to the back where Betsy stood waiting with Emmott. Slowly they walked down the aisle, accompanied by the claps and smiles of all who had gathered.

Betsy looked lovely, with yet more flowers in her hair, but Kitty was concerned by Emmott's appearance. The girl looked flushed, her gaze unfocussed and vacant. Perhaps she was dreaming of her own walk down the aisle; Kitty had heard she was to marry a man from Middleton Dale, a pretty village to the south-east of Eyam. Their wedding was set for the next Wakes Festival week when Kitty would be reunited with her own sweetheart.

As the mother and daughter reached the front of the church, John turned towards them. He smiled shyly, then took Betsy's hand and led her the rest of the way to where Reverend Mompesson was ready to conduct the short service. Emmott stepped to one side and immediately sank into the closest chair. As her mother and John recited their vows in quiet tones, she stifled a cough. By the time they were finished and presented to the congregation as husband and wife, Emmott could barely stand.

John Junior, anxious to make sure nothing spoiled his father's day, went to check on his new sister. He knelt in front of her, then slowly stood and turned to Reverend Mompesson. 'Please help!' Mompesson stepped forward, indicating to Uncle Robert and a couple of other men that they should come forward. Aunt Anne left Mary and Sarah in Kitty's care and hurried over to where Betsy was looking around anxiously for Emmott.

'What's wrong? Where's t' lass?' She noticed the huddle of men standing where she knew her daughter had been sitting. 'No!' she wailed. John caught her as she collapsed against him. Together he and Aunt Anne helped her out into the air.

'I'll take her home,' John said.

'Yes, that's best,' replied Anne. 'Betsy, darling, we'll bring Emmott along home as soon as she recovers herself. I expect 'tis t' heat and all t' excitement. She'll be right in a moment or two.' She looked at Betsy, knowing she didn't sound very convincing.

Betsy turned her head slowly, as though any fast movement would spill all the tears she was holding so carefully. 'I expect so,' was all she said, as unconvincingly as her friend.

The first days of Betsy's marriage to good John Daniel were spent nursing her last remaining child from her previous marriage. Aunt Anne and the other village women tried to help as best they could, baking and cooking, but they all knew what was coming; they had already seen it too many times before.

Less than a week after Mary had clutched her collection of wilting flowers to take to a wedding, she was gathering more for her mother to take to a funeral.

May 1666

K itty's visits to the parsonage gradually became less daunting. Mornings were spent with Catherine and the two children, leaving provisions on cottage doorsteps or gathering flowers and herbs. Catherine was knowledgeable not only about the type of plants that grew in the hedgerows or the across the stone walls of the fields, but also which ones could be used in the preparation of medicines and tonics. On one of Kitty's early visits to the rectory, she had found Catherine poring over a huge, leather-bound book. It looked a bit like a Bible but didn't seem to have quite as many pages.

'*The Complete Herbal* by Mr Nicholas Culpeper,' Mrs Mompessòn said by way of explanation. 'It's where I get all the recipes from.'

One of her particular favourite herbs was a delicate purple flower that grew in profusion everywhere they looked.

'What's this one?' Kitty asked one morning, reaching for the graceful stems.

'That's Jacob's Ladder – see how the leaves are like a ladder climbing the stem?' Kitty looked more closely at the plant she was holding and nodded. 'This is such a useful plant, Kitty. We can make an infusion of the roots by boiling them in water over the stove when we get back home. The liquid we make can be drunk by all those who are suffering. It will ease their fevers and calm their stomachs. Some of it can be applied to the skin itself, soaked in a rag and placed over the dreadful boils we saw on poor Mrs Thornley's hand the other day.'

Kitty shuddered at the memory. The previous night was the first time she'd had quiet dreams since she had seen the afflicted appendage. 'And the cough? Will it help with that as well?'

'I trust so, dearest Kitty. I have heard the racking coughs of those lying in bed even as I pass their closed windows, as I'm sure have you. They seem barely able to breathe at times.' She shook her head in sympathy.

Afternoons were spent with the reverend in his study, helping him with his research or writing the odd letter for him. Kitty never quite lost the feeling of awe when she entered such a wonderful space, but she was no longer on edge the whole time she was there.

One morning towards the end of May, Kitty arrived at the parsonage and entered without knocking, as had become her custom (at the insistence of Mrs Mompesson). She was surprised to find the main room occupied, a man standing before the unlit fire, hands clasped behind his back as he waited for someone – Kitty presumed the reverend. Lost in thought, the gentleman didn't hear Kitty come in and she was about to turn around and go back out again when she realised who it was – Thomas Stanley. Her mind raced. What was he doing there? Surely he and the Mompessons weren't friends, the type who call on one another on a midweek morning? What could have happened that would take him there?

Then she noticed a piece of paper held in his hand. Could that be the reason for his visit?

'Excuse me, sir,' she ventured. He still hadn't noticed her arrival, standing as he was so engrossed in thought. At the sound of her voice, he turned, startled, and peered at her. 'Does Reverend or Mrs Mompesson know thee is here, sir? I can run and find them for thee.'

She was glad she had met him a few times when he had come to visit her aunt and uncle and knew him to be a kind man despite the severity of his Puritan appearance. 'It's Kitty Allenby, sir, Anne Fox's niece,' she clarified for the still confused-looking Stanley.

'Oh, Kitty, how nice to see thee! What's tha doing here? Ah, I remember now. Tha's been helping out Reverend and Mrs Mompesson in their duties, hasn't thee? Good, good, I'm sure tha's going to be a big help to them in t' coming days and weeks. Reverend, there you are!' Stanley ceased his homely conversation with Kitty as the door behind her, which she had so recently closed, opened again.

'Stanley, what are you doing here? Have you been waiting long? My apologies, sir, I was visiting the Skidmore family. That poor lad, young Anthony, has taken ill and his mother's terrified he's caught this evil distemper. He's never been a strong boy, so I hate to say it, but I share his mother's anxiety.' He stepped across the room, hand outstretched in greeting.

'Mompesson, t' apologies are mine. I shouldn't have just arrived unannounced, but I have to speak with thee as a matter of some urgency.' While shaking Mompesson's hand, he held aloft the piece of paper Kitty had seen him holding. 'This, this has to be stopped. We can't let them come here to Eyam. Look – quackery of t' worst kind.'

The two men had forgotten Kitty and, not wishing to draw attention to herself while they were deep in conversation, she sank quietly to a nearby stool and waited for them to finish. She glanced at the page Stanley had now spread out across the table. In the centre was a terrifying illustration – a man dressed in a long, black coat and tall, pointed hat, but with a huge, beak-like mask covering his entire face. Kitty gasped. She hoped they hadn't heard her.

'What is this?' Mompesson wasn't sure what he was seeing, but he knew he didn't like the look of it.

'A "doctor" of t' plague,' Stanley replied derisively. 'Humph, a harbinger of fear and terror, more like! These men are leaving t' cities of t' south to come and prey on t' good citizens of t' north. I have it on good authority that they have been thoroughly discredited where they come from, and so are on their way here instead. To make money out of t' suffering of others, tha can be sure of it. They promise miracle cures, magic potions, hope to t' hopeless.'

'Why the mask?' enquired Mompesson.

'They say it keeps t' vapours away from them. They fill it with all manner of herbs and spells in efforts to ward off this evil pestilence. But we here, in this village, are people of t' Lord and we will not welcome, nor tolerate such a thing.'

'Catherine mixes herbs into all sorts of tonics which she gives to those who are suffering.' Mompesson's tone was mild, but Kitty felt some offence had been taken at Stanley's words.

'But she doesn't boil them with spells, of that I am sure,' retorted Stanley.

'True.'

'So, what will tha do? Tha must mention it in tha sermon on Sunday.' Stanley gave Mompesson no time to reply as he continued, urgently, 'Tha must tell t' congregation not to welcome any of this sort into their homes, nor waylay them if they meet them on t' highway or out in t' fields. If they need assistance, deliverance from sickness, prayer, they must call on thee, Mompesson. Tha's God's representative here in Eyam now, much as it pains me to say it.'

Mompesson looked dismayed as he realised what Stanley was suggesting. He was already swamped with visiting those who were sick. The new prayer book demanded that certain prayers and services be carried out in the home of those unwell and unable to attend morning and evening services on Sundays. If those he already knew about succumbed to the disease he would soon be conducting funerals on a regular basis again too. He had performed two already at the beginning of the month – two brothers from the beleaguered Thorpe family had died in one another's arms. If he were now to declare publicly that he was available to be called upon like some gifted village doctor, he would never cope.

'Impossible.' Desperation made him sound impatient, irritated. 'I can't perform all my duties even now, much less add numerous others.'

'That's why I'm here.' Stanley's voice was soft. 'I've come to offer my help. For t' sake of t' people of this village, I will work alongside thee. I will never agree with what tha thinks about t' king, or even t' church perhaps, but for this we can put our differences to one side. I won't use tha prayer book, but you can be assured I will use The Book.'

Mompesson was visibly taken aback. A wide-eyed Kitty was equally shocked. The two preachers working side by side – one the beloved of old, the other the unwelcome outsider? How would the reverend respond?

'Well, I...' He tried to recover his composure.

'Mr Stanley, that would be wonderful. We are immensely grateful for your offer of help and partnership at such a time as this. Aren't we, William?' Catherine had been standing at the top of the stairs, unseen by the three in the room below. Kitty expected a sharp rebuke from the reverend. Surely no wife could speak to her husband in such a manner. Instead, he went to the bottom of the staircase as Catherine descended, tenderly taking her hand in his.

'Yes, my dear, you are quite right. We – I – am indeed grateful for such a generous offer, Stanley. I can't pretend it will be easy, nor are we likely to see eye to eye on many things, but on this one thing I know we are agreed. The people of Eyam deserve our love and care at this, their moment of greatest need. On Sunday I will inform the people of our decision to stand united for the sake of their wellbeing.'

'Very well. We shall see each other many times over t' next few days. Though not, perhaps, at a Sunday service!' This said with a hint of a smile playing on Thomas Stanley's lips. After executing a small bow of farewell to each of the three of them in turn, Stanley left the cottage. He pulled his hat down over his brow and shuffled down the lane, a burdened man, but one whose burdens were now shared.

Chinese Knot out-line

That Sunday, Reverend Mompesson was true to his word.

'Dearly beloved,' he cleared his throat as his gaze swept the church. More spaces in the pews, more missing families. He knew things were getting worse; infections were rising again and there seemed to be nothing he could do about it. Fighting a sense of hopeless despair, he fixed his eyes on Catherine as he continued. 'We, the people of Eyam, have beseeched the Lord to remove this pestilence, this plague from within our midst. We have earnestly sought his favour, and we have enjoyed many months of "peace on all sides", just as the children of Israel did when they first entered the promised land. For our God is gracious and merciful, desiring that none should perish apart from him. As we have read in this evening's lesson, the second letter to the Thessalonians, I, like Paul before me, glory in your patience and faith throughout the persecutions and tribulations you have thus far endured.'

He paused, removed a handkerchief from the pocket of his long black robe and blew his nose loudly. Replacing the cloth in his pocket, he went on. 'But now, dear children, we are once more faced with a tribulation which will require our patient endurance. It is a wonderful thing that we are counted worthy in the sight of our God to suffer such trials, but let us understand that suffering is once more about to come upon us. Many in our parish lie sick with the illness even as we ourselves have been able to come to service this evening. There is little that can be done to ease their pain except pray. Which we fervently do.

'You will soon hear of supposed doctors and "men of medicine" who will try to enter our village with potions and trickery that will not ease our suffering, but rather make it worse as it is surely an abomination in the sight of God. We will resist their attempts to dupe us, to offer to us a hope that is no hope at all.'

Warming to his theme, William strode up and down the front of the church, his voice rising at the indignation he felt. 'Charlatans may come and try to steal your money with ideas of cures and remedies, but I, as the shepherd of this flock, appointed by the Good Shepherd Himself, will not tolerate them. Indeed, I will not allow them access into our community.' He stopped in front of the lectern and thumped his fist down hard, the sound bouncing off the old stone walls of the church. The flock of which he spoke sat transfixed – never had they seen the new incumbent of their country church so impassioned, so wound up on their behalf.

'And yet, my dears, I know even as my hope is to protect and guard you, precious flock, from the wolves that seek your very lives, this will bring its own hardship to you here. The Reverend Thomas Stanley and I have reached an agreement. We have put some of our differences aside in the interests of serving and reassuring you throughout this time of trial and crisis. We will take upon ourselves the roles of doctor and minister, comforter and friend. You will not be left to confront these dark times alone.'

The congregation sat utterly still. This was most unexpected. One of the women near the back sniffed. Others wiped their eyes quietly. Uncle Robert and Aunt Anne looked at each other, concern clear in their expressions. This was a worrying development, they felt sure. They were both pleased that the two men had finally reached some sort of a truce, and found a way to work together in the service of the Lord. However, the reason for their unity – a desire to protect the vulnerable from exploitation at their moment of greatest need – although honourable, was a cause for alarm. Clearly, the situation amongst the families missing this evening was worse than they had realised.

'Kitty, luv, how are things in t' village? Tha knows we've been too busy with lambing and catching up at t' mine to have had time to visit overly much lately,' Aunt Anne quizzed later as they enjoyed the last of the evening's warmth.

'Ah, leave t' girl alone. Tha knows she can't tell us more 'n t' reverend is prepared to say to us all,' Uncle Robert chided. 'Mind you, Stanley's obviously worried too or he would never have agreed for t' two of them t' work together.'

'It was him that came to t' Mompessons, not t' other way round,' Kitty murmured, not wishing to break any confidences, but also wanting to give Mr Stanley what he was due. 'He'd seen some news stories, with pictures of a doctor all dressed up, with a big beak thing covering his whole face.' She shuddered. 'I'm glad they're making sure no one like that comes to Eyam. Would frighten everyone to death, not cure anyone!'

'But is it bad, Kitty? How many families have got t' infection again?' Aunt Anne persisted.

'Well, there's more of t' Thornleys that are sick. Then there's little James and Editha Mower – we dropped some of Mrs Mompesson's special drink with their mother yesterday.'

At first the young woman was reluctant to pass on much information, afraid she was straying into the realm of gossip and tittle-tattle. But as Kitty listed the names of those she knew who were waging war against this most foul enemy, as she watched the expressions of her aunt and uncle change from curiosity to sympathy and finally to fear, she felt a burden lifted from her shoulders – as Thomas Stanley had only a few days before.

Kitty had been carrying this dreadful knowledge for several days, lain awake at night trying to imagine the suffering taking place in the cottages on whose steps she and Catherine left their parcels. She had resisted confiding in her aunt, worried lest she fear so much for Mary and Sarah that she would shut herself away, sink into herself. She needn't have worried.

'We must do all we can to help, Robert.' Anne was decisive, empathy winning over self-preservation. 'Kitty, tha must find out from Mrs Mompesson what she needs. I'll take t' girls and we'll go hunting for those plants tha keeps going on about, make up some of t' tonics. We'll make up some broth too, and help serve that to t' families in need. Robert, find out who needs help with t' lambing, and we'll get some lads together to come out t' fields and make sure it goes smoothly for everyone. I'll get in touch with some of t' family over in Stoney Middleton too. I'm sure there'd be those who could be spared to come our way and help. Robert, could tha get a message through to my brother? Get one of t' lads from t' mine to tell him what we need?'

Uncle Robert grunted that he would do so in the morning, knowing it would be pointless trying to dissuade his wife. However, he knew they would all be just as busy in the next village as they should be in this, and doubted there would be any spare labourers. Besides which, news of the pestilence must surely have reached Stoney Middleton by now, and fear would more than likely keep them away even if there were available helpers.

Kitty, however, was pleased. She knew her aunt, once galvanised, would be a force to be reckoned with. She would gather the women of the village – those who remained strong and healthy – and get them involved in looking after those who weren't. With so much to be done at this time of year, many risked the loss of their livelihoods if they remained isolated in their homes, too sick to work. Unable to take care of their flocks and crops, there would be nothing ready for harvest later in the year, and so nothing to sustain them during the winter months. But if Aunt Anne could persuade her friends to add a little more to their own daily routines, all could be taken care of without the burden being too much for any one individual or family.

Perhaps now Aunt Anne and Uncle Robert would also get to know the Mompessons better. Kitty knew her aunt and uncle had overcome much of their initial animosity towards the newcomers, especially when they saw the reverend's response to the situation as it had threatened to engulf the community before Christmas, but she knew they still didn't fully trust him. Their allegiance lay firmly with Thomas Stanley. As he too partnered with Reverend Mompesson, she hoped they would all develop a deeper understanding of one another, possibly even a friendship.

Kitty was eager to tell Catherine the good news of her aunt and uncle's involvement in helping the stricken households. She was bursting with pride and felt sure that Catherine, and even the reverend, would share her pleasure at the knowledge that others wished to toil alongside them during the coming weeks.

She ate breakfast quickly the next morning and arrived at the parsonage earlier than usual. Seeing the door slightly ajar, she gave a brief knock and stepped into the front room. Immediately she knew something was wrong. The fire had not yet been lit, the children were not sitting in their places at the table, and raised voices could be heard coming from the kitchen at the back.

'No, Catherine, I will not allow it. The children need their mother with them, especially at a time like this.' Reverend Mompesson sounded harsh, his voice edged with anger.

'And also no, William. I will not leave your side at a time like this. You need me here, with you, far more than the children need me sitting around playing silly games all summer. The women of this village need me. What use will you be if the mother is unwell and her children need taking care of? Do you know how to make and mix the preparations and tonics I send to them? Or broth? Or porridge?'

'I can look after myself. I'll ask one of the women in the village to attend to my needs – cooking and so on. I could even ask Kitty; she comes here every day anyway, so adding some extra light household duties to her day will do no harm. And she's spent her mornings with you, learned about the plants you use, how to boil them up, what to mix them with. She could do all of that very capably, I'm certain.'

'But she is still a child, William. She is here under the guardianship of her uncle and aunt, who may themselves need her should anything happen to them. God forbid,' she finished quietly.

'Catherine, my dearest, I couldn't bear for anything to happen to you. You must leave, get far away from this plague and remain out of harm's way until it has passed.' The reverend's voice was gentler now as he implored his wife to think of the consequences of staying, of perhaps herself succumbing to the contagion.

'And I, dear William, could never live with myself should anything happen to you and I not be here to care for you, nurse you if needs be. We vowed before God that only death would part us, and now here, when sickness is a threat, you wish to send me away? I will not go, William. My place is here, my promise is here. My love is here.' The final words were muffled, as though Catherine had buried her head in her hands as she uttered them. Or perhaps her husband had reached for her, enfolded her into the safety of his arms, and she had buried her head in his chest.

The conversation between the two continued, but now in lower tones so Kitty could no longer hear what was being said.

She was thoroughly embarrassed at her inadvertent eavesdropping. She was also horrified at what she had overheard. The reverend was planning to send his children away, his wife too if he could but persuade her. What did that mean for the rest of them left behind in the village? Did he feel the march of the plague would carry on unchecked, that none would be exempt from its deathly touch? What else could it mean, if he thought his family would only be safe if they fled the area?

Kitty felt disappointment cloud her earlier bright mood. More than that, there was the sharp prick of disillusionment. She had thought the Mompessons worthy of the new respect they were gaining within the small community. She had heard every recent heartfelt sermon at the Sunday services and truly thought the reverend had meant every word. And what of her developing friendship with Mrs Mompesson? Had that all been based on falsehood as well? *Really, I should have known better.* Bitter thoughts poisoned her mind. *Why ever did I think someone like me could become friends with someone of her status, background and position?*

As she stood wondering how she could escape and avoid having to spend the day in Catherine's – *Mrs Mompesson to you, Kitty –*

company, the couple opened the door of the kitchen and saw her. The reverend greeted her with a cheery, 'Good morning, Kitty,' and walked past her into his study.

'Oh, Kitty, dearest, I'm so glad you're here. And early too! Wonderful. There's so much to be seen to.' She seemed not to notice Kitty's discomfort, her erect posture a wall around a heart in turmoil.

'Well, I was coming to tell thee, I'm needed with Aunt Anne today.' The statement was bordering on rude, Kitty knew, but right then she didn't care. All she wanted was to leave, to have some time alone with her thoughts.

'Kitty? Is everything alright? Is someone sick at home?' Catherine looked quizzically at the young woman, finally aware that something was amiss.

'It's all fine, thank 'ee. I can stay to help if tha really needs me here...' her voice trailed off. She was cross with herself for having given in so easily, for not stalking out of the parsonage as soon as she had heard the gist of the fight she had stumbled upon. She had thought the Mompessons cared – about the fate of the villagers and perhaps even about her. But here they were, discussing their escape. And the reverend proposing to use her like any common serving girl rather than the educated young woman she so wanted to be appreciated as. The young woman could feel her cheeks burning as the indignation rose. She couldn't remember a time when she had been so angry, felt so aggrieved.

'Kitty, what on earth is the matter?' Mrs Mompesson was alarmed at the transformation from the kind and gentle Kitty she thought she knew to the proud, angry young woman standing in front of her. 'Whatever has happened to make you like this?'

'Nothing.' Kitty's response was sullen. Even in her anger, she knew better than to verbalise all that was raging in her head. 'What does tha need me to do?'

'No, that can wait.' Mrs Mompesson was firm; she was going to get to the bottom of this before the day progressed a minute further. 'George and Elizabeth are playing out in the woods. We'll walk and find them, and on the way you can tell me what has you all fired up so.'

Refusing Kitty the opportunity to argue, Mrs Mompesson flung a light shawl across her shoulders and started off down the path to the lane leading to the woods. Kitty hesitated, then turned to follow.

'I sent the children out early this morning as William and I needed to talk a few things over without their flapping ears nearby!' Catherine started conversationally. Suddenly she stopped walking and turned to Kitty, the colour draining from her expressive face. 'Oh Kitty, darling, did you come in and hear what we were saying? Well, arguing, more like. We did get somewhat heated in our discussion. I'm sure you would have heard much of what we were saying, especially if you had been standing there for any length of time.'

Seeing the flush on Kitty's cheeks return and the way she looked fixedly at the ground, Catherine was sure she was right. 'Oh, my dear, that was something you should never have heard. You must feel terrible, as though we are abandoning everyone here. Abandoning you,' she finished gently, reaching out a hand to touch Kitty's arm.

Kitty shrugged, trying to hold on to the strength of her anger as the kindness of Mrs Mompesson's tone threatened to release the dam of tears that lurked behind her eyes. 'Tha talked about leaving,' she accused, a slight tremor in her voice belying her true feelings.

'Yes, yes, you're right, that is what we were fighting about. But it is not what you think, truly it isn't.' Kitty risked lifting her eyes to scour

Catherine's face for any hint of falsehood, daring her to contradict what she had heard and knew to be true.

Slightly encouraged, Catherine continued. 'Yes, William does want to send the children and me away. We have relatives close by who have already indicated that we could go there for as long as necessary.' She swallowed, unnerved by the scepticism in the soft honey-brown eyes now staring at her, unblinking, as she tried to explain. 'But it is not so we avoid this contagion, it is not for fear of falling sick or even dying. It is that William needs to be able to focus entirely on everyone else during this terrible trial. He feels having the children – even me – here at home with him will be an unnecessary distraction from his Godly duties to his congregation. He wishes to be able, at all times of the day and night, to visit and pray for those who are toiling under the burden of illness and its accompanying poverty; he wishes to speak words of great encouragement to those who are still well but paralysed by fear. In short, he wants, like the Apostle Paul wrote, to be free of the restriction of family responsibilities.'

Kitty was once more looking at the ground, digging a hole with the toe of her hard wooden clog. 'So, tha's going then.' It wasn't a question.

'No, Kitty, I'm not. That's why we were fighting. I don't agree with William. Yes, I think it would be better for the children to leave. Our time will be fully occupied with caring for others, and it will be unfair for them to feel neglected as others become our priority. But I do say "our", Kitty. I don't believe William can – or should – carry this load alone. I am his helpmeet, his companion, in both good times and bad. I will not leave his side for more than a moment. He took some persuading, but he now sees things as I do.'

At this she smiled, remembering the warmth of her husband's embrace, his gratitude that she would, in fact remain with him. He agreed he hadn't really wanted to send her away but that, knowing the path ahead would be anything but easy, he wanted to give her the freedom to make her own decision. 'That must have been the part you didn't hear, dearest Kitty. We have agreed that I will take the children to our relatives and then return, as quickly as possible. And we will stay for as long as we are needed,' she emphasised.

'Kitty, truly you are my companion and friend, perhaps the only one I have here in spite of your youth. It pains me greatly to learn that our struggle to resolve our momentary disagreement caused you so much hurt. Please, forgive me and allow me once again to earn your trust and respect. Here, take this.' She held out her handkerchief to the now sniffing Kitty.

'I thought tha was leaving, that I was mistaken in there being any friendship between us,' Kitty managed to say between gulps. 'I thought tha was all full of falsehood about caring for us here in t' village, about working together with Mr Stanley, about it all. I – I thought I was just another servant to thee...'

'Oh, you silly child,' murmured Catherine, placing her hands on Kitty's shoulders. 'Look at me. There now, what a mess you've made of that pretty face of yours! One of the best things to have come out of this terrible time is that I have met you. I will need you more than ever when I get back – to help with all the work, but also to be someone I can talk to, to share my burdens with. William will be far too busy to be able to attend to me! Perhaps we could even say prayers together?' Her tentative suggestion was met with a watery smile from Kitty. 'Ah, George, Elizabeth, there you both are. Hurry dears, we have to get home and get you all packed for a little holiday!' Catherine gathered her children and gave Kitty a final squeeze of the hand. 'Follow along when you're ready.'

June 1666

Once Kitty had helped with packing both Catherine's and the children's things into the enormous carpet bags Reverend Mompesson unearthed, she was left with little else to do. She had given the children a fond squeeze of farewell as they waited for the coach that would take them first to Sheffield and then on to their relatives' home. Kitty hardly dared look at Catherine, much less say goodbye. It was the Wakes Festival all over again.

Even though it was only for a short time, she knew she was going to miss Catherine greatly. She had become accustomed to their mornings spent in pleasant, educated conversation while they worked side by side on one project or another. She loved her aunt and uncle dearly, but they would always be different to her; they had their country ways and were happy to remain the same for the rest of their lives. She, however, wanted more; she dreamt of the time when she and Master Cutler John had their own home in the city. It would be decorated with taste, and the dinners they held for Sheffield Society would be so popular that people would have to petition for invitations. She had chuckled then, knowing neither of them would ever really be so grand. A hospitable welcome and an enjoyable supper would be their preference.

The coach and horses had arrived at the door of the Miner's Arms too soon for Kitty's liking, and all was a commotion to get the luggage, the children and their mother stowed safely aboard. Once the carriage had rattled off down the road, Reverend Mompesson told Kitty she could stay at home to help her aunt and uncle for the duration of Mrs Mompesson's absence. He assured her he would be able to manage the workload on his own for that short time, and if anything extra was needed he would call upon Mr Stanley. Kitty had quietly thanked him and returned to the cottage in Water Lane.

'I've just seen a coach pull up outside t' Miner's Arms and watched people getting in!' Aunt Anne stood with her hands on her hips in the doorway as the dejected Kitty drew close. 'Don't tha go telling me that t' Mompessons have fled and gone and left us here to face this terror alone? For shame.' She tutted loudly, causing Mary to turn from her play to see what could be wrong.

'Kitty!' Mary exclaimed as soon as she saw her. 'Tha's home before tea. We can go to t' river and see if there's any fish. Can we?' Big eyes implored her mother to agree.

'In a moment, our Mary. Let Kitty draw breath and then tell me what's happening down with that coach I saw.'

'The reverend has stayed...'

'I knew she thought she was too good for us,' Aunt Anne interrupted darkly.

'No Aunt, tha's got it wrong! They've sent t' children away, but Mrs Mompesson is coming back. They're not scared or anything, they just want to be free to help as much as possible without t' young ones getting in t' way.' Kitty was distressed that one of the two most important women in her life at that moment could have so much distrust of the other. She hoped she could convince her aunt of Mrs Mompesson's motives.

'Mm, well that's good. If she does make it back of course.' Nothing further was said on the subject until a few days later when a stagecoach was again observed drawing up at the Miner's Arms and a lone figure was seen climbing out the coach and into the waiting arms of Reverend Mompesson.

Kitty returned to her duties with the Mompessons the day after Catherine arrived back. It was with some trepidation that she knocked on the door of the parsonage that morning. Would she still be needed? Or would leaving the children behind have hardened Catherine's kind heart, protecting her from the sadness she must be feeling? Kitty needn't have worried. The door was opened wide and there stood Mrs Mompesson, eyes red from crying but with arms open in welcome.

'Kitty, dearest, you are the very person I was wishing it would be. I was just saying to William, if it weren't for you, I wouldn't be able to maintain my resolve and keep the children away from us. But now here you are, and all will be well.' She ushered Kitty towards the table and gestured for her to sit.

'So, tell me everything. What have I missed? Are your aunt and uncle, and Mary and Sarah still well?'

'Yes, they are well. But t' same can't be said for t' Thornley family. Did t' reverend tell thee? Isaac passed t' other day, and Ann and Jonathon are lying in bed with t' fever. And there are other families got sick now too. I'm so glad tha's back!'

'Yes, he did tell me of the others. And this wretched heat doesn't help either. We have much work to do, young Kitty. Let's get out and start collecting so we can make up some more tonics later today and tomorrow. William won't be needing you for the rest of the day – he and Mr Stanley have their hands full visiting – so I have you all to myself.'

Despite the reason for their busyness being so desperate, Kitty found the days spent in Catherine's company passed quickly and pleasantly. Even her aunt was warming to Mrs Mompesson's influence in her niece's life, watching as each day wrought an increased care and concern for the unfortunate inhabitants of her beloved village. When she was able, Anne would join them in their hunt for flowers and plants that could be used in the various preparations that both she and Mrs Mompesson devised.

Although Anne was never quite relaxed in Mrs Mompesson's company, Mary and Sarah loved the days when they got to be with Kitty and Cat, as they called the two Catherines. Mary ran between them, arms laden with bits of grass and twigs that she had helpfully collected. Sarah, although not quite able to keep up with her sister, tottered about.

For her part, Catherine loved the interaction with the children. She would snuggle a sleepy Sarah on her lap, stroking her hair and thinking of Elizabeth. She cried out in alarm as Mary clambered up trees and slid down riverbanks, knowing her own George would do the same, if not worse. She was grateful, too, that she now had an opportunity to get to know Anne Fox better. She was one of the most influential women in the village – quiet, humble and unassuming, with an ability to lead the other women where perhaps they wouldn't otherwise want to go. She herself lacked that, was viewed as too much of an outsider, and a well-bred one at that, and so the times spent with Anne became invaluable. Besides which, Catherine enjoyed her company. Anne knew so much about country ways in general and the area around Eyam in particular, and was always eager to share her knowledge. She was kind and funny too – more often smiling and laughing than complaining or sighing.

Reverend Mompesson rarely called for Kitty nowadays. Most days he seemed to be either ministering to the sick in their now stinking hovels, Thomas Stanley at his side, or seated in the front pew in St Lawrence's, praying and imploring God to remove this terrible trial.

The burden of his position was too heavy for him to carry. As the June days grew longer and hotter, and the infection spread amongst his congregation like the grass fires that were burning out on the moors, William felt helpless. His prayers seemed to be unanswered, the pestilence strengthening rather than loosening its deadly grip. Had God forsaken these, His children? Had they sinned so greatly before his arrival that nothing could stay the punishment of heaven?

Or was it he himself who had sinned, and thus his prayers were prevented from reaching the only One who could save these poor, desperate people? Would it be better to leave them in the care of Thomas Stanley, to take his wife and join their children someplace else, taking the curse with them? But would that curse follow him to the next place and the next, wreaking destruction wherever he went?

At the end of each weary day, William would return home gratefully to his wife. In the privacy of the parsonage, he would sit at her feet, his head in her lap. Caressing his brow, she would wash him with the gentleness of her words, the softness of her touch, and he would believe peace was possible. But then, lying in bed waiting for the daylight to fade and the stars to appear, he listened to her even breathing beside him and knew the nightmares would return.

Night after night, he tossed and turned, his mind filled with fiery images of hell and eternal damnation. An imploring hand, pale and shaking, reached out to him, begging him for help. As soon as William touched the waxy hand before him, seeping blisters appeared all over it, the flesh turning black and putrid as he watched. He struggled to withdraw his hand to flee the contagion he knew he had unleashed.

The smell of necrotic decay assailed him as the hand finally let go of his own, but then it moved up towards his face. William knew what would happen next and was powerless to stop it. As the hand clamped over his mouth and nose, he clawed at his face in an attempt to release its grip, knowing this to be the hand of judgement pressing upon him, smothering him with accusations and pronouncements of guilt.

As he writhed and moaned, he broke out into a sweat as heavy as those he had seen dripping from the emaciated brows of so many of his parishioners. Finally, he awoke, gasping for air and soaked through, trembling with fear and longing for the morning.

He never spoke to Catherine of these nightly visitations, but she knew something was wrong. As the sun filtered through the window, as the birds sang their morning alarm, she would turn and find her husband already out of bed, his sheets storm-tossed and damp. Hearing not even the quietest movement downstairs, she knew he would be in his usual place within the cold, cleansing embrace of the church. She then rose and made her way over to find him, passing through the great gates of the churchyard, watched only by the tower and the gravestones. There she would find him, his head in his hands, weeping. She knew no words were necessary; indeed none were sufficient. She simply sat at his side and prayed. And prayed.

One morning he turned to her, his face drained, etched with exhaustion and defeat. 'I can do no more, my darling. It is over.' William's voice was raspy from lack of sleep, from words spoken to a seemingly unhearing God, from despair. 'We must just await our fate, with patience and fortitude. There is nothing else.'

Catherine pressed his hand to her lips and waited, knowing there was something more.

'Although...' Another pause. 'What of our friends, our neighbours – those in Stoney Middleton, Grindleford? Sheffield even? Surely there is something that can be done to save them this... this terror that has so overtaken us here in Eyam.'

'What are you thinking, my darling?' Catherine saw the flicker of a light deep in William's soul, an idea forming and growing, taking hold in the barren wasteland of his aching heart.

'We must prevent this contagion, this pestilence, from spreading beyond our borders.'

'But how, William? We cannot control the foul air, this miasma, from drifting across hills and down valleys any more than we can order the wind to blow when and where we wish it to.'

'No, my dear one, but we can restrict people and parcels from moving back and forth.' William rose, his hands animated, his stride up and down the church once more assured and confident. 'This disease arrived when George Viccars came up from London. Nothing like it had been seen around here until the moment that bundle of cloth was brought out to be dried and aired. Oh, if only we had known.' He stopped, his shoulders drooping as though they carried an unbearable load. He felt again the ghostly fingertips of his nightmares seeking their prey, and he shuddered to shake it off.

'Go on,' whispered Catherine. He had forgotten she was there, so dark was the cloud threatening to again engulf him. 'Go on, my love. What should we do?'

'Yes, yes, what *should* we do? We need to stop anyone from leaving, Catherine. We need to persuade them to stay here and wait for this to pass. No more visits to market, no more trading beyond our borders. We will be the carriers and we must ensure we carry nothing anywhere,' he exclaimed.

Catherine gasped. This was not what she had expected. How were they going to convince everyone that this was the best way forward? Surely they would simply pack up their households and leave, taking whatever they could with them. If that included disease and sickness, well, so be it.

'*Love thy neighbour as thyself,*' William quoted. 'Would we wish this on our relatives, our friends, in other regions? Would we wish for the great industries of Sheffield and Manchester to shut down and be ruined when it is within our power to prevent such a thing? No, we must look to our Lord, to His sacrifice, and follow His example.'

Silent tears ran down Catherine's face – equal parts fear for the future and pride at her husband's courage. William returned to her side. Taking her hands in his, he looked pensively around the church. The morning sun was streaming through the windows, and it was becoming hot and stuffy despite the early hour.

As he turned his attention back to Catherine, the trust and love in the eyes that returned his gaze took his breath away. Could he really go through with this? Could he forsake all he held most dear for the good of others he didn't even know, others who wouldn't ever know him or his precious Catherine? What if, God forbid, she fell sick, or worse, if she left him alone on this earth while she departed for a better place? His resolve began to weaken, his conviction to fade as fast as it had ignited.

Catherine saw it in his eyes. 'No, William, you will not put me ahead of those you are called to.' Her eyes were still bright, but the tears had ceased to flow. She stared unblinkingly at him, daring him to defy her. 'What else do you want to do?'

Again he looked around the sanctuary in which they sat. 'We have to stop meeting here, inside, now the weather is so hot. The air is not fresh. We must find somewhere out in the open, an arbour provided by the Lord Himself for our comfort and shelter.' He felt rather than saw the tremor that passed through his wife's body, but he also saw her

determination in the lift of her chin, the clench of her jaw. 'And burials. We are going to have to stop having them here, in the churchyard.'

At that, Catherine did gasp aloud, snatching her hands from her
husband's grasp. 'No, William, you can't!' She was utterly horrified.
'This is the only sacred, consecrated ground in the village. The burials
won't be Christian if they take place anywhere else, you know that.'

'Yes, darling, I do, but we have no choice. We can't delay the burial
of infected corpses for any longer than is absolutely necessary. This
way, each household is responsible for their own dead. I will of course
still administer the last rites and prayers,' he finished hastily, noticing
the blood draining from Catherine's face as he continued speaking.

'Oh, Catherine, how brutish of me. I should never have troubled
you with those details. This is for me and, hopefully, Stanley, to work
out between us. We will come up with a solution that is both acceptable and practical. Come, let us leave the gloom of our conversation
and return to the sunlight!' Taking her by the hand, he gently pulled
Catherine to her feet. Together they made their way home, the shadows of the night diffused by the light of the new day.

*Chinese Knot out-
line*

Sunday. News had travelled throughout the village that Isaac
Thornley had finally lost his battle with the fevers that assaulted his
young body. The mood was sombre as the congregation gathered in
the churchyard before entering the building. Kitty was sad to hear
about Isaac; she had been hoping their gifts of food and medicines

would have some positive effect on the poor Thornley family. She pushed aside memories of the dreadful hand as it reached for the basket, determined not to dwell on the images any longer. Mary soon distracted her, calling her over to the old stone cross in the centre of the churchyard.

'What is it now, little miss?' Kitty questioned playfully.

'Let's play hide and seek!' came the hopeful reply from her young cousin.

'Not now, Mary, t' service is about to start! Tha knows that. Now come out from behind there, I can see thee as plain as t' nose on my face.' Mary lingered behind the cross, not wanting to end the game before it had really started. For the first time, Kitty took more notice of the ancient marker. It was pockmarked, covered with deep green moss and pale grey lichen. It listed slightly to one side, as though having a momentary rest in the gentle shade of the churchyard trees before returning to duty as sentry of the dead who lay at its feet. Kitty reached out and traced her fingers around the figures and the loops and whorls engraved into the stone. It was rough and cool to her touch. She had been told it had stood here for centuries, a symbol of permanence as all around it swirled and shifted. As it seemed to be doing now.

She thought of Isaac Thornley, of Mrs Lizzy Thorpe, of others she had hardly known and yet still grieved their loss. Of still more invalids lying at home perhaps never to rise from their sick beds. What tragedies had the old stone cross witnessed over the centuries, what stories lay hidden? What words of strength and comfort had been heard and held as preachers from long ago imparted their messages of hope to pilgrims and wayfarers?

Kitty wished she could hear some of them now, be encouraged to continue in faith without fear of the future, for she was worried. She knew something had transpired over recent days between the Reverend and Mrs Mompesson, but she had no idea what it could be. For once, she was not Catherine's confidante. Instead, she observed the looks and glances which passed between them, saw a new tenderness between husband and wife whenever they were together. She also found Catherine more distracted than usual, seeming unable to focus on the tasks at hand or give clear instructions about what needed to be done next. Perhaps she was missing her children. Of course, she would be, but Kitty felt there was something more – some trouble or anguish that prowled below the surface of her mind, a monster of the deep threatening to pull her under, drown her.

Kitty had said nothing of her concerns to her aunt, although her pensive state could hardly have gone unnoticed. But then, both Aunt Anne and Uncle Robert had themselves seemed preoccupied. It was as if everyone were holding their breath, pretending all was normal when in fact each knew they were standing on the edge of a precipice from which there was no return.

'I thought you said we had t' go,' complained a bored Mary emerging from behind the cross and breaking into Kitty's thoughts.

'That I did, Mary, that I did. Come.' Extending her hand and stretching a smile across her face, Kitty did her best to be the jovial playmate her cousin wished for. 'We'll play after, maybe down at t' river, if it stays as hot as this.'

Kitty and Mary joined everyone else as they filed into the church. Unusually, neither the reverend nor Catherine were anywhere to be seen. Kitty could hear the whispers start.

'So where are they then? Followed t' children and left?' came one particularly spiteful accusation.

'And just when we were starting to like them!' was the sad response.

'No, it won't be that. They're not like that, not at all. If they were going to leave they would have done so already.'

'Maybe one of them is sick?'

Kitty hoped not. She had seen them both just two days previously and they had both been well. But then this disease was so different to anything any of them had ever known, she couldn't help but be concerned.

Everyone was seated, waiting, collective breath held again. The door to the vestry opened and out walked Reverend Mompesson. He stopped and turned, holding the door open for someone else still to come. To everyone's surprise, it was Mrs Mompesson. Why was she accompanying her husband when she never had done so before, not even at the Easter Sunday service? She had always taken her place in the front pew long before proceedings began.

Still, Reverend Mompesson waited, his wife at his side. He gestured towards the congregation and seemed to be speaking to someone still inside the small vestry. After a further slight pause, another figure appeared in the doorway – a man shorter than Mompesson, dressed in a long, black overcoat and scuffed knee-length boots. There was an audible gasp from those waiting. It was Thomas Stanley.

Reverend Mompesson escorted Catherine to her place, lingering for a moment as she gave him a look of confident affirmation. He then moved to the front of the church and motioned for Stanley to join him.

'The Gospel for this morning is John 15,' he began, offering no explanation for the man still at his side. 'Let us read this today with particular care and attention, asking the Lord to speak to us especially.'

Confused and scared, the congregation rose to their feet for the reading of the Gospel. They had never been addressed in such a way at the start of a service. Why was Reverend Stanley there? He hadn't been allowed over the threshold for years, much less welcomed by his rival. No one dared utter a word as each tried to avoid eye contact with those around them.

'This is my commandment, That ye love one another, as I have loved you. Greater love hath no man than this, that a man lay down his life for his friends. Ye are my friends, if ye do whatsoever I command you. And what, dear friends, does the Lord command us? These things I command you, that ye love one another.'

The last words rang out, echoing off the walls and columns of the old building.

'Please be seated.' The reverend spoke softly, aware of the effect the morning's proceedings were having already 'Today, we are given an opportunity to demonstrate our love for our Lord and for one another. I – we,' here he turned to Stanley 'are asking of you the greatest sacrifice of all. As you know, the Lord has not yet seen fit to remove this evil pest from our doors but rather to increase its grip upon us. We have been found worthy to suffer just as Christ suffered for us, to the point where He lay down His life.' He cleared his throat, momentarily unable to continue.

'Dearly beloved, we have a responsibility, a duty, to control this contagion as far as we are able. We must ensure no more of us are endangered, no more are lost than the Lord would Himself call home-ward. As the weather is getting warmer by the day, we have decided it would be best to conduct our services on Sundays and other holy days outside. The Reverend Stanley and I have found a suitable location – Cucklett Delph just on the outskirts of the village. There is a natural amphitheatre of sorts there where we can be quite comfortable for the duration of the summer.'

There were several nods of approval at this suggestion, many having already felt that the confines of the church prevented the free flow of fresh air and no means for the vapours of disease to escape.

'There will also be some less welcome changes. We will no longer hold burial services here at St Lawrence's. Nor shall any of the dead be interred here.' As he'd suspected, this did not go down well with his congregation. There was a clamour of voices as each person responded in either fear or anger.

Raising his hands for silence, William continued: 'We will help you find suitable areas for burying those amongst you who may yet pass away. I will be holding private prayers of committal wherever possible, as will Reverend Stanley here. There is no question that your loved ones will pass into the next world unprepared in any way. It is our Lord who is asking us to observe a new ordinance, and as such, the ground where any are buried will be deemed consecrated.'

There were a few more mutters, many not sure whether their humble parson had sufficient authority to pronounce on such matters. As if reading their minds, William added, 'I have been in touch with the bishop, and he is fully supportive of both our plan and our reasoning. Special prayers will even be said over the coming weeks by members of the parish church in Sheffield.' This latter impressed many, several of whom had never visited the city and considered its church there to be akin to the halls of heaven itself. Knowing that those within its walls would be praying for their dearly departed softened the blow a little.

Reverend Mompesson took advantage of the change of mood. He knew what he was about to say would cause an uproar. 'And now we come to the final part of our plan to save ourselves and our neighbours. Our Lord asks that we lay down our lives for the sake of others; He calls upon us to honour most highly the command to love one's neighbour as oneself. With this exhortation ringing in our ears, we have decided to shut up the village of Eyam for however long this pestilence remains with us.'

Kitty was sure she heard someone collapse behind her almost as soon as the words left the reverend's lips. There was a great commotion as men leapt from their places and manoeuvred the stricken individual outside, followed by a small retinue of women carrying their nosegays of sweet-smelling flowers which would hopefully act as a restorative.

Eventually, attention returned to the front, where the two reverends stood looking grim but determined.

Thomas Stanley spoke for the first time. 'I know this isn't going to be easy, but Reverend Mompesson is doing everything in his power, and with his considerable contacts, to ensure we are still provided for with provisions and so forth. A border has been proposed beyond which we shall not cross to leave, nor shall others cross to come in. A system of drop off and collection will be put in place so we have no need to come into contact with our dear neighbours.'

The use of 'we' was not lost on the villagers. It was the first time they felt less alone, less bereft of the love and support they felt they desperately needed if this were to work. Yes, their views on Mompesson had changed, he had gone up in their estimation, but he was still not 'one of us' like Thomas Stanley was.

No one wanted to linger after the service was finished. There was a palpable sense of a shock needing to be processed, of conversations that required privacy. Both Revered Mompesson and Thomas Stanley had stood under the church porch bidding the congregation farewell. They knew there was little they could say or do that would soften the blow they had just dealt, other than to stand in sympathy and solidarity with those they knew to be reeling.

Uncle Robert was amongst the first to shake their hands. 'Reverends. I know tha has a hard enough job without my adding to it with complaints and questions. I will support thee in whatever way I can, tha need only give t' word. God bless thee both.' Gratitude brightened both their faces; they knew this would not be the response of many and could only be glad it was Robert Fox who had approached them in this manner. If anyone could persuade others there was wisdom in their decision, he could.

'Come, Anne, let's be away home. Don't dawdle, Mary. Our Sarah, up on my shoulders with thee. It will make t' walk that much quicker.' He said nothing to Kitty. She followed quickly behind her uncle as he led his young family away. She wondered why he seemed so upset with her; no doubt she would find out soon enough.

Uncle Robert spoke to her as they walked the last part of their way home alone. Aunt Anne knew her husband wished to speak with Kitty by herself, so she had taken Sarah from his shoulders and gone on ahead with Mary, making some excuse about having forgotten to let the chickens out that morning.

'So, lass, did tha know this was coming?' Her uncle's accusation stung. How could he think she knew something so dreadful and yet kept it from them, the only family she had here in Eyam?

'No, Uncle, I swear I didn't!'

'But tha must have guessed something was going on. Tha's in and out of t' parsonage every day, child. They couldn't have planned this without much talk and arranging.'

'I was out with Mrs Mompesson most days, collecting or delivering for t' sick. I knew something was not right between her and t' reverend, but she didn't once utter a word about it,' Kitty paused as recollections of a few isolated incidents suddenly clicked together like the pieces in a game.

'There were some things that were strange though. T' reverend was in his study for hours at a time, and then he would rush out with letters or papers he said needed to be delivered. But he didn't ask for my help with any of them which he has done before. He told me I was too busy helping Mrs Mompesson to be worried about his scribblings. And then Mr Stanley did seem to visit more often and stay longer than before. Again, they would go into t' reverend's study and Mrs Mompesson and I would go out and leave them. I suppose even that was odd – she would normally stay to serve them their ale and so on.'

Kitty turned to her uncle, horrified as she realised the full importance of what she was remembering. 'This was what they were talking about, isn't it? Why Catherine kept me busy with her all day? They didn't want anyone to know what was happening until it was all decided.'

'Yes, lass, I think it was. But was perhaps for t' best. They couldn't let a half-finished plan be whispered around t' village. Tha knows what people are like. They would have packed up and left before anyone knew what was happening, and then there would be no end of trouble. For all of us.'

He watched Kitty fight the bitterness he knew she must be feeling. They had betrayed her again, in her eyes anyway. First, they hadn't told her about the children leaving and now this. Still, she had to learn. She could love Mrs Mompesson as dearly as she did her own mother, but folk in their position would never fully return that love.

'Don't they trust me, then?' she was saying now, angry at the implications of their secrecy. 'When have I ever told anyone – not you, not Aunt Anne – of anything I've seen or heard in t' parsonage since I started there? I thought we really were friends.' She ended with a tearful hiccup, anger giving way to the hurt it had protected her from.

'Ah, Kitty, happened they were doing thee a kindness by not telling thee. Think of it. Tha's not from here.' She began to protest, wanting to say she was just as committed to the people of Eyam as he himself was. 'No, wait till I'm finished. Tha's not from here,' he repeated, 'and they couldn't know how much tha's in contact with tha people back home in Sheffield. Tha might let slip that t' situation here has taken a turn for t' worse and before tha knows it t' whole of t' town's here, threatening us or condemning us because of t' curse of God that is upon us, as some see it. I don't, mind. As t' reverend said this morning, there's more love in God than most of us think. Or imagine,' he continued, 'how could tha know about t' arrangements and not speak out to someone, even if only me or tha aunt? They were saving thee t' burden of it, if tha asks me, not trying to keep it secret from thee. Perhaps thee should be grateful tha has a friend who does care for thee that much.'

Uncle Robert was right, Kitty knew. She just felt so disappointed at not being included in the discussions, felt left out and unwanted. But when he explained how it must be for them, carrying the weight of knowing they not only had to think up a way forward, but also had to persuade others to follow them, she relented. *It must be dreadful,* she thought. *The children away from home and now they won't even be able to go to them for a visit or bring them back until all is well again.*

And Reverend Mompesson having to rely so heavily on the goodwill and co-operation of Mr Stanley couldn't be easy either. The dislike of one for the other was more than personal, she knew. It was rooted in the civil war, in Oliver Cromwell, in the execution of one king and the restoration of another. It was about position and power and politics, with the clergy, the men of God, stuck somewhere in the middle. So many circumstances beyond their control, yet here they were doing battle shoulder to shoulder against a new enemy. A creeping, invisible, destroying enemy who seemed, she had to admit, to be winning the war.

The rest of the day was taken up with the usual farm and household responsibilities. Towards the early evening, when the day had cooled slightly, Mary sidled up to Kitty. 'Tha said we could go play down by t' river. Tha did!'

'Does tha know, I'd clean forgotten,' laughed Kitty. 'Let's go there now. Call tha ma and pa and bring Sarah. We'll have some fun before t' day is over.'

A delighted Mary ran off to collect the rest of her family. They were reluctant at first, tired from the day's work and the added emotion of the morning's announcement, but their daughter's enthusiasm was infectious. Aunt Anne found a wedge of cheese, some oatcakes and ale which she placed in a basket. 'We'll have our dinner down there while we're about it,' she declared, beaming at them all.

It turned out to be one of the best evenings Kitty had yet had during her stay in Eyam. Gone was the tension of the last few weeks, the fear and grief that lurked at the edges of all their thoughts. The water was cool and fast flowing, burbling and chattering as it eddied and flowed over the rocks and boulders of the riverbed.

Mary hid behind trees and bushes, popping out with shouts of triumphant glee when no one could find her. Uncle Robert lay on his stomach, peering over the edge of the bank in the hope of finding a fish in an easy-to-reach pool, or a moor hen nesting in the weeds. Aunt Anne laid out the food and ale on a patterned cloth she had taken down. Sarah plopped herself down on a grassy mound and practised the many unintelligible words she was now trying out.

For the first time since they could all remember, there was laughter. A fish got away with a great splash, soaking Uncle Robert's head and shoulders. Kitty chased and caught Mary, tickling her until she could barely draw breath. Aunt Anne cried out in delight as she discerned a 'mama' in the midst of Sarah's mutterings.

This is love, thought Kitty as they made their way home, the sun still high in the sky and the trees casting their shade across the path. *I would do anything for this dear family of mine, yes, even die if it meant they could have more evenings like this.* She was surprised at the thought, but knew she meant it. And she knew there were other families like this one, living on the other side of the fields and over the ridge and hills in the distance. Other families who deserved evenings like this, evenings untouched by the stain and stench of this terrible contagion, free from the fear of its stalking presence.

Yes, she would stay here, in Eyam, with her family and their friends. Her friends. She would trust herself to God, believing in His providence for her and for them. Of her own family back in Sheffield, she would try not to think too much. She knew the best thing she could do for them was to protect them by not going to them, no matter how much she longed to. And yes, John. Would she live to see him again, to have the future she had so long been dreaming of? She prayed so. Fervently.

Chinese Knot outline

The next morning when Kitty approached the parsonage it seemed she had arrived at an inopportune time. Again. Raised voices could be heard coming from the open study window even as she entered the parsonage gate. This time it was two men who were arguing; she caught snippets of their discussion as she pushed open the door.

'No, Mompesson, that will not work. Tha needs to think up something more practical.' It was Thomas Stanley. A habitually quiet and measured man, Kitty had only heard him speak in the gentlest of tones. Until now. His voice was harsh, with emotion, irritation and annoyance clear as he waited for a response.

'What would you have me do, Stanley? I am not a medical man, I know only that we have to make arrangements for the collection of items in a safe manner. Not to mention payment. Ah Kitty,' Reverend Mompesson had noticed her standing on the threshold, unsure whether to enter or retreat until they had settled their dispute.

'Come, child, perhaps you can shed some feminine light on our problem. Ah yes,' he continued, seeing Kitty's inquisitive glance around the cottage in search of Catherine, 'Catherine is already at the Skidmore's cottage. The poor mite, Anthony, has a fever and the start of a dreadful rash. His mother is going out of her mind with worry and Catherine, dear one that she is, offered to go round and sit with her to see how he does. He was only baptised a matter of weeks ago. Tragic.'

A pause at the sober recollection reminded the two men that their battle was not, at this time, against each other, but rather against an invisible foe who spared none, regardless of age or status.

'Apologies. I allowed myself to lose sight of our common purpose.' Stanley was gruff. Mompesson waved aside his apology, knowing his own stubbornness and pride were as much to blame as anything else.

'Kitty, please do come and see if there is any suggestion you can offer. You have come more recently from living in the city than I, and it could be you have heard of new methods or techniques, especially as your father is a learned man.'

Kitty took a couple of steps into the room where the two men stood on either side of the unlit fireplace. The desk under the window was unnaturally cluttered and untidy, papers strewn haphazardly across its surface. A quill had splattered ink over several of them, indicative of the state of the reverend's usually composed demeanour. She noticed

a sketch of the village and its surroundings, the church prominent
in the centre, other markings denoting each of the dwellings. Some
were blotted with a large black cross; with shock Kitty realised these
were the homes that were already empty and abandoned by their
now-deceased occupants.

'Morning sir, Mr Stanley,' she bobbed a brief curtsy. She would
normally not do so for either man individually – she was now so
familiar with Reverend Mompesson he seemed more like a slightly
severe uncle to her, and Thomas Stanley abhorred seeming in any way
superior to those he served. However, confronted with both of them
together, and knowing they were taking her into their confidence,
Kitty felt the need to demonstrate her respect.

'Kitty, let me get straight to the point. We are closing the village,
as you heard yesterday, in order that we can save our neighbours and
the wider community from suffering the same distress as ourselves.'
Kitty nodded, indicating she understood so far. 'However, we still
need contact with the outside world. We need to purchase provisions
for ourselves, and those amongst us who remain healthy need to be
able to sell their wares as would be usual at this time of year. We,' here
he indicated Stanley, 'are discussing the best way to do this.

'I feel we should have certain locations along our boundary desig-
nated for the purpose of exchange, whereby we can leave our goods
or payment which will then be collected by a member of the community beyond. Our dilemma is this: We are making this sacrifice
for the wellbeing of the people who will be responsible for helping
us from the outside, but what is the best way to ensure there is no
contamination from anything we may leave for collection? We know
not the finer details concerning the spread of this distemper and so
extra precautions should be exercised. The argument you no doubt

overheard arose from our trying to arrive at a solution that is both effective and practical.'

'Vinegar, sir.' Kitty was surprised two such well-educated men had not thought of this simple solution; no doubt it was due to their lack of experience in household matters. She chuckled inwardly at their perplexed expressions. ''Tis used all t' time when something bad needs cleaning or getting rid of. I'm sure Mrs Mompesson will have some in t' kitchen.'

'You're right, Kitty, she does! I did wonder why we always had such a big jug on hand.'

'Well done for using tha head, Kitty lass. ''Tis practical souls like thee, and tha Aunt Anne, that will see us through this.' Stanley gave Mompesson a derisive glance, clearly conveying his conviction that the gentry and all connected with them were good for not much beyond fine speaking and grand sounding but daft suggestions. Mompesson pretended not to notice the look.

'Tha'll need to fill something with vinegar and leave it there where t' people will meet. Money can be dropped in it and left there; provisions can be wiped down with a rag before handing over. I don't know it will kill this pestilence, but it won't harm,' she added hastily, not wishing either of them to take her idea as a miracle cure, nor hold her responsible when it didn't work.

'Yes, yes, of course, we understand that.' Mompesson was ready for action. 'Stanley, I'm going to write to the earl immediately and make sure our plans are clearly laid out so we can establish this protective ring as soon as possible. We must delay no longer.'

'I'll be off then. I must call in at t' Skidmore's, as we agreed earlier. James and Editha are another two young ones who have taken ill – I must attend to them also.' With a final shake of hands, and a pat on Kitty's shoulder as he passed, Thomas Stanley took his leave.

Kitty herself was now at a bit of a loss as to what she should do. The reverend was obviously about to write some personal correspondence to the lord of the manor, the Earl of Devonshire, and she doubted he would need her assistance.

'Have you ever been to the estate at Chatsworth, Kitty?' Mompesson seemed keen to engage her in conversation despite the task he had declared himself about to perform. She suspected he wanted to impress her with his contacts, regale her with stories of all the grand houses he had dined at. 'The earl holds a grand event every Christmas, opens the estate to all his tenants and farmers. I thought you may have been with your father?'

Kitty shook her head. No, she had never been to any palaces or mansions. And no, her father most certainly wouldn't have taken her, his thoughts on the gentry being what they were. But she thought it prudent not to say anything. Instead she prompted, 'Don't tha need to write that letter, sir? I would suspect tha doesn't want any delay in getting it to t' earl so tha can get his response before nightfall?'

'You are right, of course. It is just so pleasant to exchange the despair of today with memories of joy from other times. But, God willing, we shall see those days again soon!' He moved towards his desk and sat down. 'My, what a state I am in. Kitty, pray, be seated here with me that I should bring some order to this chaos with your calm assistance.'

Together they moved and shuffled papers, wiped split ink and eventually had enough space for a new parchment to be spread out in preparation for writing.

Sir,

I write to you this June morning with sad news as to the condition of the parish and her people here in Eyam. You will, of course, be aware that the pestilence has once more returned to our streets and homes, and even now many amongst us lie sick and dying. It is therefore with some urgency I wish to apprise you of the decisions we have taken over the last few days and to seek such assistance from yourself as you feel duty-bound to offer.

Together with my predecessor, Thomas Stanley, I have persuaded these dear, courageous folk to remain within the confines of our boundaries. In this way, we believe the contagion's spread can be restricted and contained, thus preventing an outbreak amongst those on the rest of your estate. We will shortly be erecting symbols to mark our boundary lines, beyond which neither man nor beast shall cross.

However, for this to be a successful plan, it will require the assistance and co-operation of those of you able to move freely outside this cordon sanitaire. I would therefore beseech you, my lord, to organise such parties of men you deem fit who can be prevailed upon to carry provisions of victuals and other necessary supplies to us here in Eyam. Said articles can be carried to the aforementioned boundary markers at first light and be exchanged for coins deposited by ourselves in receptacles containing vinegar to ensure there is no spread of infection. There need be no direct contact between either party; indeed, this should be eliminated entirely.

My sincere apologies for the shortness of this missive, but I must press upon you the dire situation in which we in Eyam find ourselves. The pestilence is strong upon us, and we are hourly losing members of my precious flock to its evil.

In eager anticipation of your positive response,

Yours

William Mompesson (Reverend)

Mompesson signed his letter with a flourish and carefully blotted the ink before rolling the parchment. He tied it neatly with a ribbon and quickly applied his seal to its edge.

'I must be away with this letter, Kitty, I have delayed long enough!'
He looked at his desk and noticed a few small leftovers of parchment. 'I wonder, while you wait for Catherine to return, whether you wouldn't like to write to your family? I'm sure they would like to hear news of you, and reassurance that you, and your aunt and uncle, remain in good health. Perhaps you should also tell them of our new arrangements here...' His kindness caught Kitty off guard, and she bit her lip hard to prevent her eyes from filling with the embarrassment of tears.

'Thank you, sir, that's most kind of you,' she managed.

'Very well then. I shall see you either later or tomorrow, hopefully with news from the earl.' William turned, not wishing to discomfort Kitty any further, and left the parsonage in her care.

The silence rang in her ears the moment he had departed. Despite the wide-open windows, the air was still and not a page on the desk in front of Kitty stirred. Outside even the birds seemed to have ceased their song. She pulled a piece of parchment towards her, took up the quill and wrote. Her letter writing had come to something of a standstill, owing in part to her lack of access to parchment and to her being far too exhausted at the end of each day to put words on any page. The words now flowed easily as she told stories of herself and the rest of the family in Eyam.

She reassured her family of her wellbeing, and wondered how much they had heard of what was happening. She decided to be brief in her explanation about the shutting up of the village. After all, she was only due to return to them when they visited at the next Wakes Festival; given that was several moons away still, she thought circumstances might well be different by then and it would be heartless to worry them unnecessarily.

She signed her name and then sat staring unseeingly out of the window for a few moments. She drew a second parchment to her.

My dearest John

It is with much sadness of heart that I write these words to thee. T' situation here in Eyam is dreadful. So many are sick and unlikely to recover this side of eternity. T' reverend has decided to shut up t' village, not letting anyone go out or anyone come in, so as to make sure t' infection doesn't spread anywhere else. I don't know how long it will be for, but hopefully, by Wakes it will have passed.

But John, I am so scared. I am so often in contact with those who are ill as I work with Catherine – Mrs Mompesson – who is as kind to me as ever I expected her to be. What if I get sick? And what if it is a sickness that leads to my dying? We still had so many plans, so much to hope for – what if they come to nothing?

In so many ways I wish I had not had to come here, to leave thee and wait until t' apprenticeship is complete. I could have been patient there at home, I'm certain of it. Perhaps though it is best I am here, where I can be of use. Oh, I am so torn! My head is here, where I am of service. But my heart is with thee, my dearest darling John.

Should it be t' good Lord's will that I should be taken, and so never see thee again, I want tha to know how much I love thee, and always will. Be not sad for me, should I depart, but live on my behalf all our dreams.

Forever thine, Kitty.

Her falling tears blotched the ink as she wrote, her shaking hand smudging the letters. Kitty knew she hadn't been able to put her heart into the words she wrote, but she hoped John would read and know.

*Chinese Knot out-
line*

The next hours and days were a flurry of activity. Households were visited and informed about all of the arrangements that had been made on their behalf. Lists were compiled, detailing what was needed immediately and what could wait until later. Fresh produce was collected and made ready for sale. All lead excavated from the mines over recent weeks was hurriedly dressed and despatched to the agent. Those who could write – the Mompessons, Thomas Stanley, Kitty and a few others – sat patiently while individuals dictated letters to relatives living beyond the village boundary. Many could not be sure they would ever see those family members again, and the notes were raw and grief laden.

A rota was also put in place detailing who was responsible for the daily early morning boundary visits. It was deemed better to have more than one drop-off location point so as to ensure the foul air of death could not concentrate in any one spot. When all was finalised, everyone involved gathered together. Under the leadership of Reverend Mompesson, they took a walk along the newly established boundary lines to check that all was in order. Kitty and Aunt Anne were included in the party as both would be expected to help in some way with the distribution of goods once they were brought into Eyam. Provisions would need to be accounted for and fairly shared out amongst the various households; letters and news from outside required sorting and posting. Armed with jugs of vinegar, even a small one for Mary, they took their place in the sombre procession.

'Ah Kitty, did tha see t' reverend has asked our Robert to bring his tools? He wants him to make holes in t' main boundary rock up at top of t' hill, big enough for coins to easily fit into. We're then to fill t' holes with this vinegar, and so prevent t' contagion from living on t' coins and spreading to t' person who picks them up. Clever I thought. Who would think t' reverend knew something practical like that. Maybe it was Mrs Mompesson who had the idea?' Kitty smiled knowingly, happy that her mentor was being given the credit for something she herself had suggested.

'And we're to take more of this vinegar to that little well out on t' road to Grindleford, tha knows, t' one that looks like a little pool?' Kitty nodded. That was a fair walk, and she hoped the girls would be able to keep up.

Kitty needn't have worried. The children thought the whole outing was great fun, and there were enough people to help carry Sarah for short ways when she wanted a break from the novelty of walking. First, they climbed the hills to the south of the village where the great boundary stone sat nestled in the long summer grass. Uncle Robert set to with his chisel and heaviest hammer, boring seven or eight large, deep holes into its surface. As this took some time, the others had an opportunity to rest and get their breath back.

Kitty wandered a little way off from the others, seeking a moment of solitude. She gazed out over the hills and down into the valley below. Through the hazy mid-morning sunshine, she could just about make out the main highway as it snaked through the green fields on its way to Sheffield. To home. She still had the letters to her family and John scrumpled in the pocket of her apron, not yet having had the courage to add them to the growing pile that would be dropped off later that day with the postman from Stoney Middleton. They felt like her last contact with those she loved, even though they hadn't yet received or read them, and she was reluctant to part with the folded pieces of parchment – as though a piece of her own heart would be leaving her, perhaps never to return.

The young woman knew she was being melodramatic, but an uneasy feeling of standing on the edge of some steep ridge or cliff had haunted her over recent days. Night after night her dreams took her to its highest point, the wind buffeting and rocking her as she stood, trying to brace herself and make herself steady. Then the sky would turn black, storm clouds rolling in from the distant horizon. Far away flashes of lightning slashed through the gloom, although the clap of the thunder never reached her. She grew colder, her teeth chattering and her fingers turning blue. She knew she wouldn't be able to maintain her position much longer, the storm sapping her spirit.

Someone, or something, was approaching her from behind, the foul warmth of its breath tickling her neck. She felt the presence getting nearer, closer, until suddenly she was falling from the edge of the ridge, down into an empty abyss, clawing frantically at the air as her screams rang in her ears. And then she would awaken, the half-light of early morning illuminating all but the deepest corners of her room.

'Come, Kitty luv, we're done here. Time to go on to t' well.' Aunt Anne had walked over to stand at her side, scanning the outspread landscape as though searching for her own peace in its empty vastness. 'Tha'll be home soon.' She placed a gentle hand on Kitty's arm, then steered her back to where the others were already starting to walk on ahead. Before continuing on, Kitty went to check the newly drilled boundary stone. Each hole was filled to the brim with acrid-smelling pools of vinegar. She nodded her approval, then followed her aunt as they walked to the northern side of the village and the well they had spoken of earlier.

'Mompesson's Well now, no doubt,' whispered someone behind Kitty. She thought it was a bit mean of them, but funny all the same. Yes, Reverend Mompesson would like to think he had left his mark in some way.

Once the shallow mouth of the well had been topped up with vinegar, everyone started drifting back to their own homes. The work was done, the fun of the outing was over and the stark reality of what had just taken place was sinking in. The next day they would have their first church service out at Cucklett Delph. Kitty glanced at the gathering clouds and hoped it wouldn't rain; it was a disconcerting enough day without adding getting soaked to the skin into the bargain.

Before she made her own way home with Aunt Anne and the rest of the family, Kitty dashed over to Reverend Mompesson's side.

'Sir,' she began, tugging the letters out of her pocket as she spoke. 'Could tha make sure these get out with t' rest of t' letters later?'

The reverend looked at the small pieces of folded parchment. He noticed the destination – Sheffield – on each and noticed to whom they were addressed. His heart went out to the poor child. She had come here to Eyam with the sole intention of helping out her aunt and uncle with their two children and tiny parcel of land. Instead, she had been caught up in a living nightmare of disease and decay and death. And now she was to be trapped, forced to remain here for as long as the pestilence required their sacrificial offering of health and life.

Kitty had become such a help to him personally, assisting with the ever-increasing demands of a parish at war with an unseen enemy. Her quiet demeanour and gentle spirit were a balm to his often-exhausted mind, and he knew she was welcomed by his congregation whenever she helped Catherine with parcels and provisions. Indeed, it was her friendship with his dear wife that really meant the world to him. He knew Catherine would never have survived the absence of her children if it weren't for Kitty and her daily presence in their lives. He also knew he wouldn't have been able to spare the time to be her constant companion in the way Kitty was.

He looked fondly at the young woman now. 'Yes, of course, my dear, I will personally make sure your letters reach their destination in safe hands. I trust it will not be much longer before you yourself shall be following them to Sheffield where you will be reunited with your family. And young man,' he added mischievously. Kitty blushed. Catherine must have told him about John. William chuckled and turned to leave.

*Chinese Knot out-
line*

The threatened rain held off as the villagers of Eyam made preparations for their first outdoor Sunday service. Aunt Anne located bonnets and shawls for herself and the girls, while Uncle Robert debated the wisdom of allowing Patch to follow along beside him, knowing he would love the chase for rabbits while they were out. In the end he decided against it, remembering that it was still church even it if weren't in a building. Kitty helped where she could, hoping that the morning service would go well and that the reverend could successfully lead them in such strange circumstances.

For his part, Reverend Mompesson glanced nervously over his notes and read one or two sentences aloud, experimenting with volume and tone in an attempt to make sure he would be heard when the waving trees were the only roof above his head. He hoped he would be loud enough, able to convey his message with clarity and conviction. There was no doubt, much would be demanded of him this morning.

This was the first day of the new restrictions preventing the people from leaving the confines of their village. All the letters had been collected late the evening before, and the requested provisions were even now being dropped at the two main locations out in the fields. The comfort and security associated with meeting together within the solidity of the walls of St Lawrence's Church were also being forsaken, and he knew this would unnerve many. Several had approached him during the week expressing their dismay at the arrangements, challenging him over his decision and its basis in good Church practice. He was weary from explaining and persuading, yet he knew this would remain his role for several weeks to come while his flock adjusted.

There was worse. Over the last week, the first of the home burials had taken place. To start with he'd been called to the home of the Thornleys where another two children had died, together with their widowed mother. There had been no man of the house able to dig a grave, and he'd had to find someone willing to help. Then he'd attended the Mower's home where a young brother and sister had died on the same day. The weather was stifling, the heat meaning everything needed to be done as quickly as was decently possible. He knew others might not last the day, and hoped he could at least finish his homily under the trees before he was again called upon.

William thanked God earnestly for Thomas Stanley – not a circumstance he would ever have expected, but his thanks were heartfelt. There was so much he would be incapable of doing without the older man's assistance. His was the reassuring face of familiarity that the distressed longed for, his the voice of comfort when grief overwhelmed.

Being a widower himself, Stanley empathised with individuals more than William knew he ever could. He tried, but always at the back of his mind was the relief that his children were far away and his wife, here at his side, remained well. He suspected some of his congregation were aware of how he felt and, while not blaming him, did respect him a little less for it.

His planning complete, William called for Catherine and together they took the lane out of the village centre and across the fields to Cucklett Delph. A few nervous groups of families were already gathered, unsure whether to stand or sit on the grass. Others were still making their way from their cottages, coming from all different directions. The reverend's heart was glad. He had half wondered if anyone would actually turn up, so unusual was the request to have services held in the open air. Of course, he knew it was commonplace amongst the non-conformist preachers, but he also knew that, at their core, these people were traditional in their habits and practices.

Cucklett Delph was a perfect natural sanctuary. A slight dip in the hillside created a sheltered hollow where the congregation could easily gather. A tower of rock rose from the grassy slope, at the centre of which was a natural archway where Mompesson could stand. From this vantage point, he could see every person gathered and they could both see and hear him. It was ideal.

When Stanley had first suggested the idea of taking the Sunday services outside, Mompesson had been doubtful. For a start, he couldn't immediately think of anywhere suitable. Then one day he and Catherine had taken a walk further into the countryside to see if the Lord had Himself already provided a place. He had. As soon as they saw it, they had known this was the place. Now, the harshness of the rock under which he stood softened by the profusion of ferns and mosses growing down its face, William felt certain. Here he could minister to his brave, embattled flock just as well, if not better, than he had ever been able to when surrounded by walls.

As their reverend climbed to his verdant pulpit, the parishioners of Eyam settled down into their chosen spots on the grass. Together but separate, they remained in their small family groups, not wishing to mingle and mix as they would on other Sundays. Everything was different – not just their place of meeting, but the way of meeting too. There was now an invisible barrier between them, an irrevocable change in circumstance that required an irrevocable change in behaviour.

Strangely, the bonds of solidarity and unity of purpose had grown stronger over the last few days than perhaps they had ever been, despite the physical space that now existed. Kitty felt the greetings of one to another were more sincere, more heartfelt than usual. There was a measure of relief that each had made it through the night, that the weather was fair, that good men were leading them forward.

It was proving somewhat more difficult, however, to convince the many children present that this was the solemn occasion of a church service. Mary and Sarah had joined their young friends in racing around the hollow, chasing the butterflies that flitted from one flower to the next. Uncle Robert was glad he had decided to leave the dog at home; it was chaotic enough already.

Eventually the parents of the happily playing children managed to drag them back to their place where they were instructed to sit down and be quiet. The reverend clapped his hands to gain everyone's attention and a hush fell over the standing crowd; all eyes turned to William Mompesson.

For the first time for as long as he could remember, he was nervous before preaching. Perhaps it was knowing that he would need to offer those standing before him words of courage at a time when all was changing around them. The absence of the security of St Lawrence's, and the knowledge that they could no longer travel freely throughout the countryside they had grown up in, was unnerving in any circumstance. Add to that the rise in daily infections and he knew fear and anxiety were gnawing away at each of them. He had prepared well for this morning. He had read over the passages of Scripture for the day and committed them to memory, leaving the ancient church Bible safely stored away from the elements. He knew the liturgy for morning prayer and was grateful for its structured patterns, the one aspect of this strange service that was familiar, comforting.

Reverend Mompesson was painfully aware that over the weeks to come, the number of those clustered to hear him preach would inevitably reduce in number. He wished it were not so, but he had seen enough of this contagion to know that the neighbours of those currently lying on their death beds would follow close behind to their own graves. As he looked at each of the small huddles of families gathered together, he wondered who would be there the following week, and then the next.

William felt his emotions rise, knew with certainty that these were a people he had come to love in a way he had thought impossible when he first arrived in the parish of Eyam. Their hostility had been palpable, their dislike of him and preference for their previous minister plain. He had tried hard at first but the constant rejection of him had worn him down and he had retreated to his studies, performing that which he was obligated to do and little else. If it hadn't been for his beloved Catherine, he thought, he would have written to his benefactor and requested a different appointment. But now here he stood, and whether their attitude had changed towards him or not, he realised it didn't matter. It was *his* attitude to them that had changed. He saw them as sheep without a shepherd, lost and wandering through this valley of the shadow of death, in need of direction and succour. For this he had been called here, he was sure of it.

'Dearly, dearly beloved,' his voice bounced and echoed off the rock face behind him. And he knew all would be well. He was as secure here as in his stone pulpit at the front of St Lawrence's. The people heard the empathy, the warmth, in those opening words and they too relaxed. This wouldn't be so alien after all. They were to be led and ministered to by a man they were beginning to learn to trust, a man who had chosen to remain by their sides rather than join his children in the great houses of the city. They had heard of his night-time visits to the bereaved, watched as he and his wife visited the sick with little concern for their own health. They had seen the hand of welcome he even extended to their old friend, Thomas Stanley, and were impressed by his humility and acceptance of help.

'This morning I would like to highlight a few verses from the first of our readings from the Psalter – Psalm 86, a Psalm of David: Bow down thine ear, O Lord, hear me: for I am poor and needy. Preserve my soul; for I am holy: O thou my God, save thy servant that trusteth in thee. Be merciful unto me, O Lord: for I cry unto thee daily. Rejoice the soul of thy servant: for unto thee, O Lord, do I lift up my soul. For thou, Lord, art good, and ready to forgive; and plenteous in mercy unto all them that call upon thee. Give ear, O Lord, unto my prayer; and attend to the voice of my supplications. In the day of my trouble I will call upon thee: for thou wilt answer me.

'We may not be those who sit in kingly palaces, brethren, but we are those who can enter the palace of a Heavenly King. We, like David before us, can cry out to the Lord, indeed should be doing so daily, imploring Him to have mercy during this, our time of trial. As we lift our *souls* to the Lord, we should remember that the Lord is good.

As we lift our *voices* to this, our good God, our weary souls will be restored, and our hope shall again be strengthened.'

Kitty was impressed. Reverend Mompesson seemed so out of place in this outdoor setting. He was a man of pattern and conformity, unlike the Puritan preachers who had long ago become accustomed to ministering to their flock in the fields and along the byways. Despite that, now here he was, speaking with authority and compassion in these unfamiliar surroundings. She knew he feared for the future. Not his own particularly, assured as he was of his place in eternity, but for the fate of them all as they endured the unendurable. She had overheard conversations between him and Catherine, discussing the fate of yet another afflicted family. It was no longer only Catherine's voice that carried tones of pity and sorrow; her husband too was affected by their plight. Kitty was glad when she observed the men nodding in agreement at the reverend's words, saw tears cascade unchecked down the faces of the women as the tenderness of tone touched their breaking hearts.

The first open air Sunday service was drawing to a close.

'Almighty God, who hast given us grace at this time with one accord to make our common supplications unto thee; and dost promise, that when two or three are gathered together in thy Name thou wilt grant their requests; Fulfil now, O Lord, the desires and petitions of thy servants, as may be most expedient for them; granting us in this world knowledge of thy truth, and in the world to come life everlasting. Amen.'

A unified chorus of 'Amen' rose like incense heavenwards. Kitty trusted it would be a sweet-smelling sacrifice unto the Lord.

'The grace of our Lord Jesus Christ, and the love of God, and the fellowship of the Holy Ghost, be with us all for evermore. Amen.' The congregation stood awkwardly, waiting to be dismissed. Usually, there would be greetings and a slow progression to the doors of the church and so to home. Now there was no door, no exit.

Aunt Anne woke Sarah from where she had fallen asleep on the soft grass, and Mary begged desperately to join the embrace of her playmates. Meanwhile Uncle Robert was engrossed in conversation with a fellow miner. Kitty overheard something about plans for the upcoming week and ways to keep the mine operating now there were fewer men fit and well enough for the arduous underground labour, and few women free to carry out the remaining tasks once the stone was pulled into the open.

Kitty watched as families and groups gradually slipped away, eager to return to the comfort and safety of their own homes. There was so much more to be done by everyone, helping as they were those who were incapacitated or preoccupied with nursing. There was no time to linger.

On the edge of the dell, Kitty noticed a familiar figure standing alone – Thomas Stanley. Had he been here for the whole service? She hadn't seen him, but then she hadn't really been looking around too much, waiting as she was for Reverend Mompesson to commence the service. Mr Stanley hadn't attended any of Reverend Mompesson's services aside from the one where they stood united to announce the new plans, but perhaps he wished to show his support for this, the first service to be held outside the church building. Whatever the reason, Kitty was glad to see him. The two men of God learning to work alongside each other, to respect and honour each other, for the sake of the people of the village was one of the most surprising, but most welcome, outcomes of all that was happening.

Uncle Robert finished his conversation and turned to take the sleepy weight of Sarah from his wife. 'Go on, then, lass.' He smiled at the elated Mary as she raced off to join her friends. 'Just don't get too far ahead. And don't be a nuisance!'

'Oh, look, there's Grace Morten – Kitty, we must go and speak with her. She promised to give us some eggs to take t' others in t' morning. Let us make arrangements with her.' Kitty followed her aunt; it was time to be practical once more.

July 1666

As June progressed into July, the villagers of Eyam fell into the macabre new routine of isolation and self-sufficiency. The weather was stifling, as hot as the winter had been cold. With the heat came the stench of disease and decay. Kitty felt it lingered in her hair, had seeped into her skin. Every night she returned home from her rounds with the Mompessons, filled a bowl with warm water and vinegar, and scrubbed herself almost raw. But it didn't work. As soon as she lay in bed at night, trying to ignore the horrors of the day floating like wraiths before her closed eyes, the foul scent assailed her. Although she rarely went into the shut-up homes of the sick or dying, she was enough in the centre of the village for the fetid stillness of the streets and lanes to seem to become the only air she breathed. At times she even felt she could taste it.

The outdoor Sunday services continued each week. Reverend Mompesson became accustomed to his new pulpit, and his congregation their pews, as he tried to offer hope and courage. In the absence of official funerals, he had decided to read out the names of those who had passed on over the course of each week. William felt this was the best way to honour the families who otherwise were unable to mourn with their friends and neighbours. His message was becoming increasingly hard to bear as the dell where they met became more and more sparsely populated.

On the first Sunday of July the list of recently deceased was short – only four people. William was relieved it wasn't longer. The widow Ann Skidmore had died the previous Sunday – shortly after he had finished morning prayer – leaving behind two sons. Jane Townend had died the following day and by the end of the week the boy John Swann and a second member of the Heald family was being buried. William was sure poor Emmott Heald's mother would be following her daughter to the grave in only a matter of hours. He suspected there would be more names the following week.

He was right. Mr and Mrs Lowe both died on Monday. The orphan Deborah Elliot who had been staying with her aunt, Mrs Naylor, passed on Tuesday. On Wednesday, Mompesson was summoned to the bedside of George Darby. The worst blow came on Thursday – two girls from the Talbot family died together. While Mompesson was doing his best to comfort the distraught parents, themselves displaying signs of illness, he had received a desperate message from his wife, Catherine. He was needed urgently over at John Daniel's cottage. Mrs Daniel – Syddall as she had been and Betsy to all her friends – was about to become a widow for the second time. As William stood in front of those friends on the second Sunday in July and read John Daniel's name, he watched as a few of them reached for Betsy's hands in a vain attempt to offer comfort; he struggled to continue. This was the cruellest of diseases. None would be left unmarked by its touch, of that he was certain.

By the middle of July, the daily death toll was unbearable. Mompesson and Thomas Stanley ministered last rites and offered prayers of consolation at the homes of Lowes, the Thornleys, the Talbots, the extended Thorpe families – the list was endless. Five or six would pass in a single day, whole families carried off in a matter of hours.

Some in the village no longer went out or visited anyone, deciding to simply stay in their cottages and wait for the pestilence to reach its deathly conclusion. They ventured out only for Sunday worship, standing apart from the others for fear of infection. They greeted no one and were always the first to depart for home. Both William and Catherine were worried for them; it was hard enough to be isolated as a whole community, but to be isolated within that community was unimaginable. They both tried to visit and encourage those families, but even the entreaties of Thomas Stanley fell on deaf ears.

Then there were others, like Uncle Robert and Aunt Anne who, despite having young children, were doing all they could to help and serve their neighbours. Kitty was honoured to be able to call them her family, and she worked daily to live up to their example. Aunt Anne continued to make the herbal preparations Catherine had taught her, while also developing some of her own. Each morning she took the girls to collect eggs from all the abandoned hen houses around the village. She had contemplated moving the hens nearer to their cottage but was persuaded not to by Robert. He felt it better to keep them separate, just in case any were infected as their unfortunate owners had been.

'Did tha see Margaret Blackwell there at t' service this morning?' It was the end of another long day. The two young girls were in bed although the sun was still high and hot in the sky. The three adults were sitting under the shade of the tree, Aunt Anne shelling peas as she spoke. Kitty was sitting idle, too exhausted to find something useful to do.

Uncle Robert sat nursing his jug of cold ale, his big rough hands clasped together around its middle. 'Aye, now that's a miracle right there!'

'What happened?' asked Kitty. She'd vaguely heard about the Blackwell family, but she thought they had all fallen sick and died over the winter. She was surprised to hear her aunt and uncle mention one of them.

'Well, it was only Francis, the eldest son, and Margaret who were left when t' others all passed. And it looked certain that Francis was to be left all alone as Margaret had recently become unwell too.' Aunt Anne absent-mindedly continued with the peas, engrossed now in her story. 'Well, he was called away to t' coal mine, sudden like, and had to leave his poor sister at home on her own. He'd cooked himself up some bacon to take with him and poured t' fat into a piggin so he could reuse it later – as dripping, I suppose. Anyway, young Margaret hadn't heard him leave, so worn with fever was she. At some point she woke up and was desperate for a drink. Not being able to get help from her brother, she staggered into t' kitchen and drained that whole pail of bacon fat in one gulp! 'Twas from then she got better.'

'Tha'd swear tha was there to see it all happening!' Uncle Robert said with a wink at Kitty. 'Who knows but that she wasn't starting to feel better already?'

'Well, maybe,' Aunt Anne laughed. 'There's others that have got better, like Marshall Howe. He's fighting fit again, so I hear?'

'That he is,' confirmed Uncle Robert. 'So much so he's taken to helping families with burying of their dead. Especially t' children where there's no one strong enough left at home.'

'Ah, but that's foolish for Joan and t' young one – Billy. He's not more 'n two years old. Marshall should be careful he doesn't bring others' illness back to his own family.' Aunt Anne had expressed her disapproval on the subject before; she hadn't been able to convince her husband then, and it seemed unlikely she would do so now.

'Ah at least he's helping, luv. Everyone is so scared, there's little enough help to go around. Bring down t' Bible, Kitty lass, and let's read a while.' Kitty had been only half-listening to the conversation; the heat and labour of the day made her feel listless and dozy. She reluctantly pushed herself to her feet. Her skirts clung to her legs and sweat dripped between her shoulder blades; she didn't think she'd ever been so hot in all her life.

Returning with the Bible, she sat back on the grassy hump where she had made herself comfortable. 'What does tha want me to read, Uncle?' The book was heavy and hot in her lap; she really wished he hadn't wanted her to fetch it, hadn't asked her to stir from her place of laziness. Her fingers traced the gold lettering on the cover, picturing how her father always did the same when he took it down from its special shelf at home. Then he would stroke the cover, feeling the softness of the leather beneath his scholarly palm. Kitty did the same now, noticing as she did so the hard callouses that had developed, the chipped and dirty fingernails.

As she turned the cover, her eyes fell on the names written with intricate care on the first page: Richard Allenby and Margaret Allenby, and the year of their marriage. Then her own name – Catherine Allenby – and next to it, scrawled in the untidy handwriting of her childhood, Kitty. She smiled. She had got into so much trouble the day she did that!

Everyone had been out, and she had just learned how to write her name – Kitty, not Catherine. She had pulled the Bible from its shelf, stretching up on tiptoe to reach it, and then she had proudly written her name, tongue sticking out at the effort. As she finished, her father had walked in on her. He had been furious. Didn't she know this was a holy book, not just any piece of old parchment she could scribble on? She was never to take the book off the shelf again.

Kitty had started crying, imploring her irate father to take a look at how neat her script was. Eventually, he had bent his head to look, more to silence her than with any expectation of seeing anything more than a mess covering the whole page. When he saw the effort she had clearly gone to, realised she had been doing what he himself had taught her, his face softened. He'd kissed her hair and hugged her close, stemming the tears. He had told her it was very beautiful, and it would always be special to him, but that she should never take the Holy Bible off the shelf again unless asked to do so by him.

How she wished her father were here now, with his strong arms around her and his reassuring voice whispering in her ear. What would he say to comfort and encourage her now?

'Ah, tha can choose.' Uncle Robert's response broke into her reverie. 'Anything written in t' Word is good for times like these.'

Kitty opened the book randomly. Well, almost randomly. She didn't fancy a great long list of names and places she couldn't pronounce, battles others had fought, kings rising and falling, so she chose nearer the back than the front, hoping for an encouraging psalm or wise word from Solomon's Wisdom.

Galatians. Not too bad. She skimmed the first few lines and then read: *And let us not be weary in well doing: for in due season we shall reap, if we faint not.* How long could they – could she – continue doing good without becoming overburdened and exhausted? As Uncle Robert said, there weren't many in the village who were still prepared or able to help with all that was demanded.

Aunt Anne let the peas fall into her lap as she bowed her head. It was true, they were all weary. Right now Anne felt more fear, grief and helplessness than at any other time in her life. But weary of doing good? No. She looked over at Robert. His eyes glistened with unshed tears, and he gripped his tankard so tightly his knuckles were white. His burden was even heavier than her own. Not only had he taken on the organisation of all the practical work around the village, but he also had their own small family to be concerned for. Should anything happen to Mary or Sarah, or even herself come to that, he would never forgive himself. He worked tirelessly for the community, but she knew he worried endlessly for them. *Ah, Lord,* she prayed, *help us that we would faint not.*

August 1666

K itty jerked wide awake. It had taken her a while to fall asleep, as
usual. Her body had ached from all the walking between her
home here in Water Lane down to the parsonage and from there to
the various cottages scattered around the village, all the while carrying
a basket heavy with provisions and supplies. The bottles and jugs of
tonic alone were enough to weigh her down. And then there were the
clean linens, the carefully wrapped eggs, and newly plucked pigeons
or wildfowl.

She knew that for some families Aunt Anne and Catherine Mompesson were their only providers, and although she knew she was
doing the Lord's work, she couldn't help but wish it were a little less
tiring. The incessant heat was troubling her too. By mid-afternoon on
most days, she had a headache – a dull throb that put her in a bad
mood, making her short-tempered with her sweet cousin Mary who
longed just to play with Kitty when she eventually got back from her
day's work. So that night, as on so many others, she had lain awake
on her straw mattress willing herself to relax and rest. Eventually, as
twilight dulled the sky to a soft blue, she had drifted off into a deep
and, for once, dreamless sleep.

But now something had woken her. Kitty lay perfectly still, her eyes
wide as she got used to the darkness that was now complete. *It must*

be past midnight, she thought. It didn't seem to be something from within the cottage that had disturbed her; there was no sound except the snoring of Uncle Robert in the next room, and the wheezy snuffles of Mary here beside her. Poor child, she seemed to always have a runny nose and angry, itching eyes at this time of year, or so her mother had told a concerned Kitty when the sneezing had first begun. Thankfully, no rose-red rash had appeared on the girl's skin, and Kitty had been reassured.

The young woman clambered from the bed and went to the open window. The sound must have come from outside. Patch, barking in his sleep? Or a fox hunting the chickens? She pulled down the upper window and leant out as far as she dared. The cool night air was a welcome change from the stuffiness of the day. The waning moon shed an eerie pale light over the landscape, but it wasn't bright enough for Kitty to make out more than the shadows of the trees and the distant hills. And then she heard it – something metal hitting stones or rock. A bit like when the men were deep in the mines, hammering with their chisels at the rock from which they would extract the lead ore. Even though they were far from the surface, the ring of their picks echoed and wound its way up to the entrance where the women worked.

Kitty craned her neck in the direction of the noise, but she couldn't make anything out. Whatever it was, it was just beyond her range of vision. It stopped again, as though whatever – or whoever – was making the noise had paused for a moment. And then she realised – it was someone digging a grave. But who? She was confused by the night-time echoes that distorted the noise, making it impossible to tell whether it was close or several miles away. The gravedigger returned to work and Kitty again tried to identify from whence the sound came. Could it possibly be as far away as the other side of Riley's Wood? That was a good way from where Kitty hung out of the window, but that was definitely the direction the noise was coming from.

She fervently hoped she was wrong. There were only two homes located that far out of the village – one belonging to the Talbots, the other to the Hancocks. Both farmed the old Riley land, although the Talbots were also the local blacksmiths who worked from the smithy they had built to the side of their home. Once Eyam had been placed into its self-imposed isolation, many felt it unlikely they would see either family until it was again safe to enter the village. However, much to everyone's surprise and consternation, the children from both homes had regularly trotted through the woods that separated them from their friends. In search of playmates, they had wandered throughout the village and joined in with whatever games or activities were on the go.

Sadly, it wasn't only a few fish or some new game that they took back home with them; the illness of others followed them through the dense undergrowth and the shade of the woodland trees. Two of the Talbot sisters died at the beginning of July and were buried by their devastated father on a plot of ground on the land they worked. By the end of the month their close neighbours and friends, the Hancocks, were said to have buried the broken-hearted father and, a day or two later, his last remaining son.

Now only the Hancocks remained on old Riley's land on the far side of the wood. If she was correct in assuming that the noise she heard was coming from there, Kitty knew it could mean only one thing – the Hancock family were sick, and at least one had not made it through this August night. Devastated at the thought, Kitty withdrew her head from the open window and turned back into the room. She found Uncle Robert standing in the doorway, a look of concern on his face.

'Oh! Did I wake thee?' whispered an apologetic Kitty. 'It must have been when I slid t' window down.'

'No, lass, was t' same noise woke me as I dare say woke thee – t' sound of a grave being dug?' Kitty nodded, her lips trembling. She stifled the cry she knew was about to escape – too loud for the stillness of this midnight hour. 'Come downstairs, lass, there's no point in waking t' others.' Uncle Robert led the way. They sat on opposite sides of the scrubbed table, Kitty resting her chin on her cupped hands, Uncle Robert leaning heavily on his elbows.

'It's not fair, Uncle, really it isn't. They don't even live right here in t' village with t' rest of us. Why couldn't they have just kept t' children at home with them? Told them not to wander away.' It was rare that Kitty spent time alone with her uncle without one of the girls or Aunt Anne. She liked it, sitting there in the quiet of the cottage, hearing the first of the dawn chorus warming up, the fresh notes heralding a new day. With its hopes? Or with heartache?

'*His compassions fail not. They are new every morning: great is His faithfulness.* I learned that many years ago, Kitty, when I was a lad in t' Sunday School. There'd just been an accident over at one of t' mines, t' old Glebe Mine what was up behind t' church back then. Some of my friends' fathers had been killed, but mine had escaped and walked away unharmed. I still remember him coming in that door, all black and scraped, the tears tracing clean white lines down his cheeks.

'Ma sat him down and made him tell us everything that happened – how he'd tried to warn t' others as soon as he'd heard t' first crack of the wooden beams. But it was too late, and he couldn't save any of them, only himself. We sat here all night, keeping vigil for t' souls of those who had departed. And then the first bird started up singing. My father got up from his place, went straight t' water bowl and washed his face and hands until they shone. He turned to us, and declared those very words to us, saying as how he'd been saved by t' mercy and compassion of t' Lord alone, and that he owed it to both Him and his friends to start the new day with thankfulness. He said he had been spared where they hadn't, and now he must show himself faithful to the families of the dead and find a way to provide for them. And that he did, until t' day he breathed his last.'

Uncle Robert lifted his head to look at Kitty. 'We that have been spared owe it to those that have lost so much, that are in despair, to show ourselves faithful to them – until our own time has come.' He reached across and squeezed Kitty's wrist. 'We'll make it, child, with t' Lord's help. And we'll bear up under t' strain for t' sake of those who need us. Go on now, there's still a bit of time before tha needs to be up and about tha business; try and get some more rest before t' day starts properly.'

Yawning guiltily, Kitty stood and headed for the stairs at the back of the room. 'Thank thee, Uncle. Tha's just like Pa – tha knows t' right thing to say, all t' time.' She disappeared back to bed, not seeing her uncle cover his face with his hands nor his shoulders shake as sorrow engulfed him.

*Chinese Knot out-
line*

Kitty stretched and opened her eyes. And then recoiled in shock. Standing over her, peering intently through scrunched up eyes, was young Mary. 'Oh, tha's not dead. I am glad,' Mary pronounced happily. 'I've been up for ages already, tha knows. We got ten eggs this morning.'

'No, child, I'm not dead,' laughed Kitty, grabbing Mary before she could get away, and pulling her onto the bed. 'Though I nearly died of fright seeing thee staring down at me like that! And now I'd best get out of bed I think!'

'Pa has gone out already. He went to find out about some people who live on t' other side of t' woods. He left before I was even awake – I've not seen him yet.'

'And tha ma?' Kitty tried not to let her voice betray her. Uncle Robert had been right to tell her to return to bed in the early hours of the morning. She had fallen back to sleep almost immediately, the awakening birds her lullaby, and had woken refreshed. Well, apart from the shock of Mary, of course.

But it seemed that her uncle hadn't taken his own advice, and had remained up and then headed out early to find out if their suppositions were true. Kitty fervently hoped not. She was tired of hearing of another family, another member of the community falling ill. Each new case seemed to accentuate the loneliness of their isolation, reinforce that they wouldn't be free for some time still to come.

It was already August; they should all be preparing for the fun of the Wakes Festival, for welcoming outsiders to the festivities, not withdrawing further from those they loved. Her family should have been visiting, and she was supposed to be returning home with them. Back to Sheffield. Back to John. Back to her hopes and dreams. And yet here she was, trembling inwardly as she anticipated news of further death and decay.

'Oh, aye, she's here. Told me to come and get thee up. Says tha's supposed to be going out to check on t' fields today and they won't check themselves.'

Kitty had forgotten all about those plans. She had been released from service with the Mompessons for the day so that she – along with all those who were fit and well enough – could spend time in the fields checking on the state of the crops. There was so much more to do now that the healthy villagers had taken on the plots belonging to those who were sick.

She usually relished the fresh air and hard physical work, so different to fetching and carrying and walking all day around the village. She enjoyed the camaraderie of everyone working with one purpose, stopping for oatcakes and cheese and ale in the mid-day heat. After lunch they moved to the shade of the trees alongside the river to see what fish they could catch, only returning to complete the field work when the sun lost some of its ferocity. But this time Kitty wasn't so sure. She couldn't bear listening to the stories of despair and hopelessness that coloured every conversation. She was tired of being too hot, her skin burnt and sore by evening. She clumped downstairs, her usual light-heartedness absent.

'Morning, luv,' Aunt Anne called brightly from her place at the kitchen table. In front of her were jars of preserves, bottles of ale, wrapped oatcakes that still smelt warm and lumps of crumbly cheese. Two large baskets sat at her feet, and she was carefully stowing everything on the table into them. 'It's a grand day to be out, our Kitty, that's t' truth. I've had enough of moping about and carrying our sorrow everywhere we go. We need to leave it behind us, if only for a few hours. Here, help me with this, won't thee?' Kitty knew her aunt was right. They just needed a change of scene, a different type of activity, and all would be well again. She smiled gratefully.

'When will Uncle Robert be back? Oh, here is now.' She saw him as he walked in from the lane. His head was bowed, his shoulders drooped as though his great miner's arms were suddenly too heavy to carry. 'Oh, no, we were right,' Kitty whispered.

'Aye, 'tis t' Hancocks. Morning Kitty, lass, did tha get some more rest?' Not stopping to give her time to answer, Uncle Robert continued: 'Elizabeth was up burying t' young ones overnight – young Elizabeth and John. Seems old man John wasn't well enough to help, nor anyone else close enough she could call on. Besides, who would go to her aid?'

'Imagine having to bury tha own children, without help nor comfort from anyone.' Aunt Anne shook her head.

'I fancy it will be more than t' two of them.' Uncle Robert avoided his wife's enquiring gaze. 'T' rest are all down with it. Seems they caught it from t' Talbots.'

'Oh, and I saw Mrs Wilson while tha was out,' Anne informed him. 'On her way back from early visiting, I think. She told me news of Mr Hadfield...'

'The tailor?' Kitty asked quickly, wanting to be sure of whom they were talking about.

'Yes, lass. After all this time, and him staying so well right at t' beginning. He passed during t' night – no more than a day after his old dad, too.'

Kitty wanted to shout or scream out loud, to stamp her feet and demand an end to all the death and despair that surrounded them. Surely, this was enough? She looked at Mary, solemnly sucking her thumb while the adults talked and talked. Aunt Anne was no longer singing and smiling. Uncle Robert paced the floor.

'T' picnic...' she was hesitant, hoping she hadn't misjudged the mood and so would seem insensitive and uncaring.

Uncle Robert stopped, then seemed to notice the packed baskets for the first time. He grinned. 'Ah, that's t' thing. Anne luv, let's get busy with being useful where we can and entrust t' Hancocks and others like them to t' care of t' Lord, if only for today. We're no good to them if we're all down in t' dumps and falling faint with worry!' He scooped Sarah up from where she was clinging to his leg and lifted her onto his shoulders, to the accompaniment of her ecstatic giggles. Mary ran round in circles, whooping and cheering that at last they were going, and Kitty and Aunt Anne laughed aloud at the chaos. It was good to find joy in the midst of crisis.

Chinese Knot out-line

Reverend Mompesson was limping, and Catherine was worried. Kitty could tell he had an injury by the erect posture, the tight shoulders and the determinedly forward-facing look as Catherine's husband made his way slowly up the incline to what was now his grassy pulpit. Not only was he limping, but William also winced each time he bore weight on his right leg. He hoped no one amongst his flock would notice; he didn't want to give them any more to worry about, more to be afraid of than they already had.

He wiped the sweat from his forehead, wishing the weather would break and the intensity of the summer's heat dissipate. He longed for a downpour, for rolling thunder and flashes of lightning to slash across the sky. He wanted to know the elements understood, that they felt his terror and roared in protest just as he himself was.

Outwardly, he felt he was maintaining his calm authority. He continued to visit all who fell sick, or whose loved ones lay in torment, offering words of hope – if not for this life, then for the one to follow. None would see the hopelessness, the despair that raged rampant through his mind and soul when he returned from those visits and lay down to rest at night. Only his beloved Catherine, waiting for him each day with words of comfort and a gentle touch of empathy, knew how he really felt. And Thomas Stanley.

William looked out across his reduced congregation and saw the man standing on the edge, leaning on his stout stick while he waited for the service to begin. Stanley had come to each of Mompesson's services since they had been moved from the confines of the church building to Cucklett Delph. He always arrived after everyone else and hung back, not engaging with any of the villagers, as though to do so would undermine his support of the current incumbent. His support had truly been immense all round. Mompesson was deeply grateful, not only for the practical load that Stanley was now carrying, but also his quiet understanding of how William, felt and his encouragement to remain strong and continue on the chosen path. Mompesson knew the man prayed for him daily – probably for his conversion from his erroneous theological views, but also, he knew, for the wellbeing of both his body and soul. He had come to rely on his old nemesis and rival in ways that had taken him by surprise.

'Did tha see t' reverend looking lame this morning?' Kitty asked of her aunt once they were home and sitting under the shade of the tree. She tried to sound nonchalant, as though she were talking about nothing more distressing than a passing shower in April. But Anne wasn't fooled.

'I did, lass, and I think most of t' congregation did too. That's not such a good sign, I know, but hopefully, he just caught his leg on a branch when out walking. Or something like that.'

The next day Kitty burst through the door of the parsonage, ready to demand answers. If she'd stopped long enough to think about it, the fact that the door was still closed should have alarmed her, warned her even.

Reverend Mompesson was seated at the small table in the living room, his breeches rolled high above his right knee. At his feet knelt Catherine, dipping a rag into a bowl of pungent liquid. As she turned in surprise at the intrusion, Kitty caught a glimpse of a wound on the reverend's shin that was so vile she felt faint. That was not from any branch or stick that she could think of. One look at Catherine's imploring face and she knew exactly what it was – the start of the now-familiar rosy rash.

'Don't say anything to anyone, Kitty dearest, please.' Catherine's voice was a whisper, as though she feared the words spoken aloud would in themselves worsen the infection. 'We can't have people knowing. They'll be too scared to have William come and visit. They need him now more than ever. Besides, it's getting better.' Kitty heard the desperate attempt to sound hopeful in her friend's voice, but she saw the look of pain and dismay in her eyes. The young woman shut the door carefully behind her and knelt next to Catherine.

'Here, give me that,' she said gently. 'I'll see to it.' Taking the rag and bowl, she did her best to continue cleaning the wound. The boil was red and angry, with a slight greenish tinge noticeable at its centre. *At least it isn't black*, thought Kitty – she knew black, dying flesh was a sign that the likelihood of recovery was slim.

Catherine sat back on her heels and grasped her husband's hand. His face was white and glistening with the sweat of pain as Kitty dabbed away with the rag. He didn't utter a word, just stared straight ahead, not looking at either Kitty or his wife, as though their distress would release all the emotion he was trying so hard to control. How could this have happened to him? He was always so careful, ensured that he washed thoroughly after every visit. He knew the signs, had seen them more often than he would he have liked – a seemingly healthy father standing away from his child's sick bed, but with an unnoticed sore on his own hand or wrist. A desperate wife unwilling to leave her husband's side for long enough to clean her own open wounds.

He couldn't get sick, he couldn't die, he just couldn't! This village needed him! He was called of God to be here at just this time, to lead this dear flock through the dreadful trial they were so bravely enduring. And what of his own children, missing him and their mother, longing to be reunited as a family again, not understanding their banishment. And Catherine – dear, precious, beautiful Catherine. He couldn't leave her side, leave her to cope alone without him while the pestilence yet maintained its grip. His lips moved in desperate supplication to his God, to his Saviour.

Kitty finished cleaning and dressing William's leg. He looked down at her bowed head, and once again thanked God for the people He had seen fit to bring alongside them during this dreadful time. He hid the grimace of pain behind a broad smile of thanks and unrolled the fabric of his breeches. 'Thank you, Catherine, Kitty, I feel in much less pain – of both leg and heart, as your ministrations have relieved the anxiety of my condition greatly. I must now prepare for my day's work. His grace is made perfect in my weakness,' he added sternly, stopping his wife's remonstrations before she could utter them.

Leaning heavily on the table, he struggled to his feet. Beads of perspiration appeared on his forehead as the exertion of movement reignited the pain in his leg. He tried to make light of it. 'Ha, I shall be needing a stick like our good friend Stanley's soon! Catherine, your arm momentarily, if you would be so kind.' Catherine leapt to her feet and helped her injured husband through to his little study, where he sank gratefully into the chair at his desk. He kissed his wife's hand, a gesture so intimate, so expressive of the love he had for her, that Kitty looked away.

She heard the window being opened wide, and felt the gush of outside air, still hot but fresher than the stale air of the closed room. The young woman gathered together the soiled rags and, picking up the bowl of now filthy liquid, went into the kitchen to dispose of it all. The rags went into the kitchen fire, lit despite the heat of the day, then she took the bowl to the end of the property and poured its contents as far from the wall as she could reach.

*Chinese Knot out-
line*

The next day Kitty was up early. She dressed quickly and quietly and left everyone else in the cottage still slumbering. The morning light was gentle and welcoming, beguiling the early riser into thinking the rest of the day would remain equally temperate. A soft breeze stirred the leaves of the trees and bushes as she passed, and small, unseen creatures scurried away from her approaching footsteps. The dawn choristers were in full voice, butterflies flitted around and bees lumbered from fragrant flowerhead to flowerhead.

Kitty untied the ribbons of her cap and pulled it from her head, allowing her deep brown hair to flow freely down her back. She swung the cap in her hand as she strode down the lane, humming a tune of gratitude to the morning's Maker. Her path led up the hill to the boundary stone – her destination; it was Kitty's turn to collect mail and supplies.

She wound her way up the path and over the small stile into the lush green field beyond. Sheep nibbled the sweet, dew-dampened grass, barely raising their heads as Kitty passed. Their shorn coats made them look ill-proportioned and gangly, but the fleeces they had been stripped of were safely stored in preparation for the winter task of spinning and yarn making.

Kitty hoped she would be long gone by the time that tedious task was begun. She had been excited to try her hand with her aunt's spinning wheel but had found herself hopelessly unskilled. Even Mary seemed to manage better than she did. The carefully cleaned and carded clumps of wool wouldn't run smoothly over the spindle and kept breaking or knotting no matter how much Kitty tried to prevent it. Winding the yarn into great balls of wool for use by the village knitters and crafters was easier, but so utterly boring that Kitty had found it impossible to do neatly, so desperate was she to finish and move on to something more interesting.

Summer work was definitely better, she thought as she crossed the field. She felt strong and fit, healthy despite the disease and death which floated in the air all around her. Her face and hands had also become tanned from the hours of walking and outdoor labour. She chuckled to herself, wondering what John would make of this new look when she was next able to see him. He was so pale, almost the same deathly white as those she spent her days ministering to, although of course his pallor was not from disease but rather from the hours spent underground in the mine. Now at least he had his apprenticeship and was working above ground for the first time in his life.

Kitty wondered how he might have changed in the time they'd been apart. She knew it wasn't just her appearance that was different to what it had been when they parted almost a year ago; her heart was different too. She had grown up, become a woman who now knew about suffering and sacrifice. She was no longer the girl whose thoughts were full of plans for marriage and children and the advancement of her husband's career. Here at her new home she had developed new skills, learned country ways and habits. Thanks to Catherine and Aunt Anne she was starting to recognise plants and flowers, knew which were good for health and food, which to avoid for fear of sickness. She now knew the bright red berries she had always thought would be the tastiest were actually the sourest, and that only the mushrooms with dark underbellies should be picked and eaten. She could lie still on the banks of the stream and fish for pike and perch, could lay a trap for a rabbit or hare, and then knew what to do with them once they were caught.

Did she want to remain in the country once she was free from the bonds of disease that held them all imprisoned? Probably not. But she knew she would miss this life once she returned to the city. Kitty felt needed in Eyam – not only as a result of the plague and the visiting and practical care work she was doing with Catherine, but something more fundamental. As though her presence had become embroidered into the very fabric of the community. She had become part of something bigger than herself, a patchwork piece stitched on all sides to other pieces, creating a life-quilt of vibrancy and connection she didn't think existed in the city.

Kitty imagined herself trying to explain that to John, and wondered if he would understand or whether he would laugh at her silly notions. Could they together, perhaps, create a village within the city? Could they learn to work alongside those they didn't like or trust, like the Mompessons and Stanley had done? Could they love beyond their own four walls, like Aunt Anne and Uncle Robert did? The idea excited her, gave her a glimpse of what could be after this horror had passed and she was free to return home. It also frightened her.

What if John didn't understand or, worse, didn't even want to hear? What if his plan to become a Master Cutler, a man of position and influence in the city, had become his only goal? Kitty knew what some of the rich and powerful were like because her father brought tales home from his days spent tutoring their boys. She couldn't bear that to be her destiny – to be married to a rich but arrogant man, corrupted by power and tainted by his own sense of importance.

The young woman's musings had taken her to the boundary stone without her even realising it. No one could be seen, but there was a small pile of letters wrapped in oil cloth and wedged securely under another large stone, and a basket of something which was to be taken straight to Mrs Mompesson – or so the note on its handle declared. Kitty flopped down onto the grass, wanting to rest for a few moments before returning to whatever her day might hold. The early morning cool was gone.

As Kitty looked down over Eyam, the village spread out below her like a meticulously drawn map. She could see the soaring tower of St Lawrence's, the bells long hanging silent within its walls. Opposite, she could make out the parsonage; she wondered how Reverend Mompesson's leg was. Further along, she identified the cottages belonging to the Hadfields and Thorpes, the early victims of what was now a bitter enemy. *How long ago that seems*, she thought. So many sleepless nights had passed, so many cries of grief, sorrow and revulsion as family after family were touched by the foul stench of death. When would it end? Suddenly Kitty knew she was weary from more than the walk. Her grand ideas and dreams for the future were still there, but in that moment her heart was once again raw with pity and dread; pity for those already afflicted, dread lest it still touch her or those close to her.

Sighing, she reached over and lifted the 'post stone', pulling the package into her lap to check who the letters were for, which houses she needed to deliver them to. She flipped through the first two or three, and then she stopped. The familiar, untidy but dearly loved handwriting of John leapt from the envelope, as though her thinking and fretting had summoned him before her. She hadn't heard from him in a while, and indeed had wondered if her own letters had reached him, it had been so long. She dropped the rest of the letters onto the grass and, with shaking hands, tore open the paper.

My dearest darling Kitty

How I miss thee! I will come to thee for Wakes Festival as was planned.

With all my love

John x

Two sentences and Kitty's fragile composure was shattered. She had thought herself strong, able to cope with this awful reality in which she had found herself thrust. All the bright thoughts and plans of just a few moments before were lost, dust blown away on the wind. Tears blurred her view, distorting the tower and the cottages and the streets and lanes of Eyam. She looked again at the letter, noticing the splotches of ink where tears had fallen and spoiled the words on the page. He was coming to fetch her, just as he had promised when he'd kissed her farewell to the jeers of his friends. She had survived the year and was somehow intact. Or so she had believed. Until then.

Kitty drew her knees up under her chin and encircled her arms tight around her legs. She moaned with the longing of her homesick heart, knowing John would come, but knowing too that she would be unable to leave. Even if it had been allowed, she knew that a love deeper than anything she felt for her dearest John would keep her in Eyam until the bitter end. Whatever that end might be.

As she sat there with tears running down her cheeks, Kitty heard the caw of a crow in the nearby copse. A year ago, she would have heard the noise but not recognised the bird that made it. Similarly, she identified the fields of oats and barley as they shifted lazily in the summer breeze, and knew which was which. Closer to where she sat, the brightness of the buttercups drew her attention. This place had become part of her in ways she simply hadn't expected or even fully realised; and that was just nature. The people had become her friends, her companions, through diversity and trials. Her prejudices had been blown away by the example set by the Mompessons and the rest of the village community, coming together as they had to serve and encourage each other.

The sun suddenly burst out from behind the cloud that had earlier obscured it. Kitty rose to her feet guiltily; she had been sitting there for far longer than she should have been. After dusting off her skirts and smoothing the creases, she used her apron to wipe her tear-stained face. She clutched the post in one hand and gathered the basket with the other, then started off down the hill. She couldn't think any more about the letter for now; there was work to be done and provisions to be delivered. Kitty was anxious to see how Reverend Mompesson's leg was doing, hoping and praying that the boil hadn't spread beyond that one spot.

The young woman's mood lifted as she enjoyed the walk back down into the village. The day was hot again, but the path took her through the trees and alongside the river which burbled along, blissfully un-aware of all that was happening along its banks as it wound its way through the centre of Eyam. Before she emerged onto the main street, Kitty carefully put the letters and basket on the soft grass at the water's edge and knelt to splash the river's cooling liquid over her hot and dirty face. She cupped her hands and drank deeply before finally gathering everything together and making her way directly to the Mompessons' cottage.

The door was open when she arrived, although neither the parson nor his wife was anywhere to be seen. She stepped into the cool interior and called for Catherine.

'Ssh, do please be quiet,' came a deep voice from upstairs as William, rather than Catherine, responded to her greeting. 'I'll come down to you.'

There was a shuffling followed by a heavy, uneven tread as the injured vicar of Eyam made his way carefully down the stairs and into the room where Kitty had put the post and basket on the main table. She looked enquiringly at William.

'Reverend Mompesson. How's tha leg doing? I see tha's walking a little easier this morning.' Kitty looked beyond him, waiting to see Catherine appear at the top of the stairs and follow him down. When she didn't, Kitty turned accusing eyes on William. 'Where's Catherine – Mrs Mompesson – sir? Is she out visiting? I must go and join her; she might need my help.'

'Sit down, Kitty, please.' William lowered himself into his chair, wincing as he bent his bandaged leg. Without waiting for Kitty to do as instructed, he continued. 'Mrs Mompesson has had a fitful night, my dear, and is resting at the moment. She – she is a little feverish, it would seem...' His voice trailed off and he dropped his head into his hands, as though the thoughts racing around inside it were suddenly too heavy to carry on his neck alone.

Kitty rushed to his side and knelt at his feet. 'Sir, what does tha mean, she had a bad night? Has she turned poorly? No, surely...' she couldn't continue. William dropped his hands slightly and looked at her intently, no words passing his lips. His eyes were dark pools of despair. He merely nodded then turned away, unable to watch as shock, fear and disbelief chased across the expressive features of his wife's young friend.

Eventually, he spoke. 'Yes, she has taken ill. We were out for a walk yesterday evening after you had gone home for the day. The air was heavy as always with the stench of death, a smell which followed us even as we ventured out across the fields. Catherine was in a fine mood, happy and joyful, chatting about the children and how she hoped they could be restored to our company again soon. All at once, she stopped, her eyes bright and her cheeks a little flushed. Inhaling deeply, she declared how sweet the air smelt, how fresh and clean.'

William bowed his head again, his remaining words so soft, Kitty could barely catch them. 'Of course, that was utter nonsense. We haven't enjoyed a breath of untainted air since this all began. Nothing but death and decay is absorbed through our very skin. I can taste it every time I take a bite to eat, breathe in its foul vapours in my sleep even. And this wretched, unrelenting heat! Oh, when will this plague, this pestilence leave us? When will the test be considered sufficient, the trial enough?'

A sigh more like a moan escaped from William's lips. 'I took her hand to lead her straight home after that. It was so clammy, so unlike the dear palm I had clasped just moments earlier. She followed me as though asleep, unaware of the steps she took or the sights around her. We eventually arrived back here where I took my poor darling straight up to bed. I have been sitting at her side all night, cooling her fever and imploring her to sip the tincture she has bestowed on so many others in this village. Oh, Catherine, my darling, my angel. Please God that he should have mercy on you – on me – and spare you!' The reverend's shoulders were shaking, tears running unchecked down his face and dripping pitifully into his lap.

Seeing this man she had once distrusted because of his different views sitting before her broken with grief and exhaustion, awoke Kitty from her shocked stillness. She had witnessed this scene in so many homes with so many other families over the last months, had watched as their beloved Catherine brought calm and order into the chaos of distress. She knew it time for her to take the lead and to behave as her stricken friend had shown her.

Kitty rose and, pushing the hair from her face and replacing her cap firmly on her head, spoke kindly but firmly: 'Sir, sitting here will do thee no good. Nor will it help Catherine either. When did tha last have something proper to eat?' He shook his head, trying to wave her away. 'No, sir, I won't go away. Tha needs to keep t' strength up, so tha can be there for her whenever she needs thee. I know Aunt Anne prepared some oatcakes for thee just yesterday. Let me get them, and a cooling drink of ale, while tha goes and sits on t' bench out in t' garden. Tha needs t' fresh air.'

She spoke with a finality that broke through William's deep grief and misery. He acknowledged the wisdom of the young woman's entreaty; after all, it would benefit no one if he also were to take to his bed. He thought of George and Elizabeth. How he longed to have them by his side. But, knowing this was an impossible wish, and dimly acknowledging that they might be more in need of him in the coming months than had been anticipated, he rose heavily to his feet. He shuffled out to the garden, his leg still troubling him a little although thankfully it seemed to be healing well.

William eased down onto the bench in the shade of the large beech tree that grew sturdily just inside the wall of the churchyard opposite. In between his deep breaths, he became aware of the sounds of the birds singing above, of insects and butterflies buzzing and flitting around him. As he sat there, his fingers found and idly traced the outline of each family member's initials that had been clumsily carved into the wood of the bench seat. He smiled.

They had given George a penknife for Christmas the previous year and, young though he was, he had delighted in picking and scratching at whatever piece of wood he could find. Before leaving his parents for the visit to family far from the deadly influence of the plague, George had gone into the garden and spent hours patiently gouging out each of their initials. The little boy had run proudly into the house when he was finished, pulling his mother and father away from their work and out into the garden so they could see the product of his labours.

William looked down again, the memory etched as clearly in his heart and mind as the letters were in the seat on which he sat. Though he missed the children immensely, he was glad he had sent them both away. It had been a dreadful time and seemed to be worsening every day.

But had he been right to allow Catherine to stay here, at his side? Should he have insisted that she go away too? Or at the very least put a stop to all her visits and ministrations amongst the villagers who were sick and dying? In his heart he knew he couldn't have stopped her – she was a determined woman with a faith and conviction that was at times stronger even than his own. She had always wanted to dedicate her life to the poor and the suffering, had longed to carry the comfort of her Precious Saviour to all who were in need.

William knew there were many in the community who were glad she had stayed, who had relied on Catherine's calm, practical presence during some of their most intense personal trials. He even admitted that his own burden of shepherding and pastoring the terrified flock under his care had been made lighter because of her. His wife's persistent prayers and heartfelt cries for health and safety, her gentle touch of empathy at the end of another long, appalling day, had made everything bearable.

But now, his companion, his helpmeet, his beloved, lay stricken by this foul curse from which there seemed to be no escape. He found the letters of her name, CM, and pressed his palm over them, feeling the rough, splintered edges of the marks his son had carved. He lifted his hand and looked at the indentation, a red patch with the letters standing out white and clear in its centre.

Behold, I have graven thee upon the palms of my hands. The words of Isaiah the prophet floated unexpectedly into William's mind. Here was assurance that though everyone else may have forgotten them, tucked away in the Derbyshire hills as they were, the Lord God Himself had not. William curled his fingers over the rapidly fading impression on his hand and lifted his clenched fist to his lips. He beseeched his Lord for mercy as all he stood for and believed in seemed about to perish before his eyes. Indeed, he had chosen to sacrifice himself for the cause of his parish, had chosen to stay here and walk with them through the valley of the shadow of death. Yes, he had known it would be hard – impossibly so at times; had known that he would need to draw on reserves of faith and strength that he hardly knew he possessed. But this? This was too much.

Lord, take this cup away from me, he cried, his soul tormented. He had seen the way Catherine's eyes stared sightlessly ahead of her while she lay, hot and feverish, in their marital bed; had watched as the evil rash that had begun on her neck spread and enveloped her whole body. He had held her hands even as he watched the fingers become tinged black, had smelt the vile stench of her usually sweet breath. The image of her initials faded from his palm even as her soul was fading from this life.

William had never felt so helpless. Every sermon he had ever preached, every passage of Scripture he had ever expounded on, giving hope to the hopeless, courage to the suffering, felt so trite. Who was he to offer such assurances? How had he dared offer comfort to those who traversed this abyss of despair when he hadn't even been aware of its existence, much less stood on its brink?

Yet not my will, but yours, Lord. In his pride and arrogance, he had believed himself untouchable, fulfilling a calling and mission that was so vital to the furtherance of the Gospel that nothing would hinder his efforts. After all, he was needed, wasn't he? He grimaced at the notion now. The Lord had given and the Lord could take away whenever He saw fit. His own Son had submitted to the path that lay before Him, had carried His cross and surrendered Himself to Roman nails; why was it so hard for William to do likewise? Oh, he would willingly follow his Saviour unto death, but let it be his own death, not that of the one his soul loved. *Let it be me, Lord, not her.* Deep down he knew – his was not to be the relative ease and escape of his own death and transference into heavenly places, but the much heavier burden of watching his precious Catherine go there ahead of him.

William was so immersed in the intensity of the battle that raged in his heart, that he had ceased to notice anything that was happening around him. The slight breeze had stiffened into a persistent wind that swirled and billowed in the tree branches above. Clouds were forming in the previously clear blue sky and an ominous dark shadow hovered over the distant hills. As the first rumble of thunder penetrated his reverie, he also became aware of someone calling his name, an urgent entreaty that aroused his deepest fears and caused him to leap to his feet in instant alarm.

'Sir, sir, tha must come quickly, sir!' It was Kitty, standing at the door of the rectory. 'Mrs Mompesson – Catherine – she's...'

Her words were lost as a roar louder than any thunderstorm filled
William's head. He watched as the garden gate was opened and Kitty's
Aunt Anne walked forward, in apparent slow motion, along the path
towards him. How had she got here? Who had called her? He felt
so confused, disconnected from the sights and sounds that his senses
were experiencing but that his brain refused to process. As if through
deep waters he heard the voice of Anne gently calling his name, felt the
pressure of her hand on his elbow as she attempted to guide him back
towards the house.

'Come, sir, t' weather's on t' turn and tha's going to catch tha death
if tha stays out here. And there's our Kitty, calling thee too.' A plop
of unseasonally cold rain landed on the back of his neck. It was all he
needed to revive him, to shake him from the selfishness of his torpor.
William straightened and turned to Anne.

'Thank you, Mrs Fox, I shall be alright now. Let us go inside, away
from the storm, and together face whatever storm lies within,' he
finished softly. He strode purposefully back towards the cottage, all
vestiges of self-pity and sorrow gone, as though they had been flung
off and snatched away by the howling wind. Branches were being
tossed and tangled in the tree under which William had so recently
found his peace. Lightning slashed the now dark horizon, a bright
zigzag of crackling white. The accompanying thunder sounded closer
than before, echoing off the ridge behind them. As Anne and William
reached the door, the rain poured down, cold and harsh after the
earlier heat of the summer's morning.

'Kitty, is she...?' In spite of his determination to be strong, William
found he couldn't finish.

'No, sir,' Kitty hastily interrupted. Waves of gratitude and relief
flooded through him, rivers of hope like the rivers of rain already
forming in the street outside. 'But she is asking for thee. She was

sleeping, or so I thought, and then her eyes were suddenly clear and focused. She called me by name, urgent-like. She kept plucking at her bedclothes as though she wanted to get up or something.'

Kitty looked from William to her aunt, imploring her to understand what she was really saying. 'I know tha told me not to go in t' room, sir, because of t' infection, but I couldn't just leave her. So I went in and knelt beside her, trying to hear what she was mumbling.' William nodded his understanding and approval absent-mindedly. 'And then she pushed herself up on her elbow and looked straight at me. "Fetch William, Kitty dearest, fetch him quickly." Then she lay back on her pillow and closed her eyes. So I just turned and ran down t' stairs to fetch thee.'

Kitty had barely finished the sentence before William was off up the stairs, taking them two at a time in his desperation to meet his wife's wishes, perhaps before it was too late. Kitty herself sank to the bottom step and dropped her head into her hands. She sniffed. 'Oh, Aunt Anne, thank thee for coming. How did tha know? Oh...' Kitty remembered seeing Thomas Stanley pass. He must have been aware that Mrs Mompesson was unwell and had made sure word got to Anne at home.

Anne moved towards her niece and settled down next to her, shuffling her along the step a little so as to make space. She put her arm around Kitty's shoulders. 'There, there, my luv, I'm here now. All we can do is sit here and wait. And pray, of course. T' Lord knows what He's doing, even when we don't.'

Kitty nestled against her aunt, feeling like a young child needing the comfort of her mother. Together they sat in silence, listening to the continuing storm as the wind blew stronger and the rain fell harder. There seemed no need to speak while the weather spoke for them, the external tempest a reflection of the turmoil Kitty felt as she waited for whatever would happen next.

Her day had started bright and full of promise, now it seemed to be nothing but a battered mess. First the letter from John which had so unnerved her, and then the discovery that her friend and mentor had been lying ill without her knowledge. Why hadn't the reverend sent for her the previous evening? Why hadn't she been forewarned in some way, been given a hunch or a premonition? Kitty knew she was at heart a practical, sensible child – her father had seen to that – but she had always assumed she knew the Lord well enough to hear Him whisper should there ever be something she urgently needed to hear.

Fear gripped the young woman as she wondered if she were deaf to His prompting. Perhaps her family were in trouble and she hadn't sensed it? Or John? Was that why he had written to her, saying he would come? He had bad news, that must be it – news that she had no idea about. Or was she just being silly, reading more into the tragedy unfolding in the room above where she sat than was either wise or necessary? Kitty pulled away from her aunt and wiped her face on her apron. She seemed to have done that more than once in the last few hours.

'Perhaps we should prepare some food for t' reverend in case he forgets to eat again?' she suggested to Anne. She knew finding such a chore to do and pretending to be busy was her way of putting off the thoughts that were oppressing her so badly, but it would be better than doing nothing.

Kitty began to move away from the stairs and head to the kitchen when she heard violent coughing from the bedroom. She froze, every nerve on edge, her ears straining to hear above the gale outside. She looked at her aunt who was also listening intently. The coughing soon subsided, much to Kitty's relief. She started to move away again. At that moment, there was a lull in the storm's onslaught, a pause in its violent progress through the countryside. The silence which followed was complete and unexpected.

Kitty realised she was holding her breath, unwilling to be the one who broke the spell. As she slowly exhaled, it dawned on her that the silence was as much inside the cottage as it was outside, that a stillness which she hadn't felt since arriving earlier that morning had suddenly descended. Was Catherine finally sleeping peacefully, resting as the fever left her exhausted body? A single moment of delicate peace held like a shimmering sunbeam in the air, then everything changed.

Kitty heard a low moan, as though the wind had found its way into the chimney and was trapped within the brickwork. Round and round it went, tormented and terrible. Kitty clamped her hands to her ears hoping to drown out the dreadful noise, but it continued gaining in volume and intensity. She thought she would go mad if it didn't stop soon. What was it? Where was it coming from? Not the chimney after all, but from upstairs. Had the reverend inadvertently pushed the window open, allowing the howl of the newly invigorated storm access to this haven of peace and quiet? No, it wasn't the wind was it? It was the reverend himself. That could mean only one thing.

Kitty collapsed onto the hard stone floor, a crumpled heap of grief at the loss of her friend. She couldn't move, her limbs suddenly heavy and unwieldy, so she gave up trying and lay her forehead against the cool of the flagstone. She closed her eyes and allowed herself to drift to she knew not where. Finally the moaning ceased and she was aware instead only of the pulsing of her broken heart deep inside her chest.

Kitty didn't know how long she had lain there. At some point, someone – Aunt Anne? – had wedged a piece of fabric under her head as a makeshift pillow and thrown a coarse blanket over her shivering body. She vaguely heard voices, far away and indistinct, nothing of any great importance to her. The shuffle of feet, the hollow thump of people continuously walking up and down the stairs. *Why can't everyone be quiet*, she thought? *Let me rest, let me hide. Let me pretend I am not here.* She drifted off again.

Chinese Knot outline

The next time she awoke, Kitty had been moved. At first, she couldn't make out where she was. She could hear the sound of the still-falling rain on a strip of thatch above her head, could make out a dim light from a window nearby. She rolled over slowly, her eyes adjusting in the shadowed room. She was home. Well, not Sheffield home. Not back with Ma and Pa and the little ones. Not close to her John. But home with her aunt and uncle.

Why did she feel so strange? She was thirsty as if she had been working in the fields all day without a drink of anything. When she noticed the jug of water on the table beside her, she poured some into the cup which was also there. She drank deeply and gratefully, the refreshing liquid reviving her somewhat. Putting the cup down again, she lay back against the pillow.

Had she been sick, that she was lying here in the near dark on her own? She couldn't remember having fallen unwell at any time, but maybe that was how it all started – one minute fit and healthy, the next laid low and unknowing. Where had she been before she'd been carried to her bed? She seemed to remember a storm, but hadn't that been when she first arrived in Eyam? She thought this was a different storm, more ferocious than any she had previously experienced. There seemed to have been something sinister about this one, but she didn't know what. The intensity of the thunder, the darkness of the sky perhaps?

Kitty turned as she heard the rustle of skirts. The silhouette of her aunt appeared in the doorway, a small candle held aloft. In its flickering light, she thought her aunt looked pale and drawn as though weary from a great journey or harrowing experience. Had she been that ill, she wondered? As Aunt Anne drew closer and went to sit beside her, Kitty looked at her questioningly. 'Have I been unwell, dear aunt? I'm sorry to have been a burden to thee, but I feel quite fine now.' She stopped as Anne shook her head and gently took her hand.

Rubbing her thumb across the back of her niece's hand, she asked, 'Does tha not remember anything, Kitty, luv? Uncle Robert carried thee from t' parsonage earlier.' She stopped as she saw signs of comprehension begin to flit across Kitty's face. There was a frown, a drawing together of eyebrows and a pair of darting eyes as they foraged in her memory for a truth that wished to remain hidden. Suddenly her eyelids flew wide open and her darting eyes settled on Anne's own face. 'Catherine!'

Tears welled up and overflowed, hiding the young woman's eyes again behind a cascading waterfall of grief running unchecked down the horrified face of Anne's dear niece. *Oh, the harshness of life,* Anne thought while holding the distraught Kitty close. Here was this wonderful young woman who had come to stay with and serve her family while she waited for real life to begin back in Sheffield, patiently anticipating the day when she would have a husband and home of her own.

Kitty had arrived in this countryside backwater where nothing much ever happened between one summer and the next, one harvest

and another, expecting simply to enjoy her small cousins and learn
the ways of countryfolk. Instead, she had become engulfed in tragedy
and misery that should never have been part of her story. These were
Anne's people, her friends and neighbours, not Kitty's. *The precious
child agreed to stay when she could so easily have caught the first wagon
back to the city,* Anne reminded herself. *Now here she is gulping and
gasping for breath as she mourns the ugly death of her newest and
perhaps dearest friend.*

Kitty didn't remember much about her aunt's visit that night.
Anne had waited until the worst of the sobs had subsided, then encouraged her exhausted niece to take a little warm ale before once more
settling her under the covers. She remained perched on the edge of
Kitty's mattress until the ragged breaths became smooth and rhythmic
with sleep.

Kitty awoke with the sun streaming in through the window, the
blue sky clean and clear again after the storm of the previous day. She
lay still for a few minutes, enjoying the luxury of knowing she had
been allowed to sleep in longer than usual. And then she remembered
why. She turned her head into the pillow as images flashed through
her mind. Reverend Mompesson trudging wearily down the stairs
when she had first arrived. Watching him from the doorway of the
rectory as he had poured out his soul to God in the shade of the tree.
Creeping softly up to the bedroom and peeping round the door to
catch a glimpse of Catherine. The sight of her prone form, eyes closed
while hands covered in weeping, angry sores plucked agitatedly at the
covers.

Kitty had been nervous to admit she had seen Catherine. Even at the
height of the storm, in the confusion of William and Aunt Anne arriving at the cottage, the rush of activity and then the deathly stillness,
she had known her actions were likely to be rebuked. Primarily out

of concern for her welfare, of course, lest she had inhaled the reeking air and its deadly contagion and so made herself sick in the process. But she could no more have stayed away from her friend than if it had been her own mother, or sister. As Kitty had stood at the edge of the door, unsure whether to proceed or retreat, Catherine's eyelids opened wide. She had shuffled her position a little, turning her head this way and that as though looking for something. Or someone.

'William, William.' Although weak and spoken through thick, bruised lips, her voice was determined and firm. 'Where are you, my dearest. I must speak with you.' Her eyes had continued to roam the room until, at last, they settled on the figure of Kitty half-hidden in the shadows of the doorway.

'Who's that?' Catherine called.

'It's me, Mrs Mompesson. Kitty.' Kitty had taken a couple more tentative steps into the room, concerned the patient was about to attempt to get up out of bed and would fall and hurt herself terribly. 'Stay there, I'll come to thee. Ah, tha's far too weak to be getting out of t' bed,' she admonished as she crossed the room to Catherine's side. 'What is tha wanting so urgent that tha has to struggle up? Does tha need a drink? Or making more comfortable?'

Catherine seemed desperate to silence Kitty so she could make herself heard. 'No, child, nothing. William. That's all. Please find and bring William.'

Kitty looked at her doubtfully, wondering whether it was a good idea to leave Catherine alone, seeing as she was awake and clearly trying to get some message across. Catherine watched her and smiled gently. She reached out for Kitty's hand and held it in her own. Kitty bit her lip, fighting the urge to recoil from the diseased flesh. 'Kitty, my dearest friend. You have been my closest companion these last months. With me when I was afraid and lonely, lost without my George and Elizabeth here. How I have missed them so. I wonder what they are doing now. Are they happy? Do they miss me as much as I have missed them? Oh, that they would know themselves loved and cherished.' There were long pauses after each sentence, the effort of making herself heard and understood using up what little breath Catherine had left. Worn out, her eyes closed again.

Kitty wondered if Catherine had fallen asleep, if she had forgotten that her friend was there. She gently tried to release her hand, trying not to wake the sick woman. Catherine's hand tightened on hers, not letting her go. 'No, don't go. Stay with me a moment. I like the coolness of your hand, the sweetness of your presence.' She fell silent again. 'Do look after William won't you? He won't know how to do anything, really.'

'Don't talk so. Tha'll be looking after t' reverend soon enough,' Kitty began to protest.

'No, child.' Catherine's grip began to loosen, her eyelids fluttered open and shut. *Like the butterflies from this morning*, thought Kitty. 'Go now and fetch William. And thank you. For it all, my dearest Kitty.' Catherine sank back into the bed, looking small and pale.

Kitty had flown down the stairs and out into the garden, calling William's name as she went. Why didn't he come? Could he not hear over the gathering storm? Or did he not want to hear, knowing why she was calling, knowing what awaited him if he moved and came towards her?

Kitty groaned, trying to block out the rest of the afternoon's events. It had all happened so quickly. She had been so grateful that Aunt Anne had gone to the parsonage. As Catherine's soul tiptoed away, Aunt Anne had taken charge. Kitty dimly recollected the reverend stumbling down the stairs and out into the reinvigorated storm, not stopping to gather either hat or coat. She hadn't seen him again. The next thing she remembered was the rain falling on her own face, the rough feel of her uncle's working coat and his strong arms carrying her close.

As she lay still in her bed, unable to drag herself up, she became aware of the sound of voices downstairs – two men and a woman who seemed to be making plans about something.

'...no, it can't be t' same as t' others. It wouldn't be right.' Kitty recognised the voice of her uncle.

'I quite agree. And I feel sure others will too.' Kitty struggled to identify the speaker. They didn't often have visitors, especially during the working day. And if they did, it was usually a friend of her aunt's who popped in for a chat. 'I will be happy to officiate, of course, poor Mompesson won't be up to it. I know what he's going through, remember it only too well from when my own wife passed. Not able to come to terms with what has happened, numb to everything and everyone. Awful.' There was a rustling of clothes as though the speaker was shaking his head.

'Thomas, tha has done so much for us in t' village. We're grateful, and glad tha stayed on afterwards, even though it would have been easier to leave it all behind, I'm sure.' So that's who it was – Thomas Stanley. He must have come to make arrangements for the burial. That was kind of him. Everyone else was being buried on their own land, in small private plots far from others to avoid contamination; Kitty was glad this was not to be Catherine's fate. She hoped Marshall Howe wouldn't be involved. She wasn't sure she liked him overly, but then, he had helped in circumstances where no one else would. Perhaps she should be more gracious and allow her beloved Catherine to be sent off by any who had loved her, not only those she herself liked.

Thomas Stanley had left soon after that, stating there was much to do, and time was of the essence. Aunt Anne went upstairs to see if Kitty was awake. On finding her so, she explained that Mrs Mompesson would be given a full burial service and be laid in the church grounds, albeit with a limited number of mourners in attendance. She urged Kitty to get up as she was sure the reverend would wish that she be included, even though of course he was actually in too much of a daze to be particularly aware of who was present and who was not. All he knew was that Catherine was no more.

Aunt Anne had fussed around some more, encouraging Kitty to try to eat something, if only a morsel of the pie that had been left from the day before. She had rummaged through her own meagre collection of clothes in search of something suitable for Kitty to wear; she had arrived in Eyam in her bright festival dress and carried with her only the simplest of working clothes, none of which would be appropriate.

Finally, the time came to leave the security of the cottage now called home. Kitty leant against her uncle for support as they slowly walked down the lane towards the church, she dressed in the borrowed clothing, which thankfully fitted her perfectly. Mary and little Sarah had been left at home, cared for by one of the village women. Aunt Anne walked on the other side of her husband, sombre in her dark Sunday frock, and holding a lace handkerchief to her watering eyes. Kitty briefly wondered where the dainty piece of fabric had come from, then dismissed the thought as both irrelevant and irreverent.

It was a heart-wrenching procession. They passed dwellings that were closed up and gardens that were overgrown, homes that would never again be warmed and cared for by the families who had lived in them. In other doorways, survivors stood with pale, gaunt faces, their own tales of sorrow etched deep in their dulled, vacant stares. Posies of bright summer flowers adorned a few gateposts and boundary walls.

'Please take them, please take t' flowers to t' grave,' implored several.

'She was t' kindest there ever was.'

'When Rebecca first got sick, she was here every day. Brought that syrup she makes. Not afraid to come in t' house either. Might have done her good to have been a bit more afraid...'

Tributes were murmured, acts of kindness remembered and shared. Few tears were shed; few tears were left.

All too soon they arrived at the entrance to St Lawrence's. Waiting for them at the gate stood Thomas Stanley, dressed in his formal preacher's attire. Kitty registered some surprise at this; she had only seen him in normal, commonplace clothes, sharing the look of the farmers and miners who made up his old parish. Perhaps he had decided the nature of the occasion demanded a different response. After all, he was officiating where usually Reverend Mompesson would. He was operating outside the law in doing so, but everyone knew no one would report him. He was performing a service to a family who had, in the sight of many, usurped him, but who he had come to know and care for. These were days when the laws of kindness and love superseded any law of the land.

Kitty ducked her head as she passed through the gateway and into the churchyard. To her left stood the ancient cross, witness once again to the temporal nature of life. Weathered by seasons of sun and of snow, its scarred and pitted surface looked the way Kitty felt her heart must look. Around its base, untended now for many weeks, flourished the purple and blue valerian flowers that Kitty had come to know so well on her forages with Catherine. She had learned so much from her friend, including what plants and roots could be used for different ailments, and how to prepare them so they would be palatable for the poor patient. She turned away, unable to look at something which had once signified vibrancy and promise and which now seemed nothing more than a collection of weeds and waste.

The small group of mourners made their way along the overgrown path to the centre of the churchyard where the burial was to take place. A hole had already been incised deep into the ground. *Another scar*, thought Kitty. Alongside it, ready to be lowered into its final resting place, sat the coffin. It was plain and simple; Kitty thought Catherine would approve. This was no time for frivolous expenditure or ostentatious appearance.

Standing beside the coffin was Reverend Mompesson. It was the first time Kitty had seen him since he'd run out into the howling fury of the storm the day Catherine died. He looked exhausted and dishevelled, already showing signs of widowed neglect. His hair was tangled and messy, his chin stubbled and unshaven. His usually upright stature was stooped. He didn't move as they approached, nor did he look anywhere other than at the coffin in which his wife lay.

Kitty was stirred with pity. She felt bad enough herself, still trying to process her own grief at the suddenness of Catherine's passing, but at least she had Aunt Anne and Uncle Robert to take care of her. She also had Mary and Sarah with their young, untroubled natures to lighten and brighten her moods. William had no one. She understood why George and Elizabeth had not been sent for, knew that of course there was no way they could enter the village even had they all wanted them to, but still it felt cold and lonely. She linked her arm through Uncle Robert's in silent gratitude for his presence as Reverend Stanley began the familiar liturgy for the departed.

Kitty didn't take in much of what was said during the short service. She let the tears run unchecked down her face, sniffing indecorously. Uncle Robert offered a handkerchief which she took, but merely crumpled and twisted in her hands. Aunt Anne was similarly upset on the other side of her husband. She wondered what would happen now. Would William leave and seek the comfort of his family and close friends? Endeavour to be reunited with his children? Or would he remain in Eyam, choosing to honour the memory of his dead wife by serving ever more determinedly? Perhaps he hoped to run himself into an early grave where he could be together with his love once more.

Anne had known men, and women, like that who were unable to bear the burden of grief and chose to wear themselves out with busyness instead. She looked over at Kitty; she was worried about the girl. The two Catherines had formed a special bond with one another over the short period of time they'd known each other. The continual proximity to suffering and death had accentuated the need for love and gentleness, and had enabled them to be sensitive to each other's moods and concerns.

Anne was grateful that Mrs Mompesson had taken so kindly to Kitty. She herself had been less than gracious toward the woman when the Mompessons first arrived in the village. She regretted that now. She had seen them all – not only the reverend, but the whole family – as a threat to her settled way of life, of her understanding about church and God. Reverend Mompesson were so different to dear Thomas with his austere ways and fervent preaching.

Anne had been friendly with Mrs Stanley, had liked and respected her before she passed on. Catherine had arrived bringing city ways with her. She had always seemed in too much of a hurry to stop and talk, to pass the time of day with the common women of the village. Her accent was also different – one of refined living, of dining rooms and parties held in mansions, not the quick and easy tongue of northern countryfolk.

But over recent months, as the village lay decimated by this evil that had arrived in a tailor's box, Anne had seen a different side to Catherine and, in her own way, had come to love her for it. The sick had been tended to and cared for with a compassion and gentleness

Anne hadn't expected. Catherine's knowledge of plants had impressed and surprised her as much as it had Kitty, revealing a country heart if not a country exterior. The reverend's wife hadn't once, in the hearing of anyone Anne knew, complained about missing her children after they were sent away. Anne thought of Mary and Sarah and of how bitterly she would fret if they were ever to be taken from her. Catherine might not have been one of them when she arrived, but she had certainly become so by the time of her death.

The Fox family lingered for a short while after the service but felt they were intruding on a private moment between Mompesson and his newly buried wife, and so had quietly turned for home.

The days that followed were long and tedious for Kitty. The unrelenting summer heat had still not abated, despite the storm, and Kitty found the simplest of chores near-impossible to complete. She often stopped halfway through and stared blankly into space before breaking from her reverie to wonder what she had been doing before she got distracted. She spoke little, and when she did it was in unfinished sentences and incomplete thoughts. She fidgeted constantly, picking at the hangnails that were growing in length and inflammation at the edge of her grubby nails.

The distraught young woman wanted only to roam for hours at a time through the fields and up the hillside behind the cottage, allowing the tears to fall hot and free as she strode along. She would return to the cottage as the swallows dipped overhead and the sun's shadows ran long, her legs aching and her heart pounding from the exertion. Retreating almost immediately to the attic room, she would flop on her bed, bidding her exhausted body to carry her into a deep and dreamless sleep. But she lay awake for hours, listening to the sounds of the household making their own way to bed.

Mary would creep in and tiptoe over to Kitty's bed, staring anxiously at her troubled cousin. Kitty lay motionless throughout the nightly inspection, trying to breathe as evenly as possible in the hope that Mary would believe her sound asleep and so leave her alone again. It usually worked, although one night Mary had leaned close and gently kissed her cousin's cheek. She whispered in her ear, 'Get better Kitty, please do. I miss thee.' Kitty had waited until the little girl was gone, then turned away to stare at the wall in front of her. How could she be so mean? Mary only wanted to offer comfort, nothing more.

Once Mary had settled, Kitty's next visitor was always Aunt Anne. She perched next to her niece, stroking her hair gently and whispering words of prayer and comfort over her. It was the one moment of each day that Kitty felt at peace, calmed by both her aunt's presence and her faith. A few times she had been tempted to bury her weary head in her aunt's lap and pour out the bitterness of her soul to her. But she always resisted, thinking that Aunt Anne had enough burdens of her own to carry, never mind Kitty's grief as well. Finally, she would hear Uncle Robert close up downstairs and make his way to bed, his tread weary and heavy on the stairs. She knew he would leave her alone, although he did always pause at the doorway before passing to his own room where Anne and Sarah were long asleep.

After all the people were in bed, Kitty lay listening to the sounds of the cottage – the pop of the cooling stonework or the fall of an ember in the fire lit for cooking despite the heat of the season. Eventually, her eyelids heavy despite her fevered mind and racing heart, she would descend into a restless, storm-tossed sleep, only to find herself awake again with the dawn.

She didn't venture into the village at all, nor try to contact Reverend Mompesson. Kitty assumed someone else would be seeing to his duties, and that he would call for her if he required anything in particular.

She hoped he didn't. She hardly had the energy for her own tasks, let alone those of a recently widowed rector.

There was one visit she did make that week though. A couple of mornings after the funeral, Kitty had absent-mindedly put her hand into her apron pockets. Her fingers closed around a crinkling clump of paper which she had completely forgotten about – John's letter. She pulled it out and smoothed the wrinkles so she could decipher the already barely legible handwriting. She had become so consumed with her grief for Catherine, so exhausted and dazed as long day passed into even longer night, that she had no idea when exactly John would be arriving. Had he already been, and she hadn't been there to explain why she couldn't go with him? Or did she still have time, and he was yet to come? What was it she had heard Aunt Anne and Uncle Robert chatting about the night before, when they'd thought her asleep, or at least out of earshot?

'Does tha know what this week should be, our Robert? Wakes Week! I can't remember a year when we've not had t' fair set up in fields yonder, and everyone coming from miles around to enjoy t' break from work,' Aunt Anne had said, her voice tinged with sadness and disappointment. The festival was the highlight of the year for most of the villagers, more so even than Christmas. Their family and friends would come in from the nearby towns and villages, and everyone would take a few days break from the hard work of mining and farming and cooking and cleaning. There was much rivalry between the villages as to who held the best fair, and Anne prided herself on helping to ensure Eyam's was better than most each year. 'We had such plans for t' well dressing this year. Stoney Middleton's display put ours to shame last year, and we needed to put that right.'

Uncle Robert chuckled. 'Tha's always so competitive; 'tis just a bit of fun, tha knows. Mind, I will miss t' Morris men – they're always good entertainment.'

Recalling their conversation, Kitty dashed down the stairs, clattering so loudly Aunt Anne, busy in the kitchen, looked up in alarm.

'What on earth's t' matter, Kitty? Slow down and tell me properly, I can't understand thee.'

Kitty was waving a piece of paper under her nose, talking so fast all her words merged into one breathless question. 'What'stodayandwhen'swakesandI'vegottogooutnow.'

Aunt Anne grabbed Kitty's wrists and held her firmly while looking her directly in the eyes, willing her to calm down. 'Breathe, child, breathe. Come, take a seat and tell me properly what's going on.'

Kitty allowed herself to be guided to the closest stool, closed her eyes and took a few deep breaths before trying again. 'Aunt Anne, please tell me what day it is. I had this letter from John, t' day that C atherine...' she gulped, unable to finish the sentence without her voice trembling and tears appearing as glistening droplets on her lashes. She shook her head crossly, desperate to explain herself before it was too late. 'Anyway, he said he would come for me at t' festival, just like he promised last year. But now I don't know if he's already been and if I've missed him, and he'll think I don't care, and he'll leave and go back home and he'll hate me and he won't understand and it will all be over. All of it.' She finished on a wail as she envisioned herself an old maid, living alone and lonely for the rest of her days.

'Ah, there now Kitty, tha's not missed him. Not yet anyway. T' festival should have been on today and tomorrow. Tha can still meet him. But,' and here Aunt Anne paused as she looked at her niece with concern, 'does tha think it wise to go and see him? What would be t' point? It could just make everything worse.'

Kitty shook her head vehemently. 'No, I must go, I must see him and explain.' She was already moving restlessly on the stool as though getting ready to fly out of the door that minute.

'But what will tha explain, luv? Tha knows, tha can't go with him.' Aunt Anne was gentle, knowing the truth would most likely be unwelcome.

'I know, and I wouldn't, dear Aunt Anne, really I wouldn't. I couldn't leave thee and Uncle Robert, and Mary and Sarah. Not now. Tha's t' only ones who can understand, who knew her too. With thee, I don't have to talk, or explain or anything. Back home, no one would know, and I'd have to pretend as though nothing had happened. I don't want to leave her – or thee – not right now.'

It was the most Anne had heard Kitty utter for several days. She pulled Kitty towards her and held her in a long hug. Kitty shuddered then pulled away. 'Let me go so I can see him, and then I'll come back straight away. Please.'

Anne still looked doubtful, not sure this was the best course of action, although she was touched by her niece's earnest entreaty. 'Go then,' she relented, 'and take a basket of food with thee. Spend as long as tha likes up there, but be careful. Don't let anyone see thee, in case they start to talk and think tha's running away, trying to escape t' village now tha friend is buried.' As she spoke, Anne turned away from Kitty and bustled about collecting all that she thought the youngsters might need for their meeting.

Soon Kitty was on her way, her face cleaned, and her hair neatly brushed and pinned back. A gentle breeze blew and clouds brushed past the sun, providing her with pools of shade and cool as she walked. Her heart beat in a rush as she neared the boundary stone, the basket suddenly feeling cumbersome and unnecessary. What had she been thinking? Why had Aunt Anne let her go? John would probably not even be there. After all, she hadn't replied to his letter, she realised. She had been so consumed by everything else that had happened, but he wouldn't have known about any of it. He would think she no longer cared, that she had maybe found herself someone else out here in the countryside. Or worse, he might think she was too ill to respond, perhaps that she was lying even now mere moments from death herself.

As she crested the final rise of the hill, the sun appeared from behind the cloud where it had been sheltering, and she was momentarily dazzled, unable to see. She stopped walking, waiting for her vision to clear, and placed the basket on the ground while she caught her breath and shielded her eyes from the brightness.

'Kitty!' His voice reached her before she saw him. He was laughing, walking towards her with the easiness of friendship and an assured welcome. 'Can't tha see me then?' And then he was next to her, smelling of travel and the city and home. He pulled her to him, hugging her so tightly she squealed. Her ear was squashed into his chest, her mouth muffled by the cloth of his jacket. His heart thumped in harmony with her own – hers fluttering, his strong and certain.

Kitty drew back and looked up at John, turning him so the sun was to the side rather than directly behind him. He looked even more handsome than she remembered. He had less of the underground worker's pallor, and his clothes looked smarter, less worn. She lifted his hands as they held hers and rubbed the calluses that had grown thick on the thumb and forefinger of his right hand.

'Knife work hard then?' she teased.

'Better than getting t' stuff out of t' ground, that's for certain,' he replied, grinning. 'Ah, 'tis good to see thee, our Kitty. Though tha's looking a bit peaky if tha don't mind me saying. I would have thought all this country air would've done thee more good than it seems to have done. Tha's not sickening for anything is thee?' He looked at her anxiously.

Kitty's happiness evaporated. She released his hands, dropping her own listlessly to her side. The bliss of seeing John, of snatching a glimpse of the normality that she missed so desperately had allowed her, for the briefest of moments, to forget all that lay at the bottom of the hill she had just climbed. Without any warning or forethought, words began to tumble out. Thoughts and feelings that had been tucked away and hidden were released by that one caring, knowing look. John pulled Kitty to the ground, urging her to at least sit while she unburdened herself.

The shadows grew long, and the sun burnt amber and pink and deep red as it passed over the distant ridge. Kitty talked and talked, absent-mindedly picking the daisies and buttercups nestled in the grass where she sat, heaping them in a riot of yellow and white in the lap of her apron. She dug her nails into their stems, making little slits through which she threaded the next flower she picked up, a bright chain of carefree summer growing as she spoke of winter horrors.

John, to his credit, though he lay back in the soft grass, head cushioned by his crooked elbow, listened attentively. He heard about George Viccars and the tailor's family, about disease spreading and then abating, about harvest hope and spring despair. In his mind he strode with Kitty to outdoor services, ducked through doors of shame and pain, wrinkled his nose and coughed at the vile stench she conjured with her words. He sat and took her hands in his, gently resting the daisy chain beside him, as she whispered the grief of the death of a friend. Gradually the torrent of words became a trickle, until eventually they ceased altogether.

Kitty looked at John for the first time throughout the telling, her eyes shiny with her tears. 'Thank you.' Her pulse no longer raced, her breathing was calm and even, her shoulders relaxed and soft.

John smiled. 'Ah lass, I'm glad to have been here.'

'Tha's t' only one I could talk to.'

'But tha's not coming with me, is thee.' John's own voice was low, and he avoided her gaze. It wasn't a question. A nearby thrush chirruped and chirped as it flew home to roost for the night, and the evening breeze rustled the trees.

Kitty sighed and shook her head. 'No, tha knows I can't. I'm sorry. I have to see this to t' end, whatever that might be.' She scrabbled to her feet, wilted flowers cascading to the ground as she stood. John stood too. Together they looked down the hillside at the village below; from a distance there was no sign of the horror that lurked in every lane, had stolen into every home.

'I'd best be off then.'

'Oh, John, I've not even asked thee where tha's staying? Or given thee any food to eat. Aunt Anne packed so much; here, take it with thee.' She stooped to pick up the basket and at the same time gathered up the discarded daisy chain. She held the basket out to John, and as he reluctantly took it she reached up and placed the garland around his neck. 'Remember me always, won't thee?'

John let go of the basket which landed with a thump back where it had been picked up from. He grabbed at Kitty's hands while they were still behind his neck fiddling with the chain that was, from that moment, worth more to him than any gold ornament worn by kings or princes. 'Always.' He rested his chin on top of Kitty's bowed head, smelt the sweetness of her hair and caught the warmth of her breath.

At last they drew apart. John picked up the basket again, bade Kitty thank her aunt, and gruffly muttered about writing soon and that he would be waiting. Tucking a stray hair behind Kitty's ear, he winked. 'Soon, then.' He took a couple of steps back, gave Kitty one last questioning look – which was met with the slightest shake of the head and a look of determination – smiled and turned away. Long, firm strides quickly took him away from the boundary stone and over the crest of the hill. Kitty stood watching him until he was out of sight; there was nothing else for her to do, but to stumble through the twilight back to the cottage.

Chinese Knot out-line

Aunt Anne had been extra kind and gracious to Kitty since her meeting with John. She didn't question the whereabouts of the missing basket, nor did she over-burden her niece with chores around the house or out in the fields. She knew Kitty would talk if she wanted to.

For her part, Kitty tried to get back into her normal routine, albeit without the usual trips into the village to visit and help the Mompessons. She pushed all thoughts of John out of her mind – or at least tried to. Still she would sometimes catch herself replaying their last conversation together, chastising herself for not having asked anything at all about his wellbeing. She had no idea where he'd been staying, or even when he'd arrived in the area. Nor did she know when he was leaving. She hoped he wouldn't be absent from his place of work for too long lest he got in trouble or lost his precious apprenticeship.

No doubt it would be sometime before she heard from him again. Letters hadn't arrived with any great frequency all year, and she doubted that would change much now. Kitty did, however, feel different after seeing her betrothed. She still didn't sleep well, and concentrating for long periods still tired her out, but she had begun to take a little more care over her appearance. She tried to make sure she was up at her usual time rather than languishing miserably in bed each morning, and she took more interest in Mary's idle chatter, even smiled as Sarah tottered around trying to find her feet. But she still didn't venture down into the village, nor enquire about Reverend Mompesson's wellbeing. She wasn't ready for that yet. Besides, he didn't seem to have need of her anymore. Perhaps he had tolerated her presence simply for the sake of his wife. Kitty wasn't sure she cared.

To her surprise, the reverend did call on her towards the end of the week. Anne had been down to the village to see if there was anyone in need of immediate care or assistance. Illness and death had not halted their march through the village. Poor Joan Howe hadn't been as lucky as her husband, Marshall, and she succumbed to the terrors of the plague a day or so after Mrs Mompesson was buried. The Howes' young son, Billy, died three days later and was buried by his devastated father; others were found to help bury baby Mary Abell and the last surviving member of the doomed Talbot family, baby Catherine.

Anne returned looking sombre. No one stirred in the village, no voices were heard, and even the birds seem to have become silent or flown elsewhere to enjoy the delights of song. She had called in to see Reverend Mompesson, accompanying Reverend Stanley on his careful rounds.

'Poor man.' Anne shook her head in sorrow. 'He doesn't seem to have eaten in days or moved from that chair of his near to t' fire. He just sits, staring as though there's t' brightest of flames in t' grate. Which of course there isn't. There's nothing bright in that home, not anymore. I didn't think he recognised us when we walked in; he just looked up blankly until Thomas drew close and called his name. He was ever so gentle, but tha'd think he'd bellowed t' name, t' fright it gave t' poor reverend.'

Anne paused in her story to cuddle Sarah and kiss Mary. She looked carefully over at Kitty, watching for any signs of distress as she continued. 'Once he realised who we were, he settled back in t' chair for a time. But then he started to get agitated, kept muttering under his breath about something. Seems he was thinking about t' children, because he suddenly stopped his mumbling and spoke clearly for t' first time since we got there. "Kitty, I need Kitty," he said.' Kitty raised her head at the mention of her name, turning dulled eyes on her still-speaking aunt. 'He says that he needs to write a letter, but that he wants help with it. Feels he's not strong enough to hold t' quill properly, or something like that. Anyway, he wants tha help, our Kitty.'

Kitty started to rise from where she sat, shaking her head as she tried to get away. Aunt Anne reached over and pulled her back into her seat. 'No, lass, tha needs to do this. Tha can't run away from it. Tha friend's dead and gone, to a better place for sure, and I know tha's missing her something dreadful. But tha's here in t' place of t' living, not lost in t' realm of t' dead. I know it seems harsh and unkind, but it is so. And those that live still need thee.'

Kitty wouldn't look at her aunt as she talked, each word harsh in its truth. She clenched her fists and two bright spots of angry red appeared on her cheeks. How dare her aunt speak to her this way? Was it not enough that here she was, stuck far away from home with no means of escape, hounded by an evil curse that had nothing to do with her and the only friend she had made since arriving here having now been snatched from her, without her aunt trying to guilt her into helping others some more? And Reverend Mompesson of all people!

If he hadn't taken Catherine out for a walk that afternoon, if he had let her rest at home, perhaps she wouldn't have fallen so sick, would have had the strength to fight her illness and recover.

The young woman hung her head, trying to escape the words that Aunt Anne continued to speak. Words of comfort and understanding, words that caressed her still-weary soul just as her aunt's palm stroked her hair and weary forehead at the end of each day. Despite her best resolve to remain angry and stiff, Kitty found it impossible to withstand the onslaught of love that flowed towards her. Her face crumpled and her fists fell open.

Aunt Anne grabbed a hand while she had the chance, pulling her niece towards her. She held Kitty tight, shushing her as she did Mary when she'd had a nightmare. Eventually, Kitty raised her face, now puffy with crying. She smiled wanly at her aunt who placed her hands on either side of Kitty's hot cheeks. 'There, lass, tha's been needing that for all of t' last week. Tha'll feel better now. Not fully right, but a bit better. Now, tha must be off to wash that face and get ready to go down and see what Reverend Mompesson has for thee to do. Mary,' she called loudly and cheerfully, 'take tha cousin off t' river with thee, and mind she washes her face properly. And bring back some of those water herbs and a fish or two if tha can catch any. We need something nice for tea!'

Mary raced over delightedly, flinging herself at her cousin. Wrapping her arms around her waist, she squeezed tight until Kitty cried out. 'Stop! I can't breathe.' After the release of tears, Kitty delighted in her young cousin's simple affection. She reached around and prised apart Mary's hands, grabbing both her skinny wrists and holding her at bay with one hand while she tickled her with the other. Mary squirmed and wriggled in an ineffectual attempt to escape, squealing and screaming as Kitty reached down and nuzzled her neck.

'What on earth is all t' noise?' The commotion had brought Uncle Robert from the other side of the yard where he had been attending to some broken fencing. He stopped when he saw the two girls, a tangle of arms and helpless with giggles. He smiled and looked over at his wife, mouthing, 'Well done.'

Turning on his heel, Robert returned to his work, whistling as he went. His wife was amazing. Only the night before she had been telling him of her concerns for Kitty. Together they had sunk to their knees and prayed for the child. They knew the sorrow and despair of loss, even before the present tragedy had visited them. The high peaks which surrounded them were unforgiving in the depths of winter should anyone lose their way, and the mines and caves had been the graves of many over the years as well. They also knew that comfort, the real and lasting comfort of the kind Kitty needed, came only from the Lord. Together they pleaded for Kitty, that He would help them find a way to reach her and draw her into His loving arms. It seemed He had already answered their prayers; Robert was sure it was in no small part to due to something his dear wife had said or done.

'Tha'd best be off, Kitty luv.' Aunt Anne beamed at the change in her niece and turned in time to see her husband bestow on her the slightest of winks before he strode around the corner. 'Tha mustn't keep t' reverend waiting and tha does still look quite a mess. Away to t' river with tha both while I make up some supper tha can take down with thee.'

Cleaned and refreshed, Kitty grabbed the basket her aunt had packed and turned to make the short walk she had earlier been dreading. Now, her features calm and her bearing again that of a young woman rather than an overburdened old woman of the world, she waved a cheery goodbye at the gate. Mary and Sarah raised their arms in fond farewell, Mary imploring her not to be long. Aunt Anne stood in the doorway, whispering prayers of gratitude as Kitty disappeared from view.

By the time Kitty reached the parsonage, some of her earlier trepidation had returned. She had passed by so many lifeless homes that the laughter and giggles which had buoyed her thus far were not much more than faint echoes in her rapidly beating heart. She breathed as shallowly as she could, trying not to use her nose despite it being buried in the nosegay her aunt had pressed into her hand before leaving. She gagged on the sweet pungency of death, a scent which she had somehow forgotten while hiding in her family's pleasant, disease-free hillside cottage.

Kitty paused and looked back up the lane, torn between retreating back to her sanctuary or pressing on to whatever Reverend Mompesson needed her for. Images of Catherine bending over a sick patient or gently comforting a grieving relative filled Kitty's mind, and the tears which she had thought dried up threatened to again spill over. What would Catherine have done? What would she wish Kitty to do now? Kitty knew of course. Catherine would put her own fears and griefs to one side, trusting that she would be taken care of even as she chose to take care of others. She would allow love and compassion to rise in her soul, eclipsing all else, and would set out to do her duty with peace and kindness. And she would expect no less of Kitty.

'It is our great honour and privilege, dear Kitty, to serve these our neighbours at this time. For so long my role here has been as William's wife, and the mother of George and Elizabeth, and little else. At least in the eyes of the village, in any case. Now I can be useful; I can be the hands and feet of the Saviour Jesus even as my husband is His mouthpiece. *For to me to live is Christ, and to die is gain.* Truly, Kitty, I believe that. We need fear nothing of death if we live for Christ each day, in whatever small way is presented to us!' The words of a long-ago conversation replayed in Kitty's mind, and with them came a restoration of the peace and confidence she sought. Yes, she could do this – not for herself, not even for Reverend Mompesson, but certainly for Catherine.

Walking resolutely ahead, Kitty continued on to the parsonage where the door was wide open, no doubt to invite in the early evening cool. Kitty tapped softly. 'Sir? It's Kitty,' she called out.

'Come in,' came the brief reply. Kitty stepped into the gloom of the parsonage, taking a few moments to adjust her eyes after the brightness of outdoors. She glanced around the room and smelled the fustiness in the air. All the windows were closed, and piles of dirty dishes and pots seemed to crowd the table. She briefly wondered who had been providing for the reverend in the absence of his wife, and then realised it must have been Aunt Anne and her few remaining friends who were still brave enough to venture out on their missions of mercy. She cleared a space and set down the basket.

'You came.' The voice sounded cracked and weary, like the men did when they emerged from the mine after a hard day's work. Kitty jumped; she hadn't realised that William was seated in the shadows of the alcove next to the unlit fireplace. 'I wondered if you would rather stay away.'

'I'm here, sir, for whatever tha needs,' Kitty replied stepping closer. She was shocked at the change in his appearance. He was unkempt and dishevelled, his clothes crumpled and stained. The brown eyes, usually so bright and full of fervent energy, were now hooded pools of despair. She had been right to come, she knew. Guilt nibbled at the edge of her thoughts. How could she have been so self-centred? So caught up in her own distress, to not realise that Catherine, so recently her own dear friend, was to William the love of his whole life? Why had she not come sooner, honoured her friend by caring for the one she had left behind?

'Sorry for the mess. It's all so wretched.' William waved a feeble hand in the direction of the room. His head sank, his chin resting almost on his chest. The effort of greeting seemed to have worn him out, and Kitty wondered if he had in fact fallen asleep. She was about to move back towards the table and start clearing up when he coughed and looked up at her again. 'I have to tell the children, Kitty. I need to write to them, tell them how brave their mother was, right to the end. They must remember her always as the angel she was. But I can't bring myself to do it. I keep starting towards the study, but then I see the pot of flowers she left on my desk the day before... and I can't enter... I lack the courage, Kitty. I need your help. I will dictate and you will write what I say, then take the letter to the post first thing tomorrow.'

It was the last thing Kitty had been expecting. She had thought she would be needed to tidy and clean, to keep house for a lonely widower, and write one or two letters about church matters. But this was far more personal. She hoped she would be up to the task and not be overcome by her own grief as the reverend dictated his.

William seemed to understand her silent reluctance. 'You have a younger, steadier hand, my dear. I wish the children to be able to read the letter themselves, not have it read to them. In my current, deplorable state, they will be unable to decipher a word. Your letters are clear and perfectly legible. And you won't have to think about what to say, I will tell you. Or at least I will try,' he finished sadly.

'If tha's sure, sir? I don't really feel 'tis my place, but tha knows t' children better than me, and knows what they need most.'

'That's decided then. And there's no time like the present. Fetch the parchment and quill and ink. Draw up that small table there.' Kitty did as she was bid, venturing into the study and seeing the bowl of flowers, dried up and shrivelled on the edge of William's desk. They seemed to hold something of Catherine's presence, her scent perhaps, and she could understand why the bereaved William was struggling to enter the room, much less sit in his usual place of work. She took a deep breath to calm herself and grabbed what she needed as quickly as she could before returning to the indicated table and chair.

Over the next hour or so, as the sun sank lower in the sky and the shadows of the trees lengthened, William did his best to dictate the hardest letter he had ever had to compose. There were false starts and frustrated tears, crumpled pages and repeated sentences. At last the task was completed to William's satisfaction, and he asked Kitty to read it aloud one last time. Holding the paper at an angle so as to catch the last of the light, Kitty bit her lip before starting.

To my dear children, George and Elizabeth Mompesson, these present with my blessing.

Eyam, August 31, 1666.

DEAR HEARTS – This brings you the doleful news of your dear mother's death – the greatest loss whichever befell you! I am not only deprived of a kind and loving consort, but you also are bereaved of the most indulgent mother that ever dear children had. We must comfort ourselves in God with this consideration, that the loss is only ours, and that what is our sorrow is her gain. The consideration of her joys, which I do assure myself are unutterable, should refresh our drooping spirits.

My children, I think it may be useful to you to have a narrative of your dear mother's virtues, that the knowledge thereof may teach you to imitate her excellent qualities. In the first place, let me recommend to you her piety and devotion, which were according to the exact principles of the Church of England. In the next place, I can assure you, she was composed of modesty and humility, which virtues did

possess her dear soul in a most exemplary manner. Her discourse was
ever grave and meek, yet pleasant also; an immodest word was never
heard to come from her mouth. She had two other virtues, modesty
and frugality. She never valued any thing she had, when the necessities
of a poor neighbour required it; but had a bountiful spirit towards the
distressed and indigent; yet she was never lavish, but commendably
frugal. She never liked tattling women, and abhorred the custom of
going from house to house, thus wastefully spending precious time.
She was ever busied in useful work, yet, though prudent, she was
affable and kind. She avoided those whose company could not benefit
her, and would not unbosom herself to such, still she dismissed them
with civility. I could tell you of her many other excellent virtues. I do
believe, my dear hearts, that she was the kindest wife in the world, and
think from my soul, that she loved me ten times better than herself; for
she not only resisted my entreaties, that she should fly with you, dear
children, from this place of death, but, some few days before it pleased
God to visit my house, she perceived a green matter to come from the
issue in my leg, when she fancied a symptom that the distemper, raging
amongst us, had found a vent that way, whence she assured herself
that I was passed the malignity of the disorder, whereat she rejoiced
exceedingly, not considering her own danger thereby. I think, however,
that she was mistaken in the nature of the discharge she saw: certainly
it was the salve that made it look so green; yet her rejoicing was a strong
testimony that she cared not for her own peril so I were safe.

Further, I can assure you, that her love to you was little inferior than
to me; since why should she thus ardently desire my long continuance
in this world of sorrows, but that you might have the protection and
comfort of my life. You little imagine with what delight she talked of
you both, and the pains she took when you suckled your milk from
her breasts. She gave strong testimony of her love for you when she lay

on her death-bed. A few hours before she expired I wished her to take some cordials, which she told me plainly she could not take. I entreated she would attempt for your dear sakes. At the mention of your names, she with difficulty lifted up her head and took them; this was to testify to me her affection for you.

Kitty paused in her reading. It had been easy so far. She took a sip of milk from the cup at her elbow and looked over at the reverend. His eyes were closed, his head leaning against the back of his chair. Was he asleep? A shuddering sigh and a weak 'Do continue,' assured her that he was not.

Kitty took a breath and swallowed. Now was not the time to indulge her own rising emotions.

Now I will give you an exact account of the manner of her death. For some time she had shown symptoms of a consumption, and was wasted thereby. Being surrounded by infected families, she doubtless got the distemper from them; and her natural strength being impaired, she could not struggle with the disease, which made her illness so very short. She showed much contrition for the errors of her past life, and often cried out, 'One drop of my Saviour's blood, to save my soul.' She earnestly desired me not to come near her, lest I should receive harm thereby; but, thank God, I did not desert her, but stood to my resolution not to leave her in her sickness, who had been so tender a nurse to me in her health. Blessed be God, that He enabled me to be so helpful and consoling to her, for which she was not a little thankful. During her illness she was not disturbed by worldly business – she only minded making her call and election sure; and she asked pardon of her maid, for having sometimes given her an angry word. I gave her some sweating antidotes, which rather inflamed her more, whereupon her dear head was distempered, which put her upon many incoherencies. I was troubled thereat, and propounded to her questions in divinity.

Though in all other things she talked at random, yet to these religious questions, she gave me as rational answers as could be desired. I bade her repeat after me certain prayers, which she did with great devotion – it gave me comfort that God was so gracious to her.

A little before she died, she asked me to pray with her again. I asked her how she did? The answer was that she was looking when the good hour should come. Thereupon I prayed, and she made her responses from the Common Prayer book, as perfectly as in her health, and an 'Amen' to every pathetic expression. When we had ended the prayers for the sick, we used those from the Whole Duty of Man! and when I heard her say nothing, I said, 'My dear, dost thou mind?' She answered, 'Yes', and it was the last word she spoke.

My dear babes, the reading of this account will cause many a salt tear to spring from your eyes; yet let this comfort you – your mother is a saint in heaven.

Now, to that blessed God, who bestowed upon her all 'those graces', be ascribed all honour, glory, and dominion, the just tribute of all created beings, for evermore – Amen!

Kitty looked up from her reading, the page trembling in her hand. William had moved slightly and was now, staring into the empty grate. 'That will have to suffice.' Exhausted from the effort, his voice was little more than a dull whisper. 'Go, child, and take the letter up to the boundary tomorrow, then come back here. I have more that needs doing.'

Kitty folded the letter and prepared it for posting the following day. She stole away as quickly as possible, an intruder eager to depart; William seemed not to notice her leaving.

*Chinese Knot out-
line*

Kitty was up shortly after dawn the following morning, eager to discharge her duty on the reverend's behalf and get the letter on its way to his distant children. How she felt for them. Catherine's passing had been hard enough for her, but at least she had enjoyed the companionship of her friend over these last few months. George and Elizabeth had been separated from the family, from their mother, for the whole of the summer. How would they react to the news? Kitty hoped the relative with whom they were staying would be gentle and kind. She prayed earnestly as she strode hurriedly up to the boundary stone.

Out of breath from the stiff climb up the hill, Kitty paused and turned to look back down the valley at the village below. The air was clear and fresh. Fluffy white clouds scudded across the sky as a breeze blew down from the ridge behind her, casting shapes and shadows over the homes clustered together, united in grief and mourning. Kitty pulled the letter from her pocket, smoothing the creases which now marred its surface.

Memories of her last visit to this place crowded into her mind, chasing all thoughts of the motherless children far away. She heard again the sadness in dear John's voice as he acknowledged that her place was still here, in this stranded and stricken community, rather than at his side, safe in Sheffield. She smiled as she remembered the daisy chain she had hung around his neck, her arms lifting involuntarily as she relived her actions. The smile faded as her heart again felt the tearing wrench of farewell, recalling his departing figure, strong and tall despite the rejection she knew he must be carrying.

Her own descent back to the village on that day had been miserable; vision clouded by tears threatening to trip and send her flying head-long onto the uncaring stones of the path at her feet. Even now, dread and fear made her heart beat faster again, despite having rested. Dread that John would lose patience with her and would decide instead to pursue one of the other girls from the neighbourhood, maybe even one of her own friends; fear that she would herself become sick and unable to recover, that she would never again see his face or hear the calm of his voice.

Kitty gave herself a shake as she tried to dismiss such thoughts, turning as she did so to place the letter underneath the sturdy boundary stone. She knew someone would be along shortly to collect it. Thoughts of her own anguish vanished as she again imagined how the letter would be received by the Mompesson children. Poor dears. Had they known their farewells to their mother would be their last? Kitty straightened and pushed her hair away from her face with a sigh. She needed to get back to Reverend Mompesson and see what else he needed her to do for him.

By the time she arrived at the parsonage the air was stifling and still, oppressive after the freedom of the hillside. Kitty noticed the flowers alongside the pathway were drooping and fading. *If Catherine had been here, she would have rushed out with some spare laundry water and given them a long drink. But Catherine isn't here. And the flowers will die, along with so much else this horrid, hot summer,* Kitty thought.

Kitty found Reverend Mompesson exactly how she had left him the previous day. He seemed not to have moved at all. There were no empty dishes to indicate he had eaten, nor were any words written on the papers spread in front of him to suggest he had become caught up in some important work or other. William's face was grey and drawn, his eyes blank and unseeing, even when Kitty gently called out to him, 'Sir, 'tis Kitty. I came as tha bid. I've been and dropped t' letter for t' children up at t' boundary; it's sure to have been collected by now.'

William turned his head slowly and with what seemed like much effort. He licked his dry lips and coughed slightly. 'Wait, I'll get thee some water,' Kitty said as she moved towards the kitchen at the back of the house. She found a little water left in the jug which she had filled before leaving the day before. So he had moved a bit then, if only to fetch a drink. She found a clean tankard and poured the remaining water into it, returning quickly to William. He clutched the proffered cup between both hands, the tremble of distress visible despite his effort to control it. Kitty looked away as he took deep draughts of the liquid, listened to him gulping and slurping, embarrassed at how this usually overly fastidious man had become clumsy and unmannered.

'Can I get thee some food, sir? I see tha's not had anything – tha must be famished.' She looked enquiringly at William who merely wiped his mouth with the back of a dirty hand and shook his head.

Placing the tankard on top of the pile of papers before him, he replied, 'No, child, I shall not eat. For what is food to me at a time such as this?' Kitty tried to remonstrate, urge him to think again. He held up his hand to stop her from speaking. 'No,' he said firmly, 'I need to suffer in body as well as in mind, for a few days at least. It is when I suffer that I am united with my Lord. And with she whom He has taken. This shall pass, I assure you, but for now, let us get to work and then you may leave until I call you again, perhaps in a few days' time.'

William rose from his chair and began to shuffle around his small study. 'I need to write to my lord, the earl. Today. I shall again dictate to you, and you shall record my thoughts. And then, if you could once more be so good as to take the completed letter out for collection tomorrow.'

Kitty settled herself in the recently vacated chair, realising that protesting or trying to change the reverend's mind was a fruitless exercise. Catherine had often chuckled at the stubbornness of her husband, saying it was his only failing and vice. Kitty thought there were perhaps a few others, but definitely agreed on this being one. She straightened the pages as she moved the empty tankard to one side, dipped the quill in the ink well, and began to write.

By the time they were finished, Kitty's hand was stiff and cramped. Blotched pages were strewn across the table, letters begun and abandoned. William had seemed unable to convey all that he felt; his usual eloquence had left him. He walked back and forth, running his hands through his hair, or else he stood behind where Kitty sat, staring out of the open window to the garden beyond. He muttered and mumbled before embarking on another sentence which soon faded into unfinished silence. Eventually, the letter was completed, and William read it over one last time.

Satisfied, he leant over to sign and seal it ready for sending. Passing a hand over his weary eyes, he motioned for Kitty to leave. 'Thank you, I'm sorry it took so long to complete. I won't need you to come tomorrow, or even the next day. Stay at home with your family.' He gave her a slight smile and slumped in the more comfortable armchair near the fireplace Kitty heard his breathing relax and deepen, even suspecting a snore or two as she quietly left the cottage and made for home.

September–October 1666

Summer dragged into autumn with little discernible difference between the two. Days remained hot and dry, fevers continued to rage, and death maintained its grip on the village of Eyam. Reverend Mompesson slowly recovered from the loss of his dear wife and resumed his duties around the parish. His Sunday sermons were now tinged with the empathy and compassion that arose from his personal grief. His concern for those who suffered a similar fate to his own was gentle and tangible. Only in the evenings did he retreat from the community, closing the door of the parsonage and drawing the curtains across his windows. None disturbed him during those private hours and called instead on Thomas Stanley when in need.

Stanley had taken on the responsibility of completing the parish register, and his spidery handwriting listed the sorrows of death and the occasional joys of birth for most of the rest of the year. Kitty knew he prayed for each family as he recorded their tragedies or delights; she had overheard him one afternoon when she'd visited St Lawrence's and found him labouring over the great book.

Her visits to the parsonage were now few and far between. Reverend Mompesson rarely called for her, seeming to prefer to maintain the privacy of his home. He greeted her each Sunday as they gathered under the drooping trees of the dell, patting her shoulder affectionately as they parted company. They didn't mention Catherine, or the children, or the letters that had been written. The pain was clearly still too great, and it was a time he obviously preferred to forget, at least when in the company of others. Kitty was content with that.

Once again Kitty immersed herself in life at the farm with Aunt Anne and Uncle Robert, finally mastering the tricky art of spinning and taking that task upon herself, much to the delight of Aunt Anne. She had spent too many years of her life stooped over wheel and spindle, she maintained, and it was about time someone else took a turn. Uncle Robert winked at his niece every time this was said, both of them knowing that Anne loved her spindle and the delicate yarn she cajoled from its grip. They also knew that she passed on the task to Kitty not because she was particularly skilled, or the lumpy uneven thread she created of much use for selling, but rather to keep her occupied, focused on a task instead of dwelling on her grief.

Uncle Robert seemed determined to keep Kitty busy too. He called for her early each morning, requesting her presence as he strode out to check on sheep scattered across the hillsides, or as he inspected the mine entrances for any signs of damage or interference. 'We don't want someone getting in without us knowing,' he explained as they cleared a particularly stubborn patch of brambles from one such entrance. 'We need to keep it clear so we can see that no one has gone down there under cover of all this undergrowth.' He tugged and pulled, grunting as he worked.

Kitty tried her best to help but seemed only to get viciously scratched by a multitude of tiny thorns each time she reached into the tangle. Eventually she sat back on her heels, content to watch her uncle work while she scratched behind Patch's ears as he lay beside her. She knew she wasn't really needed for this task but was grateful for the opportunity to leave the village for a few hours every now and then.

Kitty had grown tired of the constant baking and cooking and packing of baskets that Aunt Anne continued with; she was tired of visiting homes that were sombre and dark, tired of waiting to hear if the latest victim had pulled through to life or passed on into death. 'When does tha think this will be over, Uncle?' she frequently asked.

He would turn and look at her, brows furrowed and eyes serious. 'Ah, only t' Lord knows,' he invariably replied. 'Pray, Kitty, all we can do is pray.'

And pray she did. Kitty, Aunt Anne and Uncle Robert continued to spend their evenings together after the girls had gone to bed, the large Bible spread out before them on the table as they cried out on behalf of their fellow villagers. Each individual was named and committed to the care of the Lord. Some grew strong and slowly recovered. Others didn't.

'Young George Frith was buried this morning.' Uncle Robert spoke softly as he recalled the large eyes and smiling face of the church warden's youngest child. 'That's eight of the family since Francis himself passed last month.'

'And Baby Townend isn't going to make it.' Aunt Anne dabbed her eyes with the rag she was holding. 'With her mother just gone, there's no one to nurse t' poor mite. Ah Lord, we pray for Grace, and George and Margaret, for their health and wellbeing, and for Francis as he tries to bring them up without much help from anyone. Poor dears.' Aunt Anne picked up her knitting again. There was silence except for the clack of her needles and the crackle of the fireplace.

'Sarah Hawksworth, widowed at only twenty-something. And them only married a year.' Aunt Anne seemed to be thinking aloud, pondering the names and fates of those she had grown up with. She had known Sarah as a young girl. Kitty shuffled on her stool. She was tired of this macabre roll call. Each night there was someone else added to the list; she wished it would end.

At times they sat in silence, staring into the flames of the fire which it was finally cool enough to light. Grief paralysed their conversation, stilled their fingers as neat balls of spun wool sat unused in their laps.

The dark of evening was descending earlier each day, the morning dawn withholding the brightness of the sun longer each morning. Outdoor tasks, so helpful at distracting not only Kitty but also the rest of the family, could no longer be dragged out if they were to be completed while it was light enough to work. Aunt Anne bustled around all day long, the yearly ritual of preserving harvest fruit in full swing once more. The cottage again smelt of sugar and woodsmoke. Kitty's fingers became calloused and ugly from the hours spent at the spinning wheel; her shoulders ached from stooping and her eyes watered from the strain of trying to see what she was doing in the dimness of candlelight. The howl of the autumn wind whirled and danced around the cottage, a pack of hungry wolves waiting to enter and devour. Rain clattered on the door and windows, hissing as it fell down the chimney onto the hot coals below.

Chinese Knot outline

Last October seemed so much better than this, Kitty thought. There had been the excitement of being part of her first harvest, and the camaraderie of all the neighbours working together to bring in the precious crops before the weather turned and livelihoods were ruined

in one bitter storm. First those living close to the tailor and his family
had fallen mysteriously ill and suffered terribly, then several in the rest
of the community had succumbed to the same deadly disease. And yet
still there remained the belief that the illness was a passing distemper
of the weakest amongst them – an unfortunate but temporary fact of
life. Some had whispered and speculated as to what dreadful sins were
being punished, confidently assured of their own righteousness and
escape from a similar fate.

But now? Now there were only a few families left to huddle in the
fortresses their homes had become. The streets were deserted, grass and
weeds growing in wild profusion along the middle of the previously
busy lanes and pathways. The village square stood empty and forlorn,
bereft of the laden stalls and bunting that coloured every vibrant
market day. St Lawrence's church bells hung silent and neglected, the
remnant of her congregation now huddled in small family groups
under the stark, bare branches of a once-pretty dell. Each week those
small family groups grew smaller, were depleted and decimated by
infection and death, until the patch of ground – the family pew, Kitty
thought – was empty of all but damp grass and wet mud. Those who
remained would avert their eyes and grasp the hands of those close to
them more firmly.

Around the middle of October Kitty noticed Betsy Syddall, as her
aunt still called her, was missing from the service. She had noticed the
reddened eyes of her aunt and some of the other women as they'd all
greeted each other earlier, but hadn't known the cause. Now she knew.
Was it possible that anyone still had tears left, could still feel the stab of
grief for a lost friend? Kitty recognised how cherished each friendship
must be; she hoped she would love like that again one day.

Everyone around her looked pinched and worn, with hollow cheeks
and dark rings under their eyes, as though they hadn't eaten properly

in weeks. Perhaps no one had, thought Kitty, suddenly aware that many families were nothing more than a collection of orphaned children. She would return home each Sunday with a renewed vigour and determination to work alongside Aunt Anne for as long as it took to pack basketsful of nourishment for distribution over the course of the week. Each morning she took Mary and collected eggs from every henhouse they could find, carried pails of milk back and forth from wherever there was a cow or goat or sheep that could be milked. Aunt Anne churned and pressed and separated curds and whey, making the hard, crumbly cheese she was known for. Uncle Robert gathered firewood and split logs, delivering bundles to cold homes, then hauled bales of hay and straw to each animal stall and shelter abandoned by its owners.

Consumed as they were by their very survival, few in the village concerned themselves with news from outside. So it was with some surprise that a flushed-looking Uncle Robert burst into the cottage one October morning. A mist hung in the valley, too thick for the sun to penetrate, and despite the blazing fire in the grate, Kitty's fingers and toes were almost numb from cold.

'Shut t' door, Robert! I don't want any of that damp coming in here so soon after I've got t' place warmed through!'

'Ah, sorry, luv.' Robert pushed the door firmly closed. 'There's been a fire!'

Kitty looked up. 'A fire, Uncle Robert? Is that where all this mist is from then?'

'There's no smell of smoke though,' Aunt Anne observed. 'And I've not seen flames, even when I was out when it was still dark earlier.'

'No, no, not here – London.' Uncle Robert sank into the nearest chair and began unbuttoning his coat. 'Stanley heard from some rel-

ative or other. T' whole city's burnt to t' ground. Lasted days apparently.'

'But when?' Aunt Anne had turned pale. She had never been to
the capital, didn't know anyone who lived there, but still she was
horrified. This was the centre of England, the home of the king; surely
nothing could touch it? It couldn't have been destroyed; it simply
wasn't possible.

'September, so Stanley stays. It's taken that long for letters to reach
here.'

'What happened?' asked Kitty. Having grown up on the densely
built streets of a rapidly growing industrial town, she thought she
could guess. Something had caught fire and gone unnoticed. She'd
seen it happen before. Within a few hours, the flames would have been
soaring to the sky, sparks and embers dancing in whatever wind may
have been blowing. Before long, the roof of the next building would
have caught, and then the next, and then the next. But how had it been
allowed to get so out of control? Surely Reverend Stanley's relative was
exaggerating the tale.

Uncle Robert shrugged. 'T' letter Stanley got said it started in t'
bakery district, then spread too quick to control.' He paused, trying
to decide whether to tell them the worst of it. They should probably
hear it from him rather than someone else, someone who might have
got the story wrong. 'And St Paul's...'

'T' big church or whatever it is?' interrupted Aunt Anne.

'Aye, t' cathedral. It caught fire too. Nothing left of it, so they say.'

'Well!' Aunt Anne turned to the fire and gave it a poke. She piled
on more wood. 'I'm mighty glad we live far from London then.'

'But what does it mean, Uncle?' Kitty wasn't going to let the conversation end that quickly. 'Is it punishment for t' way t' king has been
behaving since he came back? Pa told me all about it!'

'I bet he did!' Uncle Robert chuckled, then grew serious. 'I don't know, child. There's been so much happen this last year to all of us. Perhaps it is a punishment. Only t' Lord knows.'

'But...' began Kitty.

'Tsk, enough now. We have enough to trouble us here, Kitty, tha knows that. We don't need to look for everyone else's trouble as well. Help me with making food before tha uncle has to go back out into t' cold again!'

A chastised Kitty got up from her stool and took out the dishes. Aunt Anne was right – they had enough trials of their own, they didn't need to worry about the king and his concerns. All they could do was pray, beseeching God for this terrible suffering to come to an end.

November 1666

†

A nd suddenly it did.

Hallowe'en gave way to All Saints' Day, but there was no procession, no dressing up, no joy. Kitty walked hurriedly through the drizzling rain to the dell where Reverend Mompesson would hold the usual service. The few remaining householders stood in obedient resignation as rain dripped from hats and mud-soiled hems. Blank expressions indicated everyone felt this day would be just like any other, only colder and wetter and more dismal.

Strangely, neither Reverend Mompesson nor Thomas Stanley was present. There was much shuffling of feet, blowing on cold hands and anxious sideways glances. Why were they delayed?

Eventually, they arrived together, faces lined with exhaustion. Reverend Mompesson stood in his usual place under the great stone arch that had become his pulpit. Without explanation or apology, he began the service.

Once the opening formalities were completed, he pulled from his pocket the Bible Kitty knew had belonged to Catherine. William perched his glasses on the end of his dripping nose and flipped towards the back.

'And after these things I heard a great voice of much people in heaven, saying, "Alleluia; Salvation, and glory, and honour, and power, unto the

Lord our God.'" Mompesson's voice boomed through the quietness of the gathering. He had removed his spectacles and was staring out as though engaging a multitude. He spread his arms out wide, the pretty feminine Bible small in his large palm. Kitty looked up, startled. She hadn't heard him speak with such vigour and passion for months. Even before his wife died there had been a hint of tired desperation to many of his sermons, as though what lay ahead was more daunting than his faith might prove up to.

"And after these things I heard a great voice of much people in heaven, saying,

"Alleluia; Salvation, and glory, and honour, and power, unto the Lord our God.'" Mompesson repeated the verse, intent on ensuring that everyone was alert and paying attention. They were.

'Dearly beloved, precious flock of Christ the Good Shepherd, today we rejoice.' He continued, even as the flock he addressed looked at him with puzzled scepticism. 'Today we rejoice, for today our trial draws to a close! The Reverend Stanley and I,' he nodded in Thomas's direction, 'have attended the burial of Abraham Morten.' At this, there was a murmur amongst his listeners. Many had known Abraham wouldn't live much longer, but they were still saddened to have their suspicions confirmed. It was also unusual to celebrate another's passing in this manner. Kitty noticed Uncle Robert remove the cap from his head, a mark of respect for an old friend. The reverend continued: 'Although this is, of course, sad news for us all, there is also good. Reverend Stanley and I have conducted a full survey of the village and concur there are no new cases of plague amongst us!' He paused dramatically to allow the news to sink in.

There was a ripple of voices as everyone spoke at once. Kitty turned to Aunt Anne and Uncle Robert. Tears coursed down Anne's face as she pulled Mary and Sarah into her arms. Robert looked around, signalling to the other men standing in their family groups that this was indeed the case. Kitty recalled his absence the previous evening. He had gone out soon after they'd eaten, while she and Anne were clearing up and putting the girls to bed. He had returned so late that they had been unable to wait up for him, and Kitty had fallen into such a deep sleep she didn't remember him re-entering the cottage at all. He had been the first up in the morning as well, bustling everyone along to ensure they weren't late for the service. Now she understood why. He had obviously been with the two ministers as they made their discovery. She marvelled at his self-control, knowing that she would have burst if she had been forced to keep such a secret. When Kitty looked over at him she was surprised to see him give her the slightest wink. No! He hadn't been able to keep it a secret after all. He must have woken Anne on his return and told her the wonderful news. Kitty laughed at him, her own tears now overflowing to join with the rain that continued to fall.

'Ahem!' Reverend Mompesson was positively beaming, trying to regain order so he could finish speaking. At last everyone settled and turned their attention to what he was saying. 'We now have much work to do, dear ones. In order to ensure this evil has no more foothold amongst us, we must destroy with fire all that has been, or could remain, contaminated. You are to return home immediately and take out of your houses everything that is soft or porous or which could harbour pestilence. Leather, cloth, bedding – everything. You may only keep back what is necessary until new items can be procured. A few of us shall take it upon ourselves to enter the shut-up homes of the departed and shall bring to light all that we find there.' Aunt Anne looked at Uncle Robert at this, biting her lip. He nodded impercepti-bly. So he was one of the helpers. Poor Aunt Anne, to have a husband who so loved his community that he would put himself in the way of danger in its service. But Anne smiled, reaching up to kiss Robert on the cheek. Maybe she wasn't so poor after all, Kitty realised.

'Each of you shall make a pile of all such materials, and then set it ablaze where it shall be a sacrifice of thanksgiving and re-dedication to the Lord. We who remain, dearly beloved,' William's voice sank to a near whisper, 'have much to be grateful for, even if at this moment it may seem that much has been taken.' He seemed unable to say any more. Lifting the small Bible to his lips, William kissed it gently, then he bowed his head, all his previous energy and triumph deserting him as memories of Catherine clearly rushed upon him. There was a pause as each person watching bowed their own head, in respect and sympathy.

Thomas Stanley moved to William's side. Placing a gentle hand on his friend's shoulder, he looked around the small gathering. 'There is much to be done, and not much day left in which to do it. Be away home and attend to all that is necessary. We shall reconvene at St Lawrence's Church at day's end! There we shall offer our collective thanks to t' Lord. Tha will hear t' bell ringing when it is time.' With that, he led William away to one side, speaking softly to him as they went. Everyone else made haste to return home to the task that awaited them.

There was great joy in the Fox household as the family made their way back to their cottage. They rushed around gathering together everything they could find that needed to be burnt. Robert worked alongside the women and girls for the rest of the morning, then took his leave after a light lunch of bread and cheese. They knew he was going to the homes of the deceased, and the farewells as he left were solemn. Anne, Kitty, Mary and Sarah soon recovered their happy moods, however, and the pile in their field at the back grew quickly.

'Must I really burn Mr Bunny?' Mary was gripping a rag doll by its long ears, dragging it along the ground as she spoke. 'I don't want him to get hurt!' she wailed.

'Shush, darling, of course, Mr Bunny mustn't be burnt. He's part of t' family, isn't he?' Kitty knew it was strictly against the rules as she looked pleadingly at the child's mother.

'Well,' responded Anne, 'I'm not sure really. What will we tell t' reverend when he asks?'

'We'll say he's my friend and he can't be burnt,' responded Mary firmly. 'He'll not mind.'

'I think tha's right, my luv. He'll not mind.' Anne smiled at her daughter as she hugged Mr Bunny tightly. It reminded Kitty of the straw doll she had given her sister at the Wakes Festival the previous year. It seemed so long ago, a distant memory after all that had taken place since. Could it really be that she might soon be returning home, to be reunited with her own family? With John?

As if reading her thoughts, Aunt Anne spoke quietly, making sure Mary couldn't overhear, 'We'll miss thee when tha heads for home, our Kitty. Tha's been a great friend to us all here. To me especially. I couldn't have done this without thee here. No, don't pretend it was nothing. Tha could have left at any moment, even a few weeks ago when John came to visit and take thee away with him.' She laughed, seeing the surprise on Kitty's face. 'Aye, we knew he was coming for more than picnic and visit. What does tha think t' letter in tha mother's handwriting was if it weren't to warn us? Your uncle and me were getting ready to lose tha then, and we were that surprised when tha came back after all. I'm sorry, luv, this has been so hard on thee, but now it's over and we can learn to live again!'

The rain eventually stopped, and a weak winter sun appeared from behind the grey clouds. It was still cold, but somehow the sight of the sun warmed Kitty as much as her aunt's words had done. She was going home!

Robert arrived at the cottage shortly before dusk, looking grim-faced and weary. 'Well, that wasn't fun,' he commented as he walked through the door. 'But this should be!' And he picked up both Mary and Sarah in his strong arms, whirling them around and around until they could hardly breathe for giggling. Returning them to the stability of the floor, he found a switch of twisted paper and pushed it deep into the already lit fire. Once it had caught, he pulled it out and rushed out of the house towards the pile of bedding and belongings that awaited its touch. The girls ran squealing after him, asking where the Guy was and singing songs more associated with the festival due to be held in a few days' time.

'Tha's confused, girls,' called Anne, following her family out to the bonfire site. 'This isn't about Guy Fawkes! Although they'll probably remember it more, and it be more important to them,' she said to Kitty as the girl came alongside her aunt.

Uncle Robert thrust the still-burning switch into the edge of the heap where some dried papers and fragments of an old apron were visible. With a few soft blows and some loud encouragement from his assistants, the flame took. Soon it was a roaring blaze. Sparks rose and swirled high into the darkening sky. Cracks and pops emitted from the burning mass as it moved and shifted. Kitty looked out over the village, mesmerised by the orange glare of other fires, other sacrifices. She could make out the shouts and cries of families like her own as they mourned the loss of people and possessions, celebrated the start of what they trusted was a new, happier beginning.

Just as the fires began to dim and collapse, as rank smoke clouded the now clear air, the bell of St Lawrence's began to toll.

'Time to go.' Robert wiped the sweat from his face as he made the fire safe to leave.

Clucking the girls along, Anne wrapped them in warm scarves, hats and thick knitted gloves. 'From t' wool tha spun,' she smiled at Kitty. Kitty smiled back, delighted that her labours and frustrations had been useful for something.

Together they walked down into the village and turned, for the first time in months except for Mrs Mompesson's funeral service, under the arched gateway of St Lawrence's Church. The simple wooden cross at the head of a grass-covered mound was all that indicated Catherine's place of rest. The pitted stone cross of the ancients stood sentinel, unperturbed by the passage of time or the events by which it was measured. The doors to the church were flung wide open, light from all the newly lit candles gleaming over the steps and onto the path beyond. The greetings between the remaining villagers that night brought fresh tears to Kitty's eyes. They were survivors of a brutal war that had suddenly been won. Arms linked arms as together they stepped back into the sanctuary they had once taken for granted. Inside, the church smelt musty and stale. A vase of flowers had been left behind, forgotten in the suddenness of the church closure. The flowers' petals had withered and turned a dull brown, the leaves fallen to scatter over the windowsill and spill to the floor.

The dwindled congregation shuffled along pews that had once been full, but which now stood bleak and bare. The gathering was forlorn and forsaken, yet somehow victorious.

Reverend Mompesson appeared from his vestry, resplendent in full ecclesiastical dress. Vestments he had not worn since closing the doors of the church, kept safe in the unopened closet of the vestry, had been retrieved and aired. Behind him followed Reverend Thomas Stanley, still wearing the simple, dark clothes they all knew. Together they strode to the front of the church. Together they mounted the steps of the pulpit. Together they squeezed behind the great lectern and together they prayed.

'Look around, dearly beloved,' spoke Reverend Mompesson, his tone grave and sombre. 'Mark every empty pew, every missing family, every departed individual. We know not the reason for this plague, nor the purpose of the Lord in visiting upon us such distress. But we know that Yea, though we have walked through the valley of the shadow of death, He has been with us; His rod and His staff have surely comforted us. Let us not forget these souls as we step forward and outward, let us carry them with us always. And let us be grateful that we ourselves have been spared, knowing that one day we shall all be reunited.'

'Blessed be God, even the Father of our Lord Jesus Christ, the Father of mercies, and the God of all comfort; who comforteth us in all our tribulation, that we may be able to comfort them which are in any trouble, by the comfort wherewith we ourselves are comforted of God.' The gentle, familiar voice of Thomas Stanley echoed through the chamber, releasing all present from the numbness of grief. Sorrow that had been walled in, dammed up, hidden away, now poured out in deep, heart-wrenching sobs. Wave after wave of sadness left Kitty gulping for air. Eventually, stillness returned to the whole congregation.

'I will extol thee, O Lord; for thou hast lifted me up. Lord my God, I cried unto thee, and thou hast healed me. O Lord, thou hast brought up my soul from the grave: thou hast kept me alive, that I should not go down to the pit. Sing unto the Lord, O ye saints of his, and give thanks at the remembrance of his holiness: Weeping may endure for a night, but joy cometh in the morning.'

The strong, assured voices of both Reverend Mompesson and Reverend Stanley brought calm and peace to the gathered assembly as they recited the few verses of the psalm. A few sniffs and coughs broke the ensuing silence.

The bell rang again, its clear note ringing out across the near-deserted village and on into the hills beyond. It continued to ring late into the evening as Kitty climbed into bed.

The next morning was strange. Nothing had changed – the same people still needed to be provided for, the same chores and duties needed to be completed – and yet everything was different. As the pile of ash from the bonfire of the night before was cleared and scattered over the last of the year's growing vegetables, Kitty was aware of a new lightness in the atmosphere. Uncle Robert whistled contentedly as he worked, repairing the roof of the henhouse which had been damaged a few days before. Mary and Sarah danced and raced around as though it was the start of spring rather than the beginning of winter. They puffed clouds of cold air into each other's faces, collapsing into fits of laughter every time. Aunt Anne added a little extra sweetness to her preserves from a pot of honey she had kept to one side all year.

'Kitty, dear,' she called. 'I need thee to deliver this pot of blackberries down to Mrs Wilson. I spoke to her about it last night, said I'd be sending her some. I can't leave this new batch, or else I'd go myself,' she finished happily.

'Of course,' Kitty replied, taking the proffered pot and tucking it securely into the bag she carried.

'Take as long as tha needs, luv, no need to hurry back.' Aunt Anne waved her off and Uncle Robert stretched from where he was bending over the hens. He grinned mischievously before returning to work.

Kitty paid no attention; she was pleased to be given the chance to escape the worst of the day's tasks and wander around the newly liberated village. As she walked down the familiar lane, she thought back over the last months, and wondered when she would feel ready to pack up and find a way to return to Sheffield. She didn't want to discuss it with her aunt and uncle yet; it was too soon, although the butterflies flitting in her stomach indicated she was already getting excited at the prospect.

She was delighted to see houses that had been firmly closed now open, their windows and doors flung wide as they breathed in the cool fresh air. She could hear voices – neighbour calling out to neighbour. At one house children played around their mother's feet while her husband leaned his elbows on the wall. Many were pale and drawn, some still showing signs of sickness. Several were weak and slow to respond to her greetings, but respond they did. It was like watching a caterpillar emerge as a butterfly, Kitty thought, chuckling at her newfound country knowledge.

As she made her way towards Mrs Wilson's cottage, Kitty noticed a figure in the street ahead of her. The light was behind him so she couldn't make out who it was, but something about the way he walked seemed familiar. Her heart began to beat faster, pulsing loudly in her chest as the figure drew closer. Surely not? How could he be here so quickly? Hadn't the opening of the village only been announced the previous morning? Kitty stopped, blinking and raising her hand to shield her eyes from the glare of the sun.

John. He had come, as he said he would. Kitty didn't know how he had made the journey so quickly, but she didn't care; she could ask questions later. His pace quickened and, within a few steps, she was enfolded in his arms, the bag with the pot of jam pressed uncomfortably into her side. Oh, how wonderful and devious and secretive were her beloved aunt and uncle. As she pulled away from John's embrace, Kitty thought she saw movement in the churchyard to her right. Glancing that way, she saw two men seemingly deep in conversation studiously ignoring her presence. William and Thomas. Had they played a part in this as well? She suspected so.

'So, is tha going to show me round, lass?' John put his arm around her waist and pulled her towards him again.

'Come and meet everyone,' she replied.

Epilogue

E ach person who suffered and died in Eyam between September 1665 and November 1666 is recorded in the parish register. Their names are read at an annual memorial service held in Cucklett Delph by the presiding revered of the same church where Stanley and then Mompesson were incumbents – St Lawrence's Church. Plaques have been hung on the walls and doors of villagers' homes where the worst sort of nightmare became real. Traditionally it's believed that out of a population of 350 or so, 260 were to succumb to the plague (more recent studies have suggested the total population was closer to 800 or 900). Was their sacrifice, the terrible price they paid, worth it? The citizens of Sheffield, Stoney Middleton and Chesterfield would reply with a resounding 'Yes!' because they remained blessedly free of the dreaded plague.

Reverend Mompesson left Eyam in 1669 to take up a position in Eakring, Nottinghamshire. Although his friend and benefactor, Sir George Saville, had recommended him, news of the events in Eyam preceded Mompesson. His new parishioners refused to allow him to live in their village for fear he carried the plague with him. They instead provided him with a small house in Rufford Park where he lived in seclusion for some time. In 1670, Mompesson married Elizabeth Newby, a widow and relative of Saville's. Mompesson moved again when he became the prebendary of Southwell, Nottinghamshire, where he lived until his death in 1709.

Thomas Stanley remained in Eyam until he died in 1670. To many, he is the unsung hero of Eyam, overshadowed by the public figure that was Mompesson. It is likely that without Stanley's help and influence, William's plan to quarantine Eyam would never have succeeded. Whether they ever became friends or found theological agreement, is debatable, but that they laid down their personal preferences and animosities for the sake of their congregation is certain.

Margaret Blackwell and her brother Francis were the only survivors of their family. Margaret, after being one of only a few who caught the plague and recovered, lived until 1699. Her nine-time great-niece still lives in the village of Eyam where she speaks to parties of school children and other visitors to St Lawrence's Church, sharing how hope in God sustained her ancestors.

Another plague survivor, Marshall Howe, also lived into the 1690s. He died at the age of 60 in 1698.

Robert Fox lived for another twenty years after the end of the plague that ravaged his community. He died on 12 May 1686; he was survived by Anne, Mary and Sarah. Anne passed away at the age of 66, old for the times she lived in. There are no records of marriage or death for either Mary or Sarah. Perhaps they moved from Eyam to one of the surrounding villages, taking with them stories of tragedy and triumph.

Kitty Allenby, living on in this author's fertile imagination, married John shortly after her return to Sheffield. Together they had four children – William, Thomas, Robert and Catherine. Kitty returned to Eyam each year to see her aunt, uncle and two cousins, timing her visits to coincide with the anniversary of Catherine Mompesson's death. A fresh posy of blue valerian appeared on Catherine's grave early each morning of Kitty's stay.

11 March 2020. The World Health Organisation (WHO) declared a global pandemic. The previously unknown coronavirus – Covid-19 – had been spreading from person to person and country to country with a virulence and speed which surprised and frightened everyone. Governments banned travel and ordered their citizens to stay at home. Schools, shops and businesses closed their doors, unsure when they would next be able to open. Churches moved out of their buildings and met with their congregations in a new, internet-enabled space. Insecurity grew as the death toll rose.

Amidst the panic and confusion, a centuries-old story resurfaced. The story of the villagers of Eyam, a small hamlet in the Derbyshire countryside in northern England. A story of how the plague arrived in a bundle of cloth in September 1665, of how households were ravaged with disease and death stalked the streets, and of how two men, themselves vehemently divided by doctrine, united a community around one common goal – to save the lives of their neighbours by laying aside their own. In 2020 newspapers in Britain, Ireland and as far afield as Australia and the United States carried articles about Reverend Mompesson and Thomas Stanley, about the church which met outdoors and the *cordon sanitaire* which was imposed. As history seemed to repeat itself, questions were asked: What can we learn in our present crisis? Can we be so brave?

Did any in Eyam – the Hancock family, the Thornleys, the Thorpes, or Catherine Mompesson – have any idea that their stories would be told and retold three hundred years later? As they collected supplies from the boundary stones, as they nursed the sick and buried their own dead, would they have thought beyond the immediate terror they faced? The ripples of their sacrifice, of their love for those they didn't even know, have reached through the centuries to inspire courage during a worldwide plague in 2020.

Greater love hath no man than this, that a man lay down his life for his friends. The applause of heaven rings loud over the villagers of Eyam.

THE END

Notes from the Author

E yam has been a special place to me ever since the first school field trips that I went on as a girl. I remember running around with pieces of paper flying, locating the plague cottages and listing the names of those who had lived – and died – within their walls. We raced around as only children can, barely mindful that this was a real place where real people had suffered more than we could ever imagine.

Years later, when I was in high school and living in Cornwall, England, I took a friend to visit the village. We hiked across the fields from a nearby youth hostel, crossing what had once been a forbidden boundary. We found the marker stone with its vinegar holes, we peered into Mompesson's Well, and we trudged out to the Riley graves, last resting place of the Hancock family. We tried to imagine what had taken place and found we couldn't.

More years passed, and I was in Eyam again, this time with my South African husband and our six-month-old daughter. I told the stories and pointed out the memorials. Trip down memory lane complete, we left for home.

And then came 2020. And a novel coronavirus. And lockdowns and 'stay in place' orders. There was global panic, global grief, global hopelessness. In the chaos of crisis, a story began to resurface – a story of a small village situated deep in the heart of the Derbyshire Peak District that had been ravaged by a plague. It was the story of Eyam.

I wanted to write more than a few lines of newspaper print in honour of these heroes who are part of my own history. I toyed with different ideas, eventually settling on a novel as a way to bring a long-ago tale to life. And so *Given Lives* was born.

I now live in South Africa, which is many miles from Eyam in the UK! With international travel prohibited due to both countries' lockdown restrictions, I began to wonder whether my idea was a good one. Would I be able to conduct any research, not just detailing a list of facts and figures, but really be able to turn the characters of the drama into real people who suffered immeasurably? I would not be able to walk the streets of Eyam, other than in my memory. I would not have the opportunity to absorb the atmosphere, to enjoy the sunshine or feel the rain.

I was greatly helped in my endeavours by technology; I rediscovered lanes and paths I had previously walked, thanks to Google Maps. I gazed at photographs others have shared. I sent out emails and received wonderful responses. I emailed Eyam Museum and St Lawrence's Church.

I am immensely grateful to several people and organisations who assisted me in my task.

Firstly, the wonderful Eyam Museum, whose website provided me with a great deal of information. You can browse the museum website at *https://www.eyam-museum.org.uk/* and will find it populated with lists and images and maps. There are worksheets for kids (very like the ones I ran around with in 1984), old photographs, and background details that I would have struggled to find, all made available at the click of a mouse. I also made direct contact with Lynette Sidhu from the museum, who agreed to help me by sending early copies of the novel to some of her museum volunteers. I am grateful to both her and them for their feedback.

A similar website is the official Eyam village website *https://www.e yamvillage.org.uk/*. The local history pages are particularly useful, not just for details about the plague, but also for information about local industry and agriculture.

The second organisation I contacted was St Lawrence's Church in Eyam. I was delighted to receive a response from Joan Plant, who also agreed to read through the manuscript. Joan is a direct descendent of Margaret Blackwell, the teenager who drank her brother's leftover bacon fat and recovered from the plague.

After our initial contact, Joan and I were able to have a Zoom call together. It was incredibly special to be sitting on my verandah in Durban sharing stories with Joan from her home in Eyam.

One of the biggest problems with writing anything set during the 1600s is the lack of written documentation that can be used for research. The diarists Samuel Pepys and John Evelyn are perhaps the most well-known chroniclers of the period. Pepys' diary is a fascinating read, describing as it does everyday life in London. But therein lies the problem – he was based in London and surrounding counties, as was John Evelyn. Both relate the suffering of the plague as it ravaged London, but neither mentions the dramatic events unfolding in an obscure Derbyshire village roughly 160 miles north of London.

No doubt Reverend Mompesson and Thomas Stanley would have been far too busy attending to the needs of their desperate congregation to commit anything to paper. Instead, oral tradition has led to the telling of the tale from one generation to the next. While this preserves in memory this most remarkable of histories, it can of course lead to embellishment and the rise of myths and traditions which may be far from accurate. *The History and Antiquities of Eyam*, written by William Wood in 1842, was the most comprehensive account of the entire Eyam story that I could find. Even though it was composed almost 200 years after the fateful years of 1665 and 1666, it makes for a fascinating – and poignant – read. A version can be found at

http://places.wishful-thinking.org.uk/DBY/Eyam/History/index.ht ml where it has been helpfully grouped into chapters for easy reading. I have used this as one of my primary sources (see Copyright).

For a wider reading about the 1660s and the Restoration period, I recommend *The Time Traveller's Guide to Restoration Britain: Life in the Age of Samuel Pepys, Isaac Newton and the Great Fire of London* by Ian Mortimer. This is a social historian's delight, a time capsule of detail and anecdote. It provided much of the 'colour' I needed to create a novel rather than a dry historical textbook.

Acknowledgements

Thank you to **Craig**, **Caragh** and **Leal** for your patience and for cheering me on during the mammoth November first draft writing. Thank you for the cups of tea and coffee, and for the nudge to get on with it!

Thank you to **Alison Theron** for an excellent first draft reading. Your corrections and comments were invaluable.

Thank you, **Gwethlyn Meyer** for your friendship and wisdom when I mention my wild book ideas to you.

Shirley Corder, thank you for your mentorship and encouragement as I dipped my feet into the world of fiction. Thank you also for all your time and effort spent helping me promote and launch *Given Lives* into the world of many books.

Thank you to **Marion Ueckermann** for your advice and endorsement of my writing; it means the world. You will be missed.

Thank you to **Sheena Carnie** for the prayerful support, expert editing and use of blue ink. Our Father is kinder than we know!

Thank you to **Chantel Cromer-Wilson** for allowing me to learn from you and for helping me develop my cover design and other artwork.

Thank you to **Lynette Sidhu** and the friends of **Eyam Museum** for all the material you have shared online, which I have gratefully devoured. And thank you for reading and commenting on the first draft of *Given Lives* even as your own 'lockdown' began to ease and you were again busy with visitors.

To **Joan Plant** – what can I say? Thank you for reading and commenting on my first draft, and for being so incredibly encouraging in your response. The tears were real when I received your email. Thank you for being so excited about *Given Lives* that you were telling others about it.

Thank you to those at **St Lawrence's Church**, Eyam who read and responded to my emails and messages and then put me in contact with Joan.

When I started out with this novel, I had no idea where it would lead me or who I would meet along the way. I am so grateful to God for His hand on every aspect, from the initial idea through to its final completion.

As you read of these given lives, may you know yourself part of the greatest story ever written, by the author of life Himself, Jesus.

The Ripples Through Time series

Ripples Through Time is a series of novels telling stories of the past and showing how they inspire our present. Stories of how God takes the ordinary and transforms it into something extraordinary. The smallest of stones, tossed into smooth water, will create waves; concentric circles spreading outward to reach beyond the immediate or seen. So too, the seemingly insignificant actions of today can leave ripples that are felt into eternity.

There is the village of Eyam and her inhabitants' love and sacrifice which saved a generation, the Bletchley Park codebreakers' dedication to fight a war far from public praise, the adventure and ingenuity of diamond hunters settling in the impermanence of the Namibian desert, and the discovery of a 2000-year-old fishing vessel believed to date to the time of Jesus and his disciples. Campaigns and conflicts, castles and cottages – tales to uncover and histories to unfold.

These are the pebbles and the ripples they leave.

The *Ripples Through Time* series is dedicated to my personal mentor, author Marion Ueckermann, who sadly passed away on 25 June 2021. She included a devotion entitled *Reflections in Pebbles* in the multi-author boxed set, *In All Things* (a set which I also contributed to). I would like to leave you with this quote from Marion:

'God has chosen you to be His pebble in the sea of humanity. What ripples of hope could emit from the splashes of your life? What giants could tumble from the impact of one small stone, one random act of kindness?'

May you, like Marion, become a pebble in the hand of God, leaving ripples in the world as you pass.

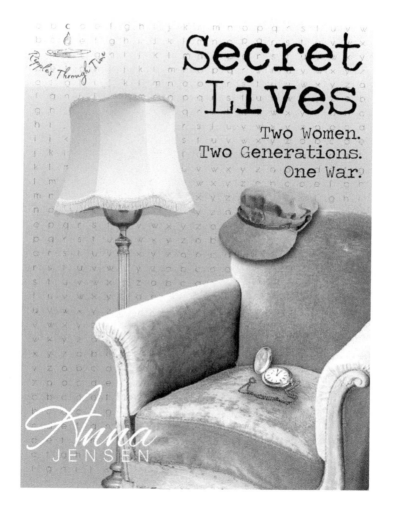

Secret Lives

Two Women.
Two Generations.
One War.

Ripples Through Time

Anna
JENSEN

Secret Lives - an excerpt

Alice

February 1942

Alice clutched her suitcase until its handle bit into her icy flesh. The mid-morning sun didn't reach the station platform where she waited. She wished she'd remembered to wear gloves. She wished a lot of things.

She patted her hat with her free hand, sure the soft bottle-green fabric must be crumpled and smudged with soot from the train ride. The gentleman sitting opposite her had insisted on keeping the window open for the whole journey. Smoke had billowed in on a bitter wind as they traversed the Fens from Cambridge, causing Alice to alternately cough and shiver.

She was glad to finally arrive at Bletchley Station. The gentleman, whose name she never asked, helped her get her suitcase down from the rack above their heads. She staggered under its weight towards the door and down the steps to the platform. *What on earth did I pack in here?* Alice tried to appear at ease with her burden as her audience of one waved goodbye.

Now she was alone on the platform, all her fellow travellers having been greeted and whisked away by friends or family. What should she do? Alice had been told she would also be met at the station and taken to the boarding house that was arranged for her. But there was no one left on the platform, except for an elderly-looking stationmaster preparing for the next train to arrive.

Stuffing her hand into the pocket of her overcoat — a coat several sizes too big on account of it having been borrowed from her brother — she wondered what to do. She could ask the stationmaster for directions, but she didn't know where she was staying. She could find the waiting room in the hope that there was a fire lit for her to warm herself. But she was worried whoever came to meet her wouldn't know that's where she was and so might leave again, thinking she had decided not to come after all. Or she could remain standing here and contemplate the many ways a person could die from exposure, and calculate how long it might take given certain atmospheric conditions.

Alice chuckled at that. Father was always saying she was a walking abacus, performing sums of varying complexities on everything she encountered. She knew mathematics was her refuge, the safe place she always ran to when confronted with the realities of a sometimes hostile world, but it was kind of Father to encourage her. Even if he didn't understand her.

Once more looking up and down the deserted platform, Alice wondered what she had let herself in for this time. It had all been such a lark when she finished that prize crossword from *The Daily Telegraph*. Egged on by Mavis and Vera as they timed her with an old stopwatch, she felt certain she must have solved it far quicker than anyone else her age. Dropping the completed entry into the post box outside college, Alice felt a flush of pride. The whole episode was quickly dismissed from her mind as studying for impending exams took priority over everything else.

That was until Professor Wilkins called her into his study a few weeks later. Alice was both mystified and terrified. Had she made some terrible mistake on one of her papers? Was she to be 'sent down' for not making the grade?

She dressed carefully for the appointment, borrowing from Mavis a neat tweed skirt and jacket. Alice hated such outfits but felt the occasion warranted it. Smoothing the newly-set waves of indignant blonde curls, she knocked on the Prof's door.

'Come!' came the immediate response.

As she opened the door and entered, Alice inhaled the smell of pipe smoke and old papers. The rush of familiarity calmed her. Although she had been in the Prof's study just once or twice, the atmosphere was so reminiscent of her father's study at the vicarage she felt immediately at home.

Professor Wilkins stood from behind his desk and motioned to a chair in front of her. As Alice sat, she became aware of someone standing in the shadows of the room, far from where the sunlight streamed in through the open sash window. Willing herself not to look at whoever it was, she focused her attention on the now-seated Professor. He was fiddling with his pipe, puffing and blowing while he held a match to its contents. Pungent smoke billowed upwards. Satisfied, he looked up. For some moments there was silence while the brightness of his eyes searched the darkest recesses of Alice's soul. Or so it seemed.

'Well, Miss Stallard,' Wilkins began. 'I understand you have been indulging in a little competitive frivolity in your spare time?' As he spoke he shuffled through the papers strewn across his desk, plucking from amongst them what looked like a piece of old newspaper. A piece of old newspaper with a completed crossword visible.

Alice groaned. *Was that what this was about? How had he heard about that? And more to the point, how has my entry ended up on his desk?* She would quiz the wretched Mavis and Vera once she was back at their rooms.

'Um,' she mumbled.

The professor waved her explanation away before it even got started.

'No matter. What is done is done.' He looked at the paper in his hand once more, then turned to the figure still standing in the shadows. 'A good score, you say? One of the quickest you've seen? Yes, yes, I suppose Miss Stallard does have a certain aptitude for these things.'

As he spoke, the figure took a step or two into the room and Alice could see him for the first time. He extended his hand in greeting.

'Good morning, Miss Stallard. I must congratulate you on your excellent crossword skills!' His voice was rich and educated. Alice could easily imagine him ordering around soldiers on the battlefield...

Recalling herself to the present with a start, Alice realised someone was talking to her. She hadn't heard anyone approach but now turned to see a nervous-looking young man, this one in uniform, staring at her. Gosh, was she talking out loud? She did that quite often, her thoughts on display for all to hear.

'Oh, I'm so sorry, miles away. I didn't hear you walk over, what did you say?' Her words tumbled out in a rush of embarrassment and nerves.

He took a step backward, removing his cap as he did so. 'Beg pardon, ma'am, but would you be Miss...' he glanced at the piece of paper he held, 'Miss Alice Stallard?'

Miss Alice Stallard nodded.

'Ah, I'm glad you're still here,' the soldier smiled, looking surer of himself now her identity was established. 'I'm Corporal Fitch, sent to pick you up from the train and take you to your digs. Got delayed — sorry — a supply train came through at just the wrong time and I got caught at the crossing. Had to wait for ages. Here, let me take that.' He reached for Alice's suitcase, which she relinquished with a sigh of relief. She massaged her frozen fingers with her other hand.

'Is it always this cold here?' she asked, while hurrying to keep up with her chauffeur. Thank goodness she wasn't wearing the ridiculous shoes Vera wanted her to wear. She would have been flat on her face if she had.

Corporal Fitch didn't reply. He was hurrying towards a muddy green car — *a Ford something-or-other?* — parked underneath the stationmaster's office window. He slung Alice's suitcase on the back seat and glanced at his watch.

'Miss Stallard, I'm afraid I'll have to take you to where you will be staying and then ask you to make your own way to the Park. I have another engagement which I will be late for if I wait while you get settled in.'

The Park? What park? 'That's no problem. Do I have time for a cup of tea? Don't worry, I'm joking. I'll run upstairs and leave my suitcase on the bed then run straight back out again. How will I know where to go?'

'You can ask your landlady for directions. It's not far; the other side of the railway line.' Fitch negotiated his way out of the parking area and into the narrow lane. Almost as an afterthought he added, 'Don't tell her why you want to go to the Park though...'

'Don't worry about that. I don't know why I'm going there myself. No one's told me anything, just to catch that train and meet you and then find a Mr Saunders.'

Fitch didn't look surprised. He gave a curt nod. 'Mm, sounds about right. Oh, before I forget — you'll need this to gain access to the Park later.'

He dug around in his breast pocket with one hand while he kept the other on the steering wheel. He pulled out a green sheet of paper, folded in two.

'Your gate pass.'

Alice took it from him and stowed it in her shoulder bag. *Where am I going, that I need a gate pass to get in? What is this place? And what am I going to be doing there?*

Knowing that only time would provide answers to her many questions, Alice looked out of the window. After crossing the railway line, Corporal Fitch drove past the Park Hotel. She could make out a couple of people sitting in the hotel lounge — a man reading a newspaper, a lady knitting. They continued on for a few more streets then turned left into Albert Street.

'Right, here you are then.' He climbed out of the car and came around the front to open the door for Alice.

'Thank you. And thank you for carrying my suitcase at the station. I can manage from here. You'd best be off!'

Fitch ignored her and grabbed her case. He strode up to one of the houses and knocked on the shiny red door. Net curtains covered the downstairs windows on either side of the entrance. The one on the right twitched, a face appeared, then the curtain fell back into place. Within seconds the door was opened by a plump, middle-aged woman in a flowery apron and fluffy pink carpet slippers.

'Well, it's about time, young man. Really, why you young people can't tell the time, I'm sure I don't know.'

'Sorry Mrs Anderson, train was late...' Fitch blushed, looked down at his polished shoes. Alice chuckled. *Has the confident Corporal Fitch met his match in this Mrs Anderson? Perhaps he doesn't have somewhere else to be; he just wants to escape.* 'This is Miss Stallard. Miss Stallard, meet Mrs Anderson. You will be billeted with her for the duration of your stay.'

Alice stepped forward, held out her hand.

'Good afternoon, Mrs Anderson. My sincere apologies for the delay. I think there was a problem on the line.'

'Well, you're here now. Come in and I'll show you to your room. And as for you, young man, be off with you. You look like a cat on a hot tin roof, jiggling around so.'

Corporal Fitch didn't need to be told twice. He directed a half-salute at the two women, murmured a hasty farewell and climbed back into his car. He coaxed the engine into life, performed a perfect three-point turn and roared off down the road.

Mrs Anderson ushered Alice into a tiny hallway which smelt of old boots and wet carpet. The wallpaper was a diamond pattern of an indeterminate colour on account of the dim light bulb dangling from the ceiling. A narrow table, cluttered with keys and pens and a ration card, took up most of the floor space. Above it hung a gilt-framed mirror, splotchy with age. Turning to close the door behind her, Alice was confronted with a row of pegs on which hung several coats, a bright purple scarf and the familiar brown box containing a gas mask.

To the right of the hallway, Alice glimpsed the sitting room. Chintz-covered armchairs were grouped around a fireplace beside which stood a Bakelite wireless radio set. The mantelpiece sported several framed photographs. A carriage clock sat in pride of place, ticking rhythmically in the quiet house. A painting of a girl sitting on a stool hung from the picture rail of the chimney breast. *Little Miss Muffet sat on her tuffet...*

The door to the left was closed. The parlour? Kitchen? Alice wasn't sure. And she wasn't about to be given a chance to find out.

'Don't dawdle, child. I don't have all day.' Mrs Anderson lumbered ahead up the stairs, steadying herself on the bannister rail as she went. Her lungs wheezed in protest.

'Sorry, yes of course. Corporal Fitch told me I have to hurry as I have an appointment at the Park. I was hoping you might tell me the quickest way to get there?' Alice grabbed her case and followed Mrs Anderson to an upstairs landing.

'Here's your room.' Ignoring the question, Mrs Anderson pushed open a door the moment Alice reached the top of the stairs. She squeezed past, inhaling her landlady's generous spray of perfume as she did so. 'Breakfast at half past seven every morning, unless you're on nights and don't get back in time. A plate will be left in the oven for you. Lunch at the Park. Dinner at 5 o'clock sharp. Again, a plate will be put aside if you're late. No smoking. No drinking. No visitors.'

Alice nodded. Rules were alright. Bit of a nuisance, but alright.

'I'll leave you to arrange your things.'

Alice plonked her case down on the orange candlewick bedspread. The room faced the street, windowpanes taped up in case of bombing raids. Blackout curtains hung from the rail. A dark wardrobe brooded in the corner. Next to the bed was a nightstand; a chipped jug and bowl for her daily ablutions and an ancient-looking table lamp with fringed shade crowded its surface. The faded blue wallpaper was peeling in the corners. On the floor, a threadbare carpet of mustard yellow completed the appalling colour scheme.

Knowing she would have to leave unpacking until later, Alice was relieved to find the jug was full of water. She splashed a little into the bowl, rolled up the sleeves of her coat and blouse and pushed her hat further back on her head. Scooping up the water in her cupped hands, she splashed it over her face, the shock of cold making her gasp. She grabbed the stiff face towel from a hook on the wall and patted herself dry. She was going to need some of that face cream Mavis always used if she didn't want to look like an old lady by the time this was over.

Poking around in her shoulder bag for the compact mirror she carried, Alice checked her appearance. Her lipstick needed a touch up. She played around with the hat until her curls looked less squashed. A last look around her new home and Alice was ready.

The wireless was on in the sitting room. Alice knocked on the closed door.

'Mrs Anderson? I'm off. I wonder — could you give me directions to the Park?'

A chair creaked and Alice heard the shuffle of slippers. The door opened so suddenly it made her jump backwards in surprise.

'Follow where that young corporal went racing off to earlier— up the street and then use the footbridge over the railway. The Park is on your left. Big iron gates. You can't miss it.'

'Thank you. Oh, er, Mrs Anderson? Sorry to disturb you again. I don't have a key...'

'Under the mat. Make sure you put it back when you've used it.'

Alice exited the claustrophobia of Mrs Anderson's hallway. The rush of fresh air revived her as she stepped out onto the pavement. Checking there was indeed a key hidden under the mat before slamming the door closed, Alice turned left and followed the directions given to her.

Alice

The Interview

Alice soon reached the footbridge over the railway line. There was no one around. She watched a robin, his red breast bobbing in and out of the bushes. She glanced over the side of the bridge, checked for any activity at the station below. There was none. A thin streak of smoke rising upward from the chimney was the only indication that the station master was still on duty.

Stumbling down the metal stairs on the other side, Alice felt the flutter of butterflies in her stomach. For the second time in a few days, she began to wonder what on earth she was doing. *Here I am, going to a job — is it a job? — I know nothing about, with no one I know. Or anyone who knows me. 'Courage, Child!' as Father would say.*

A few yards further and Alice was in front of the ornate iron gates to the Park. A guard hut stood off to one side. As she was wondering what to do next, a man in military uniform stepped out and approached her.

'We're not open to the public, Miss. Move along.'

'I — I was told to report here, for an interview?'

'Oh, I see. Do you have a gate pass?' Although mollified, the guard still regarded Alice with suspicion. He took the piece of paper and unfolded it with care. 'You are Miss Alice Stallard? Of The Vicarage, Wisbech? Your identity card, please.'

Alice rummaged in her bag for the green cardboard document and handed it over to the guard. It had seen better days — the corners were curled and there was a coffee stain on the back cover.

'Sorry,' she muttered, hanging her head in shame.

'I should think so too, young lady. These are vital documents during our troubled times. You should take better care of it.' He held the identity card in one hand, the gate pass in the other, scrutinising each paper in turn. He appeared satisfied. With a nod, he returned the identity card to Alice; the gate pass he carried into the hut and, as far as Alice could tell, added it to a pile of similar slips of paper.

'Right you are then, Miss Stallard. If you'd like to follow me...' He pulled a bunch of keys from his pocket. Leaving the hut open and turning his attention to the gate, he used one of the larger keys in the lock. He beckoned Alice through.

She stepped through the gap and waited for the guard to close and relock the gate. An ugly, red-brick house with arched entranceway loomed ahead, fronted by an expanse of frost-tinged lawns. Black smoke curled upwards from a couple of brooding chimney stacks. The blackout curtains were not yet drawn, although lights were switched on in several of the rooms. In the centre of the lawn the iced-over water of a pond glistened.

Alice turned back to the guard, impatient for him to finish fiddling with the gate and escort her somewhere warmer.

With a jingle of keys, the guard marched off down the path to the right without saying a word. Alice hurried to catch up with him. Within a few more strides, they reached a small hut, not much larger than the one at the gate.

In response to a sharp knock on the peeling green paint, a muffled command to 'Come!' bid them enter. Stepping in ahead of Alice, the guard announced her presence to the hut's occupant.

'Good, good, well move aside, let the poor girl in. She must be freezing out there.'

Alice was shivering from more than the frigid air. The sound of the man's voice terrified her. She imagined him to be tall and ramrod straight, his greying hair cut neat and sharp.

He was none of those things. He wore a brown, loose-fitting cardigan over a blue and white checked shirt. The top button was undone, a red tie loose at the neck. His hair, far from being either grey or neat, was a busy halo of dark curls framing his face. He wore a pair of round spectacles — held together on one side with a piece of string — which magnified his brown eyes. *You look like an owl who needs his feathers trimmed...*

'Do sit, Miss Stallard. Corporal, shut the door behind you, be a good man.'

He settled back into his chair and reached for a pile of papers which he shuffled through for a few moments, jotting notes on some with a worn-down pencil. Alice sat in silence. How the man could sit there without a hat or coat on, she wasn't sure. It was no warmer inside the hut than it had been outside. The only difference was the lack of fresh air. A musty, closed-in smell permeated the room. She twisted her fingers together, hoping he would hurry up.

Eventually the man looked up.

'Allow me to introduce myself, Miss Stallard. I am Mr Saunders. My job here at the Park is to run through the basics with all our newest recruits, make sure you know what arrangements are made, that sort of thing. I understand you did rather well with that crossword puzzle?'

How does everyone know about that?

'I believe so, yes. Bit of luck, really. I'm reading mathematics at Cambridge — well, I was — but I do love to play around with words too. Sort of number patterns with the alphabet, if you know what I mean?' Words tumbled over one another in their nervous rush to escape. A blush rose on Alice's neck and across her cheeks.

'Oh, don't be shy, Miss Stallard. There are plenty more just like you here. And they all love to share their achievements, if you see what I mean...' He glanced back at the papers. 'Anyway, to business. You have already met Mrs Anderson, I believe? Yes, I see from your expression that you have. Anyway, your remuneration will be £150 per year until you turn 21 — you are currently 19, I understand — out of which you must pay Mrs Anderson the going rate for your board and lodging.

'You will be allotted a few days of leave, although depending on whatever crisis is on at the time, they may be withdrawn. At short notice, I might add.

'There are three shifts here at the Park; eight in the morning until four in the afternoon; four in the afternoon until midnight; and midnight until eight in the morning. As you are billeted in Bletchley itself and therefore quite close to the Park — you're lucky with that, I must tell you — you will provide your own transport back and forth. There are several dedicated buses which run, but these are reserved for those living in outlying areas. I suggest a bicycle might be a good option.'

Alice nodded.

'I must impress upon you the need for *absolute* discretion about your position here. Is that understood? No one must know that you work here, at the Park, nor must they know what you do here.' He held up a hand before Alice could interrupt him. 'You will inform your friends and family that you are working with a group of academics near Oxford. Nothing more. Your postal address will be issued to you in due course. Please do not use any other address than the one provided.

'On your first day of active duty, you will attend a series of lectures providing more details about security procedures and so forth. You will also sign the Official Secrets Act. Be under no illusions, this is not a mere 'rubber stamp' affair; there are serious consequences should you break any of its conditions, ranging from dismissal to prison and, ultimately, death.'

Alice raised her hand an inch or two, as though still at school and nervous to ask the teacher a question.

'Yes? Is there something I have not made clear?'

'Well, sir — Mr Saunders — I appreciate all the information you have given me. But, um, there seems to be something you have left out...'

He removed his spectacles and squeezed his temples.

'Miss Stallard, I thought I made myself abundantly clear about everything that concerns your time here at the Park.'

'Well, yes, sir. But you haven't mentioned what I will be doing here. You know, what job I'm here for.'

Mr Saunders replaced his spectacles with a sigh.

'No, I have not. Nor shall I be doing so. You will receive notification when you are to return here. At that time, once the aforementioned Act has been signed, you will be told your duties.' He took out his pocket watch and checked the time. 'May I suggest you make your way back to Mrs Anderson's billet? You will probably have missed dinner already, but I understand she keeps something to one side for her boarders. Do you have a torch with you? I'm sure it will be quite dark. Must close the blackouts, while I think of it.'

He rose and busied himself at the windows. He waved a hand of dismissal at Alice.

'Thank you, sir, yes I do have a small light with me. Thank you for your time, sir.'

Alice let herself out. The man was right — it was dark. The blackouts were up at all the windows of the mansion, tiny chinks of light showing where they didn't quite fit. She flicked on the small torch she'd brought with her, keeping its beam low and close to her body.

Groping her way back to the gate, she mouthed a silent prayer of thanks for her dear father who had managed to get hold of the torch especially for her.

The click of her heels on the paving sounded loud in the quiet stillness of night and she wasn't surprised to find the guard waiting for her. He held the gate open as she passed through.

'Goodnight, Miss. Mind how you go.'

Continue reading Secret Lives. Out now in paperback and Kindle – FREE in Kindle Unlimited. Scan or click the QR to buy now.

About Anna

I'm a British expat who has lived in South Africa for a little over twenty years. My husband and I live with our two teenage children on the east coast, a few miles north of the city of Durban. We overlook the Indian Ocean where we have the privilege of watching dolphins and whales at play.

My first book *The Outskirts of His Glory* was published in May 2019. The book is a Christian devotional and poetry collection, exploring the many surprising ways that God can speak to us through His creation. I have drawn on my travels in and around South Africa, as well as further afield, to hopefully inspire each of us to slow down and perhaps listen more carefully to the 'whispers of His ways' (Job 26:14) that are all around us.

Since publishing *Outskirts*, I have had the privilege of speaking at a number of local churches and even have a weekly slot on a Christian radio station. I have also continued writing by contributing to a variety of blogs and online writing communities as well as developing my own website and blog.

Want to know more? Check out my website at www.annajensen.
co.uk

Cornwall, September 1742

*Tin mining is in Jem Pearce's blood.
For as long as he can remember, the
subterranean caverns of the Cornish
mines have been his world — just like
his father before him. Intimate knowledge of the maze of tunnels and pas-
sageways lights the way in the underground darkness, as sure as any
lantern.*

*So why, when mine owner Mr Roberts announces plans for a proposed
expansion project, is Jem so uneasy?*

*Compounding his anxiety is his son Edward's eagerness to experience
the thrill of the blasting preparations.*

*Can Jem persuade the mine officials to change their plans, and so
avert disaster?*

*Meanwhile, Mr John Wesley has returned to this remote part of the
country with his vibrant Gospel crusades. Thousands gather to hear his
simple, hope-filled teaching, including Susanna Pearce, Jem's wife. Can
she help her husband discover the true light that shines in the deepest
darkness — the light that is Jesus?*

Make it easier to hear about all things Anna and sign up for my
free more-or-less monthly newsletter. You'll receive a gift of the ebook,
Seeking Light, a Cornish tale inspired by my years living in Cornwall
when you do. You'll also be sent an invitation to join my Subscriber
Family Birthday Club. Sign up today at www.annajensen.co.uk/news

Follow me across my various social media platforms. Or email me
directly at hello@annajensen.co.za I'd love to connect with you.

Scan the QR code to access clickable links.

St Saviours Seasonal Stories

The seasons of the church calendar are important to Richard, vicar of St Saviours, a thriving church community in the heart of London. Christmas, Easter, Advent and Lent — all have a special place in the Reverend's heart and actions.

Book 1:

A Candle for Christmas
Four candles. Four stories. One Christmas Day.

The vicar of St Saviour's is preparing for Christmas. Four Sundays,
four services, four advent candles to light.
Richard loves Christmas. And he loves the ritual of the advent candles.
Only this year is different. Memories and regrets threaten to spoil his
favourite season.
Joelle is tired. Tired of the streets; tired of the weather. Tired of being
unseen. Could the preparations for Christmas at St Saviour's herald a
new beginning?
Tamara knows this Christmas is going to be different. She's been
planning for weeks. But will it be in the way she expects or is there a
surprise in store?
Ellen realises her new-found freedom isn't as wonderful as she expected it to be. Can she retrace her steps and find restoration? Or is it too
late?
Christmas Day. Richard ignites the final candle...

Book 2:

The Nine Readings of Christmas
Nine lessons. One Christmas story

Christmas is fast approaching.

The congregation of St Saviours is caught up with Christmas preparations and parties — not least amongst them their vicar, Richard.
The service of Nine Lessons and Carols has been months in the planning. Everything is in place for the evening to be the highlight of this
year's church calendar. Until Richard receives a telephone call; his
soloist has a sore throat. Can The Service still go ahead? Will Richard
seek to find his own solution? Or will God have His way?
Marjorie is baking up a storm; containers full of every Christmas treat
occupying all available space. When a Christmas card from afar arrives
with unwelcome news — and a gift — Marj is forced to reassess the life
she has chosen. Is she where she should be or has her focus on family
and church been misdirected?
Ellen, studying and involving herself in the local community, is experiencing dreams of Africa. What do they mean? And does an email she
receives have anything to do with them?
Tamara has made her peace with the single life she now leads. But is
there more? Are a young girl, a homeless woman, and a Christmas
party the key to her happiness?
Joelle has a new home, with a comfortable bed and two cooked meals
a day. She also has a family — the family of St Saviours. Can she help
Ellen decipher her dreams and discover her heart? Or show Tamara
that they are more alike than she may think? Christmas at St Saviours.
Nine lessons; one story.

Book 3:

One Passing Easter
Seven special days. And the lives they changed

Shrove Tuesday.
The annual St Saviours Pancake Relay is in full flip. Runners and
spectators alike are wild with excitement.
Until an accident occurs and an ambulance is called.

Reverend Richard has a full schedule of services and events planned
between now and Easter Sunday. Will he be able to continue as
arranged, or will circumstances dictate otherwise?

Tamara, persuaded to go on a blind date by a friend and colleague,
is desperate for change. Abandoning the shallowness of yet another
meaningless relationship, she seeks something deeper this Lent. Can
she find the love she longs for? Or will past experiences and hurts keep
her in their grip?

Joelle harbours a secret. Does she have the courage to share it with
Marjorie? Or is time running out?

Elsewhere, Ellen has found her calling. Or so she hopes. But when
disaster strikes her community, bringing with it an unexpected con-
frontation, can beauty rise from the ashes?

After this one passing Easter, the lives of the St Saviours community may never be the same.

More From Anna

The '14 Days of Devotions' Series

A Seat in a Garden

14 days of reflections and poems from seven gardens of Africa

What better place to enjoy the presence of God than from a seat in a secluded garden? Take a moment to wander with Anna Jensen through seven of her favourite African gardens in this book of 14 daily devotions.

Discover with her the delights of quiet contemplation, finding glimpses of the Creator in every leaf and flower. Pause and rest for reflection on a 'bench' – a space created through poetry and prayer.

Rugged Roads

14 stories and poems from seven journeys in Africa

Take a journey off the beaten track and enjoy the drama on seven journeys of adventure and discovery through South Africa and beyond. Take the warned-against route from Harare to Victoria Falls, Zimbabwe, or discover the twists and turns of a mountain pass into Lesotho. Stumble through the sand of a Namibian desert or feel the adrenalin rush of being charged by a rhino or threatened by an elephant. In this collection of 14 daily devotions, reflect on the whispers of God heard when driving off-road. Through stories and Scripture readings, poetry and prayer, find the joy of choosing 'rugged roads'.

Poems and Prayers

14 reflections from a year of change

The year 2020 started like any other – full of promise and hope. Within a few months, it was clear this was to be no ordinary year. By March, the World Health Organisation had declared a global pandemic of the hitherto-unknown coronavirus Covid-19. For Anna Jensen, it was a time of bewilderment, but also an opportunity; an opportunity to press in afresh and hear all that God wants to whisper.

In this collection of 14 daily devotions, Anna reflects on those early months of the pandemic, articulating her thoughts through poems and prayerful reflections.

A Gratitude Challenge

14 days of choosing thanks

In November 2020, Anna Jensen embarked on her first 'gratitude challenge', a series of social media posts giving thanks on a daily basis.

Anna found herself being grateful for the serious and the silly, and everything in between (on one of the days, she was thankful for shoe shops, after her son climbed into the car from school with a 'flapping sole', which needed an urgent remedy).

This book of 14 days of devotions is the pick of Anna's month of gratitude, shared with you in the hope that you will see the delight in the daily and the mundane. There really is so much to be thankful for.

Other books by Anna

The Outskirts of His Glory

Join Anna Jensen and her family as they travel to seek out and experience the odd and unexpected of God's creation.

Captivated by the Creator (paperback only)

Be inspired afresh by the voice of the Creator through the beauty of His creation. Be guided by Anna Jensen as she describes her own journey of discovery through articles and poems. This beautiful journal contains pictures for you to colour and space for your own thoughts and prayers.

Twenty Years an Expat

Read about Anna's experiences when she left her native land and learned to embrace the different and the new as she settled in South

Africa. At times funny, at others poignant, the one constant is God's love and purpose for Anna in all she experiences.

Find all my books on Amazon